WHAT IF I NEVER

NEW YORK TIMES BESTSELLING AUTHOR
LISA RENEE JONES

ISBN-13: 979-8795499024

To obtain permission to excerpt portions of the text, please contact the author at lisareneejones.com.

All characters in this book are fiction and figments of the author's imagination.

www.lisareneejones.com

PLAYLIST

"Girl Like You" by Jason Aldean

"Live Like You're Dying" by Tim McGraw

"Best Shot" by Jimmie Allen

"What If I Never Get Over You" by Lady A

"I Hope You're Happy Now" by Carly Pearce and Lee Brice

"I Don't Drink Anymore" by Jason Aldean

CHAPTER ONE

The small package with the pink ribbon arrives on a Thursday, the first week of October.

I'm at my desk at the Nashville's Frist Art Museum when Carrie, our receptionist, sets it in front of me. "A courier service dropped this off for you two weeks ago. I'm so sorry. Apparently, the temp we had up front had stuffed it in the drawer and just remembered it."

"Oh," I say. "Well, no one has complained that I haven't responded to whatever it is, so no worries."

"It looks personal to me." She laces her fingers together and presses her hands beneath her chin and rocks just a little. "A gift from someone special, maybe?" she asks, oh-so-coyly, but the phone panel lights up next to me, which means it's lighting up at the front desk, as well. "Dang it," she says, "I have to go back to my desk but I'm *dying* to know what's inside that box. *Please* come show me." She wiggles her eyebrows and adds, "*If* it's not *too* personal." She dashes out of the office.

I laugh at her silliness, and how can I not? I've been here for three months, and already Carrie feels like a kid sister, who big sister wants to protect. My little clone, too short not to wear heals, with dark brown hair and green eyes. Funny how thirty-two feels old compared to Carrie's twenty-four, but then again, the past few months have aged me in ways beyond my years, as well.

As for the package, my brows dip as I study the box with the card that reads nothing but, "*Allie.*" That nickname, used by those close to me, certainly explains why Carrie assumes this to be a personal gift, and of course, so do I. I go by Allison on the job, but while Carrie assumes this is some kind of romantic gesture, I do not. I'm not dating anyone right now, nor have I dated any time in the recent past.

I quickly open the box to find another box inside. A long, slender velvet box with a pink ribbon.

That ribbon, symbolic of breast cancer, jolts me, and how can it not? Cancer is the beast my mother has battled these past few months, and finally, conquered. I still can't believe this is our reality, her reality, but she's good now, I remind myself. And she has my stepfather by her side, a man who's both loving and loyal, a real hero fireman. I could easily return to my real dream career at the world-renowned Riptide Auction House right now, if I so pleased, but I just can't seem to leave.

I slide the ribbon off the box and then open the lid, sucking in a breath at the sight of an expensive diamond necklace. I mean, holy wow, it's gorgeous, the overhead lights catching on what my career at Riptide tells me to be high-quality sparkling stones. The necklace is a choker, a long strand of star-shaped diamonds, meant to grab attention. A card is taped to the inner lid that reads, *"Forgive me."*

CHAPTER TWO

There are only two men that would ask me to forgive them: my father, who is a retired professional football player, and my ex, who has been my father's agent of ten years. I also found out the hard way, that Brandon, said ex, is far more my father's son than I am his daughter and I'm the only one of the two of us actually related. I shove aside that thought before I fall down the rabbit hole of a big ol' bunch of yuck. Bottom line, I'm in this headspace for one reason: both Brandon and my father have proven that they believe gifts and money are replacements for honesty and love. Brandon Montgomery really is a chip off the old block, AKA my father. And I am *not*.

Irritated at the pinch in my chest with this idea, I shut the box, intending to send it back to whichever one of them hopes to slide back into my life. I grab the paper that was around the box to eye the return address but find none. That's when my gaze catches on the recipient's information. It reads "*Attention: Allison W,*" but the address is for the powerhouse entertainment law firm a few blocks down the road. I know this because our address is 365, and theirs is 355, so we frequently get their deliveries. I quickly grab my phone and look up the firm's reception number.

I punch the call button and listen as the line rings.

"Hawk Legal," a female greets, the infamous Tyler Hawk being the primary founder of the firm, but there must be hundreds of attorneys on staff that don't even get a name on the door. "How can I help you?" she asks.

"Can I speak to Allison?"

"She's not in. What can I do for you?"

"I need to speak with her directly," I say, afraid of spreading her personal business all over her office. "I've received a delivery that belongs to her. We have the same name and I work a few blocks down from your building."

"I can leave her a message," she says, robotic, unconcerned, though I am. This is a very expensive necklace. "Or you can have it delivered here?" she asks.

I'm back to the necklace being extremely expensive when I say, "I'd rather hand deliver it. Will she be in today?" I ask.

"I really don't know. You can try back later."

"Right," I say. "I'll try her again later. Thanks." I disconnect and set my phone aside, opening the box again to read the card. "*Forgive me.*"

For what, I wonder? What did someone do to the other Allison that justified a gifted necklace worth what experience tells me to be thousands of dollars? And how has this necklace sitting at our front desk for two weeks impacted that forgiveness? Concerned, I glance at the clock. It's almost one. Maybe Allison is just at lunch. I can meet her at her office this afternoon. Decision made, I toss my half-eaten egg salad sandwich in the trash and lug my oversized, Louis Vuitton bag over my shoulder. It's the only gift my father gave me that I kept, mainly because I received it during the one time in my life I thought I had a relationship with him. I guess, some part of me still clings to that façade.

But the bag also reminds me that expensive gifts don't erase bad behavior, and I wonder if the other Allison has learned that lesson. Or maybe she's about to learn it now. Or, I scold myself, the necklace sender is a good person, worthy of forgiveness. The men in my life might have been trouble, but all men are not. My stepfather has been the showcase of humble goodness in my mother's life and has driven that point home. And as a heroic fire chief, Barry has also proven to me that power and money do not define a man, good or bad.

But character does.

And anyone with a good character knows that you can't buy love, not even with diamonds.

CHAPTER THREE

On my way to the exit of the museum, I motion to Carrie where she sits behind the front desk, calling out, "Back in a few!"

She flings her hands in the air in exasperation, but she'll have to wait to find out what's in the package. I exit into a warm, rather than a hot October day, my basic black pumps that match my basic black suit dress hitting the sidewalk. I miss fall in New York, which feels like fall, not just a slight break in the heat index, but as a truckload of people singing "Friends In Low Places" passes, my lips curve. I do love the unique energy of downtown Nashville.

That song, and those happy people, are with me throughout my short walk to the Hawk Legal high-rise, waving goodbye to me as I halt to greet my destination. I laugh, and wave back at the group, before entering the luxurious lobby with fancy furniture and sculpture-like lighting hanging from the towering ceiling, feeling right at home.

Money all but sings like that busload of people outside in this place, but thanks to Riptide, I have a comfort level in such luxury that defies growing up poor with a single mom. Certainly not because of my father being a retired, two-ring Super Bowl quarterback with a restaurant empire. I barely knew him until a few years back, when he'd promised he'd become a family man.

A promise that went south quickly.

I head to the security desk where I sign-in. Apparently, Hawk Legal is not the only tenant in the building and I'm directed to the twentieth floor for reception. The elevator bank is filled with at least eight

11

cars, and the one to the left opens. I dash inside the first empty car. I've just punched my floor when a man, smelling of spice in that perfect way some men do, joins me.

He reaches for the panel and lowers his hand, glancing in my direction, his light brown hair longish, but not so much so that it hides his remarkable, light blue eyes. "Seems we're going to the same place."

"Yes," I say, aware of his tall stature, his well-built physique. "I guess we are."

He smiles a charming smile, then faces forward, as do I. And good lord, I thought I liked a man in a suit, but I've been proven wrong. This man in denim, boots, and a stylish tan leather jacket screams masculine perfection.

The car starts to move, floors ticking by us, and the small space seems to shrink.

Elevators are truly tiny boxes where strangers crowd inside and end up ridiculously close while pretending we are not close at all. Most of the time, it's an easy task to achieve, but not always. Not today. I'm oddly hyper-aware of me and this man alone, the scent of his earthy cologne teasing my nostrils. He smells so darn good.

Too soon, the car halts, and a long way from our destination. Anticipating a new passenger, I am both hopeful and regretful that my alone time with this stranger will soon be over. And I'm right. A stunning blonde, the kind of bombshell my car partner belongs with, joins us and does so with a blast of insanely strong perfume. She reaches for the panel and impatiently punches the tenth floor.

Choking, I step backward, as far away from the woman and against the wall as I can manage, covering my hand with my mouth. I'm choking on fumes. My God, she smells like she poured my grandmother's sharp, tangy perfume all over herself. I loved my grandma, but I broke out in hives when I was around her from that perfume. Lord, help me, I'm going to start coughing. Please let her get off soon. And please, don't cough, I tell myself. *Don't cough.*

I can feel the man watching me, but I don't dare look at him. I swear if my body is reminded of the hot guy nearby, it will surely betray me and force the coughing spell. Finally, a lifetime later it feels like, the car halts and the doors open oh so slowly.

The perfume factory rushes out of the car, and while her cologne lingers, the intensity shrinks by half, and air from the corridor makes a slight welcome intrusion. The minute the doors shut again, I sink into the corner of the car and sigh, my hand falling from my face. Without intending to do so, I find myself staring into the amused eyes of the man who makes denim look as delicious as chocolate.

"I was dying," I admit.

"Agreed," he says. "Apparently she doesn't know she could hold up a bank with that smell."

I laugh. "No. No, she does not, but to her credit, neither did my grandmother. I'm fairly certain it's the same perfume."

He leans a shoulder on the elevator, his body fully facing mine now. "Did you tell your grandmother it was strong?"

I gape at him. "Are you kidding? Never. It would have hurt her feelings. Grandma was a very sensitive woman. If you hurt her feelings, she'd refuse to cook for you."

He laughs, a low, deep baritone, and asks, "And that would be bad, I assume?"

"Oh yes. She made cookies during the holidays and shipped them to everyone in the family. I lived for that holiday box of goodies."

The car halts again and he pushes off the wall.

My short encounter with this man is over, a stab of disappointment filling me. Only it's not over. I eye the number board and the elevator is on eighteen, not twenty. The doors open and a huge group is waiting to enter. And enter they do. They file in like sardines lining up in a can, and to my surprise, the man, whose name I still don't know, steps in closer to me. Really close, as there is no room in the car. Suddenly he's right in front of me and someone shoves him forward. He catches himself on the wall above my head.

"Sorry about this," he says softly, and I swear his eyes are warm with mischief. "I didn't want to shove you into the wall. This seemed the best solution."

He has, in fact, protected me from the crush of way too many people in one tiny elevator. "Thank you," I say softly, wondering how he'd react if he knew this is the closest I've been to a man in just shy of two years. Or if I told him that he smells better up close than far away. Or if my hands accidentally on purpose settled on what appears to be an impressive chest? The temptation is real, but that would be highly inappropriate. He didn't place himself in front of me to seduce me, but rather protect me after being shoved. I ball my fingers into my palms by my sides, forcing them to stay right where they are.

The car halts and someone screams out, "Why are we on twenty? We're going down, people."

"That's us!" my hero stranger calls out, lifting one hand in the air. "We need off."

"Off!" Someone else shouts. "Everyone off. Give them space."

"Off!" Another shouts, "Off now."

Bodies move out of our personal space and the stranger clears a path for me, motioning me forward. I hurry into the hallway, the group of people, all with badges on that seem to indicate they're part of a business event, all around me. I find myself wanting to wait on the man, but several of the people from the elevator are between our exit now. They step aside just as a gorgeous blonde in a red dress and black heels grabs the stranger's arm. It's a familiar, intimate touch, not that of a business acquaintance. "Thank God, you're here," she gushes. "Let's go get a drink. We're both going to need one to talk about this contract."

He turns to her, and while his look is not doting or loving, the contract topic bringing business back into the mix, I am the awkward third wheel here. I'm just an elevator dalliance, meaningless and short, a whisper in a dark night never heard. Embarrassed that I'd thought it might lead to something more, I hurry away and enter the open double doors of Hawk Legal. My little flirtation in the elevator is over, if it was even a flirtation at all. I don't really know what it was or was not. It's over. As if proving that point to myself, I step to the reception desk, and despite my silent plea with myself not to, I glance behind me. The man and his blonde goddess are gone.

LISA RENEE JONES

CHAPTER FOUR

"I'm here to see Allison, please," I say when the receptionist finally offers me her full attention.

"And you are?" she queries.

"Also Allison," I reply, offering her my card, not the card for the local art museum but rather my card for Riptide, which I know will garner respect. "Allison Wright."

She glances at the card and then at me again, and she's clearly not impressed. She's pale-skinned, blue-eyed, and a brunette, with an air of privilege that her position does not demand nor for that matter, should anyone hold over someone else.

"Allison isn't in right now," she says, handing me back my card.

"Will she be back soon?"

"Not today," she says. "Can I help you?"

I consider bringing up the delivery again but decide she'll just do what she did earlier, and ask me to leave it here. Which I'd do if it wasn't such a personal gift. I don't want to spread this "other" Allison's personal business around the office. "I just need to talk to her. Can you give her my card?"

She glances at it fully this time, and then me, "Wait. *Riptide*? Her brows dip. "*The* Riptide?" She doesn't wait for a reply. "I thought Riptide was in New York City?"

"It is and I normally am as well."

"If you can tell me what this is about, I can try to direct you to someone other than Allison."

"I appreciate that, but I really need Allison, just Allison."

"All right then," she says. "I'll be sure to tell Allison when she returns to work."

There's nothing more that I can say. The necklace is too expensive to leave in just anyone's hands. And I can certainly call the courier, but I'd rather deliver the package to Allison myself, so that I know it's done safely. Reluctantly, I turn and walk through the lobby toward the elevator, feeling let down in a major way. When I step onto the elevator, it's with a sense of unease I don't understand. Allison will be back and she'll call me. Or I'll call her. Soon, I'll meet her and hand over her beautiful necklace.

CHAPTER FIVE

Three days after my visit to Hawk Legal, I still haven't heard from Allison, despite my numerous calls and another drop by the office. Instead, I'm sitting at my desk when Carrie buzzes into my office and announces, "There's a Mark Compton on the phone."

My heart races with the name.

Mark is one of the principal founders of Riptide, and I usually deal with his mother, who we jokingly call "Queen Compton," or her right-hand person, Crystal. Both of whom are easy to talk to, but Mark is another story. He's intimidating—a force of nature, a man who is all power and control and demand. It was his mother who let me take a leave of absence and keep my job, and I can't help but fear that's about to end.

"Put him through," I say, and I swear my hands are clammy as I pick up the phone. "Mr. Compton. This is unexpected."

"Yes, it is, Ms. Wright," he says. "Can you tell me why you're getting an invitation to Hawk Legal's annual party as a representative of Riptide?"

"Oh. I—that's strange. I did leave my card at the front desk. I guess someone got me confused with a client."

"Why were you there *at all*?" he asks, getting right to the point. "Are you looking for a job? Or, worse, are you in some kind of trouble?"

"No," I say quickly. "God, no. Riptide means the world to me and I'm not someone who gets in trouble."

He's silent, which leads me down a dark hole of speculation. Perhaps my reply doesn't sit right with him. Or maybe it just doesn't answer his question sufficiently enough, and thus doesn't justify his response. Or as he does, perhaps he's luring me into a deep, dark empty hole that entices me to fill the space with a confession. And yet, despite knowing this about him, I do just that.

"I received a package that was meant for someone at Hawk Legal," I explain quickly, and since I did tell Crystal about the temp job at the museum, I add, "The museum is just a few blocks down."

"Right," he says dryly. "The *museum*." There's disdain in his voice that tells me the museum is beneath him and that means me. I think that's a compliment. Maybe. I don't know with him. "When exactly will you be back?" he asks, obviously feeling the need to confirm what he already knows.

"January," I reply. "Is that still okay? Do you need me back sooner?"

He ignores my question and asks, "How is your mother?"

"Better, thank you," I say. "She's pulling through this. She's in remission."

"I'll hold you to that, Ms. Wright," he states, and while there is a crispness to his tone, there's also an emptiness to the words that I know has nothing to do with me or my mother. It's about his own. His mother, Queen Compton, the founder of Riptide, the boss of us all, is also fighting cancer. "How is she?" I ask, knowing we both know who I'm talking about.

"Not good," he replies succinctly. "But as you know, she's a fighter."

"Yes, she is," I say. "She has superpowers. I believe that," I add, and I mean it. His mother was the reason I'd ended up at Riptide just shy of two years ago now. I'd been in a bad place, only a month after a break-up with my father and my ex. My career had stalled. Then one day I'd stepped into a coffee shop at the same time as her, and the two of us had started chatting. That cup of coffee had changed my life. She'd seen something in me, I don't even know what. She'd called me a diamond in the rough and recruited me from my job as an editor at a publishing house and stunned me with a hefty raise. More so though, she'd made me believe I could do anything, be anything, rethink my life, and make it bigger and better at a time when I'd needed to believe those things. She'd believed in me when I'd been at my lowest. I need to be there for her now. "I can come back," I offer quickly. "If you need me, if she needs me—"

"Stay with your mother," he says. "That's what she would want. Enjoy the holidays with her. But," he adds, "if at any point you staying with us comes down to you needing to relocate her here, and/or take advantage of the doctors at our disposal, we'll make it happen and we'll pay for it. That is also what she would want."

I blink in surprise at the offer, emotions burrowing in my chest and taking root with his generosity. I'd only been with Riptide a year when my mother was diagnosed with cancer, and while I knew I'd performed well and that I'd pleased Queen Compton, Mark is a hard read. I was never really sure he noticed anything I did right or wrong.

"I—that's very generous," I say, my voice cracking.

"It's self-serving," he replies. "We need you back in the New Year."

"Absolutely," I say, and in this moment, my loyalty to Riptide has never been stronger, which stirs an idea. "Can you fax me the invitation?" I ask. "Maybe I could actually go as a Riptide representative? There was a reason they thought inviting me was a good idea. Maybe they're interested in working with us?"

"I like the way you think, Ms. Wright. Go. Do. Make things happen. I'll give you a thirty-percent commission on anything you bring in that cashes out. I expect an update." He disconnects. Just like that. No goodbye. Nothing else. He just hangs up.

And so do I, and I do so with a dry mouth.

Thirty percent of anything that's Riptide-worthy is a lot of money, money I need considering my mother's medical bills are piling up and so is my rent in New York, hence the temp job. And until now, I've never earned more than five percent and a Christmas bonus, but then, I wasn't dealing with customers until the last few months before I took my leave, either.

My computer pings and I quickly pull up the email from Mark, downloading the attachment. And sure enough, there's an invitation addressed to me. I'm cordially invited to the annual Hawk Legal cocktail party at the Grand Hyatt rooftop bar. And I'm going to attend. There's a hint of excitement inside me that I cannot deny. I've spent months fearing my mother's outcome. She's alive and well, and now, I'm starting to breathe again. My mind goes to the man on the elevator, and I can't help but wonder if he'll be there, but as soon as I have the thought, I dismiss it. I remember the blonde holding his arm and demanding his attention.

He is clearly not for me, but the party is another story.

I'm going to attend. I'm also going to give myself permission to enjoy myself. And maybe just maybe, I'll meet the elusive Allison. The other Allison. The one who was really supposed to receive the necklace.

CHAPTER SIX

The party is on a Friday night, at the rooftop bar of the Grand Hyatt. During the three days from when I received my invite and the actual evening of the event, Allison remains elusive and just plain impossible to reach. At this point though, I'm committed to the party as part of my role at Riptide.

I'm attending.

This is non-negotiable.

If by chance Allison attends, or I find a way to reach her through the party, that will be a bonus.

The evening in question arrives, and so do I. I enter the hotel dressed in business attire, rather than the invite's indicated cocktail attire, which fits my conservative, cautious nature. In this case, I've paired a figure-hugging black Chanel skirt with a black silk blouse with a cut-out neckline that manages to offer the illusion of showing a little skin while showing nothing at all. My strappy heels are Gucci. They, like the other items I'm wearing, are outrageously expensive and part of a shopping spree I'd found a necessity with my first Riptide bonus.

Dress for success, Queen Compton had told me the day she'd promoted me to a more visible role in the auction house. Our clientele can spot a brand a mile away, she'd added. It was a lesson proven right when one of the customers told me I was surprisingly far better at my job than I was at choosing my wardrobe. You'd think that snobbery would make me hate the job, but it really didn't. The one-of-a-kind treasures Riptide inventories daily are much like a perfect book you fear you'll never find again: invaluable. And Riptide has managed to offer me an identity I seem to be losing while here in Tennessee. Maybe that's why I'm so eager to be here, reconnecting with my job in some way tonight.

And all thanks to the mysterious other woman named Allison.

I'm walking through the lobby when I spot a sign directing guests of the Hawk Legal party to the elevators. Once there, I find yet another sign directing me to a specific car, which has a young, rather handsome couple in evening wear waiting for it as well. The doors to the appropriate car slide open and I join the couple inside, as does a man with smoke-gray hair and an expensive suit. As the ride begins with each passing floor, I can't deny my nerves.

The truth is that I'd arrived at Riptide beaten and bruised emotionally and professionally, a sense of control nowhere to be found, and for reasons I share with no one, Riptide helped me find my self-confidence and my footing again. But being here in Nashville, afraid for my mother, connected to that bad history more than most might think, has set my world spinning again. My mother, my best friend, could have died. She's in remission, but her cancer could come back. I'm definitely not on solid footing. I'm definitely not in control when I have nothing to think about but her illness.

My mother's doctor said that if I see my mother's death around every corner, so will she. I have to live so she can live. Tonight is me reclaiming my life. I live. She lives. With that in mind, I start thinking about my goals. First and foremost, I'll find Allison and give her the necklace that's inside my cute little Christian Louboutin Paloma studded leather clutch. It was a birthday gift from Queen Compton, and I use it every chance I get. It's red inside, and one day I'll splurge on a pair of red-soled

Christian Louboutin heels to match. I'll earn them all by my lonesome. Because I can. I know I can.

The car halts, and I'm feeling empowered.

The handsome couple exits first, and the distinguished man motions me forward. I give him a nod and exit with him on my heels. Each of us ends up to the left at a hostess stand where we present our invitations. When I'm next, I recognize the hostess as the receptionist for Hawk Legal, who I now know to be Katie.

"Hi Katie," I greet and when I see the recognition on her face, I offer a small smile. "What are the odds I actually meet Allison tonight? I know she took time off, but I thought—maybe, just maybe—she'd be here tonight?"

"She's not going to attend, sorry. But I'm glad you made it. I told my boss about your connection to Riptide. He wants to speak to you."

"Oh," I say, and since I have questions, I motion for the man behind me to go ahead. He nods his appreciation and when he's checked in and moved along, I join the receptionist once again. "Who's your boss?"

"Tyler Hawk, the principal in Hawk Legal, and he's Allison's boss. I'm sure you'll get any information you wanted about our upcoming charity auction from Allison from him."

In other words, they've assumed I'm contacting Allison about an auction I didn't even know existed. A detail that could make this invitation a good thing for Riptide, which is also, a good thing for me. "Just to be clear," I say. "You're actually auctioning off items, correct?"

"Right. Exactly. Hawk Legal is gathering donations from our high-profile clientele and auctioning them for this year's named charity. I assumed that's where Riptide comes into play."

"Yes," I say quickly and sincerely. "Yes, it very well could. I think we could be a match made in heaven, but I did think Allison would be my contact. Is she still with the company?"

Her lips tighten and I get the idea the question is oddly uncomfortable, and I can't imagine why. "You'll need to talk to Tyler."

That doesn't seem good, I think, but I leave it alone. "How do I find Tyler?" I ask.

She motions to a tall, good-looking man with sandy brown hair who reminds me of Mark Compton in his carriage, and the custom, outrageously expensive suit he's wearing. And of course, the assumed ownership of the room that radiates from him with a confidence that borders on arrogance. And yet, somehow works for him.

"Thank you," I say to Katie. "I'll talk to him."

I step around the hostess stand and enter the bar, which is a really spectacular place. There are windows everywhere and a city view from pretty much any place you might stand. The bar itself is situated to my left, and there is an outdoor area fanning out beyond that. To my right is an enclosed seating area but of course, the view is still miles of dark sky lit by a Nashville honkytonk of city lights. As for the guests, cocktail attire is now defined by dresses, suits, cowboy boots, and jeans. Not a surprise really since I'd guess that Hawk's client list probably includes at least half of the country music's royalty.

I home in on a familiar woman in a gorgeous black dress with pink cowboy boots—a country singer, I decide, though I can't place her name. Gotta love Tennessee, and I do, I really do. It just doesn't have enough books for the editor in me, who went to New

York for a publishing career, even if that's not where she's landed.

I guess I'm just not ready to let go of that part of my life.

Glancing at Tyler, I decide he's in too deep of a conversation with a couple of men for me to interrupt him right now. Since I have time to kill, I accept a glass of champagne from a waiter carrying a tray filled with bubbly. From there I head to a wall of open windows, stepping outside where there are heaters lit up, but they're really not needed. It's a mild October evening, while I'm certain New York City would not be so kind. I lean on the railing and stare out at the city. A part of me doesn't want to leave, and I know it. Otherwise, I'd already be back in New York and yet, I love my job at Riptide. Don't I? God, why am I even asking myself that. Of course, I do. Any hesitation I have to return to New York is about my mother.

"We meet again."

At the sound of a familiar male voice, there is a flutter in my belly and a rush of heat in my blood. I know even before I turn that this is the man I'd almost met in the Hawk building a week ago. The man from the elevator.

CHAPTER SEVEN

I turn to find him standing just behind me.

He's not in a suit tonight like Tyler Hawk, but he's also not all cowboyed out, like so many of the other guests. He's wearing dark blue jeans, paired with a black turtleneck and a brown suede jacket with sleek matching boots.

And yes, he's him.

The man who'd smelled good and charmed me in the elevator. The man who's leanly muscled and quite handsome and I noticed these things all too easily because he'd stood too close to me and yet somehow, not close enough.

"We meet again," I repeat, confirming our prior encounter.

His light blue eyes tell me that he's pleased with this answer, as if my memory of our encounter pleases him, as if he actually doubted I'd remember him.

"I blinked, and you were gone," he comments, inching nearer, and resting his arm on the railing next to us.

"I was swallowed by the crowd," I remind him. "I guess I lost you."

His lips quirk slightly, a hint of amusement in his expression as if he knows why I disappeared and, in fact, knows her by name, while I only know her as "the blonde woman."

"And now you've found me," he comments.

"I actually think you found me," I counter, remarkably comfortable with our banter when I'm usually not good at banter at all. Not with men. I'm not cool that way.

"I guess I did," he replies. "And how did that happen? Are you a new client of the firm?"

"Oh gosh, no," I say, waving off that idea. "I don't need legal services, and I'm not an entertainer. I don't act any way but badly, and I'm the worst singer ever."

"I'm going to have to wrestle you for the title of worst singer ever," he teases.

"I'd still win," I promise him. "Thus why I know to keep my creativity behind the scenes. What about you?"

His eyes light with mischief. "Some might call me creative. Others, not so much."

"Do *you* call yourself creative?"

"No," he says, still appearing amused. "I don't think I'm creative at all."

Now I'm really curious—beyond curious, really—but before I can push for more, I hear, "Ms. Wright."

My gaze shifts to find Tyler Hawk standing beside us. I straighten. "Mr. Hawk."

The man from the elevator, whose name I still don't know, straightens as well and gives a slight incline of his chin to Tyler. "Tyler," he greets.

"Dash," he replies dryly. "You're here, I see."

Dash, I repeat in my head.

The name is familiar, but before I can fully digest why, Tyler eyes me and says, "Please tell me he wasn't boring you with ghost stories."

My brows dip, and I glance at Dash. "Ghost stories? What does that mean? Who are you?"

"A dead man walking," he says, his lips curving ever so slightly before he eyes Tyler and then backs up, walking away. *Gone.* And I don't want him to be gone.

"Pain in my ass, that one," Tyler murmurs. "If he wasn't a bestseller—"

My brows furrow, and I glance at Tyler. "Wait. Bestseller?" Realization begins to hit me. "Is that—who is he?"

"He didn't tell you?"

"No," I say. "He didn't get a chance."

"Dash Black. He's the author of—"

"The Ghost Assassin," I supply, my heart fluttering excitedly. "Also known as *The Dead Man Walking*," I add. "My *God*. He's not just a bestseller. He's an international phenomenon. There are two movies about his character, Ghost. And I—" I cut myself off before I admit that I edited one of his books. Granted, I was a junior editor at the time, doing a simple copy edit, but I binged his entire twelve-book series after doing so.

Tyler arches an arrogant brow. "And you what?"

"I—just don't know why he didn't tell me who he was."

"Because he's Dash," he says, whatever that means. He doesn't explain. He moves on, and suddenly his full attention is fixed on *me*. And while Dash holds a rugged appeal, Tyler is refined, more classical in his good looks, but there is also something almost predatory about him, something that I find both familiar and uncomfortable.

"What business did you have with Allison, Ms. Wright?" he asks, making it clear he knows exactly who I am and how I came to be here tonight. "I must tell you right off the bat that she's taken a leave of absence and I'm afraid our December auction is in jeopardy."

This announcement jolts me to full attention. Allison is not here, nor will she be here, and I'm still in possession of her necklace. "Do you know how I can reach her?"

"I'd rather you focus your attention on me, Ms. Wright."

And while I find no blatant invitation in his words, there's a distinct shift in the energy between us that I can't quite explain. But he's also watching me a bit too intently, expectantly, I think.

This is the moment when I could tell him about the package meant for Allison, but I hold back, tormented by the idea that this is a personal item that belongs to her and her alone. This man is her boss. Or, what if— what if he's actually her lover? What if me telling him that I know about the note and the necklace has a negative impact on a Riptide partnership?

And as guilty as I feel about my motives, I can't help but consider my financial situation as well. Therefore, I stick to business, and business only. "I'd hoped to talk to Allison about your auction."

"Which you know about how?" he asks.

I blink at the unexpected question that sends me into yet another mental scramble. "I found out from a friend of Allison's," I say quickly, telling myself it's not a lie. I *hate* lies. I've lived with their bite and I don't like how it feels. But Allison's "friend" sent me the necklace and that led me here and technically to the auction. And because he could push for more, I quickly sidestep, ignoring his question. "As you might or might not know, the Riptide name alone pushes up price tags."

Thankfully he allows my diversion, staying on the current topic with, "I'm also aware that Riptide is neither fast nor cheap."

"We'll make up our commission and then some," I argue, certain I am correct. Riptide is the most elite of auction houses, as Dash Black is the most elite of suspenseful fiction.

"This is our second annual holiday charity event," Tyler states. "Not only have we committed to our donors and clients, we've committed to a charity that one of our clients was allowed to choose. Based on these things, we will *not* deviate from our timeline. If you can make that work, we can talk right now."

"Riptide prefers time to hype the auction. If you'll allow us—"

"Another year." His tone is absolute. "We're committed to the timeline this year. And Allison has left me in a bad spot. What I need right now is someone to coordinate and manage the event. If Riptide can do that for me—"

"We don't rush," I say. "That's not how we operate."

"Then we're done here," he states. "Enjoy the party, Ms. Wright." He starts to turn.

My heart races and for reasons I can't fully name, I'm not ready for us to be done at all. I can't let it end here and I blurt, "Riptide won't do it, but I will," before I can even think through the offer.

He pauses and turns to face me. "You will?"

"I'm on an extended leave through January."

He arches that brow of his again, obviously asking a question. How am I here on leave, and representing Riptide?

"My mother had cancer," I explain. "She's in remission, but I'm staying here through the holidays before I return to New York. My boss at Riptide has been generous with my time off, but he's well aware I'm here tonight. He sent me the invitation."

"I need someone working on this full-time."

"I can do that," I assure him. "I've trained under Riptide's founder. I've learned about every aspect of the auction business. But if I do this, I'll be filling in for Allison, on your payroll," I add, surprising myself with my boldness, *thank you, Queen Compton.* "And I need to have the go-ahead to exploit any opportunity for Riptide."

33

"Only if run by me first," he negotiates.

"Fine. Done. I'll see if I can get Riptide to sponsor the auction. That alone will bring in bidders and drive up prices. It can be a win-win for everyone. And I'm working at the art museum right now. I'll need to give them two weeks' notice."

"I'll handle the museum." That absoluteness is back in his tone.

But I don't accept his push. "They need me," I argue.

"I'll make it worth their while to do whatever you do without you. I'm on their board. What else?"

He's on the board. Of course, he is. My chin lifts slightly. "I need to have my Riptide salary matched."

He doesn't even ask the figure. He simply says, "Done."

We stare at each other, a push and pull of energy between us I don't quite understand before he says. "You're hired, Ms. Wright."

"Allison," I say quickly.

"Allison," he says softly, almost too softly. "I'll see you Monday morning." With that, he turns and walks away.

My mouth parts and I turn away from him, downing my champagne and setting my glass on a small table. *What am I doing?* I ask myself as my fingers close around the railing. I've just accepted another woman's job while holding her necklace in my purse. It's as if I want to be her and not myself, but I quickly swipe away that idea as silly. I'm not trying to live another woman's life. I'm trying to live my own. As the Tim McGraw country song says, "Live Like You Were Dying."

CHAPTER EIGHT

I have to tell Mark Compton I took another job and still manage to keep my job at Riptide.

I'm already holding my phone, preparing to spill the news to him, my finger hovering over his number when I recognize the urgency of approaching this smartly. This pitch needs to tell Mark Compton how this move benefits him and Riptide. And I can't do that when I haven't even had time to think this all through. Or when I'm still not fully convinced I'm actually taking the job at Hawk Legal. It's time to step back and think. In other words, it's time to go home before I get myself into any more trouble.

With that in mind, I hurry inside and across the room, weaving through random groups of mingling people. Fortunately, the receptionist who's been playing hostess is chatting with someone and doesn't notice me when I pass her by to head to the elevator. Once there, I quickly punch the elevator call button. Almost immediately the doors open, and I rush into the empty car, still holding my cellphone. Which would be all fine and wonderful if I didn't fling my phone across the elevator.

"Yes, wonderful, indeed," I murmur.

It's in just that moment, that Dash steps into the car, snatches the phone from the floor, and steps close, right in front of me. "At least you weren't throwing it at me," he says, punching the lobby level button before he offers it to me.

The air between us is charged and scented with his deliciously male cologne. My heart races and I reach for the phone. "Thank you," I say, and our fingers collide.

The impact is electric—heat rushes up my arm and across my chest. My gaze collides with his, and there is awareness in the depths of his potent stare. He knows I reacted to his touch, he knows, and I know. What I can't read is his own reaction. Maybe he felt what I felt. Or maybe I've entertained him or flattered him, but nothing more.

Afraid I've just made myself look like a silly fangirl, I quickly cut my gaze and slide my phone inside my purse. I expect him to step away from me, but he doesn't even pretend to move. He stays right where he is. Right in front of me.

"I assume you're leaving?" he asks, and just that easily, my gaze is drawn back to his, offering him a window view of each and every one of my reactions.

"I'm not really a party person," I say, trying to stay cool and collected when I feel hot all over, so very hot. "I don't like mingling or drinking all that much. That leaves eating, and that's not a good idea."

"Agreed," he states, and his voice is warm as he adds, "I don't like parties either, but I tolerate them for the right reasons."

I have no idea why that statement feels intimate, but it does. And yet, there is nothing intimate about the words, not really. The look in his eyes is another story, I decide, and this time I'm fairly certain that means something. Or not. I'm not good at the game of flirtation, which is probably why I choose now to say, "I know who you are."

"Then it seems only fair I know who you are," he replies, and I swear he sways in my direction.

"Allison Wright," I say, offering him my hand by way of a habit, and just as soon as I do so, I wish I could pull it back. "I—ah—" I try to lower it before he takes it, but it's too little, too late.

WHAT IF I NEVER

His strong hand closes around mine, an intimacy to the touch that goes beyond casual communication, and I all but melt right there in the elevator as he says, "Nice to meet you, Allison Wright."

His voice is a low, masculine baritone that seduces me as easily as does his hand on my body, even if it's *just* my hand. The elevator dings and halts on the lower level. Our ride is over, and reluctantly it seems, or perhaps that's my wishful thinking, he releases me. Disappointment fills me at the certainty that soon he will be gone again. Perhaps forever this time and I cannot help but feel regret with this idea.

He backs up, holding the door for me. I exit and automatically turn to face him. It is, after all, the polite thing to do.

"I'll walk you out," he offers, pausing in front of me.

"Since you're going that way," I tease, "I'll let you."

He winks, and my stomach does a somersault, and yet, there's no denying the comfortable banter between us or the ease with which we fall into step together. "You didn't want me to know who you were, did you?" I accuse, casting him a sideways look.

"I would have told you," he assures me.

And yet, somehow, I'm not sure he would have. I get that he's a megastar, especially since the movies came out, and that affects people's reactions to him. But I'm not that person for reasons I won't share with him, one of which is my father. Instead, I stop, and we turn to each other again as I confess, "I edited one of your books. I worked for your publishing house for seven years." Several people are headed toward us, and we move in unison to the side of the main walkway, near a sitting area.

"How do I not know that?" he asks in earnest.

"Ellen didn't want you to know," I say, referencing his editor. "She was out for three months with a medical issue. But bottom line, I edited your book. That made me judge the book, not the man. Liking or hating your book doesn't make you a likable person. And to that point, I have edited several wildly successful authors who've sold millions of books. I don't like a few of those authors, one in particular. But I like that author's books."

"Do I dare guess who that is?"

"You can ask, but I won't answer. That would be rude and not the point," I add. "The point is that the fact that you pen the *Ghost Assassin* books doesn't change one single first impression I have of you," I say. "And it doesn't make me like you. That would be shallow of me. Nothing about my first impression of you has changed."

He studies me for several long beats and then asks, "And what, Allison, is your impression of me?"

That charge is in the air between us again and my mouth goes dry. I could say so many things, but I don't. I say, "You smell good, and I feel that's a trick question, so that's all I'm saying."

"I smell good," he says, his eyes lighting with a boyish mischief I find quite charming.

"Yes." I dare to admit. "You do."

"So do you, Allison," he replies, and I swear my name comes out a raspy suggestion. "Do you want to know my first impression of you?" he asks.

That question jolts me, and I hold up my hands. "Please, no." I turn and start walking.

He laughs and falls into step with me again. "Chicken."

"Oh yes," I agree as we reach the front doors of the building.

He laughs, this low, sexy laugh that I feel in my sex, as silly as that probably sounds. That's how affected I am by this man, which is crazy. I've been around powerful, rich, sexy men often. They don't affect me like this one. He's different. I'm different around him. We reach the automatic door and I go in first with him following, aware of him behind me—nervous about our goodbye which is about to follow.

Once we're outside, the cold washes over me, the reminder that I left my coat in the car oh so clear. I shiver and hug myself. Dash is right there almost immediately, handing off his ticket to the bellman. "Do you have a coat?" he asks. "We can give them our tickets and go back inside to wait."

"No ticket," I say. "I parked down the road and stupidly left my coat in the car to avoid struggling with it."

"I'll walk you to your car," he offers.

"Not necessary," I say quickly. "Thank you, though. I'll be fine. I made sure I was under a streetlight, and this area is highly populated."

"I'm walking you," he says, shrugging out of his jacket. "I'm wearing long sleeves. You can wear this."

Before I can object, he's in front of me, sliding his jacket around me and pulling it closed, his wickedly wonderful scent all around me now. "Thank you," I say, softly.

"No thanks needed," he assures me. "Let's walk."

"What about your car?" I worry.

"I tipped well enough when I arrived that they won't mind waiting on me. Which way?"

I motion to the left and then hold onto the jacket, and there's no question now. Dash Black is walking me to my car and I'm wearing his jacket. I can't help but feel a little thrill in the moment.

CHAPTER NINE

My car is parked on the east side of the museum where I've been working, and not far from the craziness of the strip of bars and restaurants off Broadway. As Dash and I begin the walk, we pass a bus playing loud country music and filled with drunk people dancing and acting stupid.

"Ever been on one of those?" he asks.

"Oh gosh yes," I admit. "I grew up here. I was happily stupid, drunk, and dancing many a time."

He laughs. "Would you do it now?"

"You'd have to get me drunk first," I promise him. "What about you?"

"I've never been on one, nor do I want to be on one."

"Well, at least they're not drinking and driving," I say. "There's always that."

"Yes," he says, sobering on the reply, his gaze shifting forward, and there's a distinctly sharper quality to his mood.

We stop at the intersection and I turn to him. "Did I just say something wrong?"

"Not at all," he says, but the light changes, and he motions me forward, offering nothing more.

I'm suddenly awkward with him for the first time ever, but fortunately, I don't have to wallow in the weirdness. As soon as we cross the walkway, he seems to soften again in a palpable way before he asks, "Are you still in publishing?"

"No. I left a little over a year ago." A thought hits me and it's not a good one. I stop dead in my track and rotate to face him. We're in front of the museum now, a bench right beside us. Another party bus goes by, but I

41

tune it out. "I'm not here for your publisher or any publisher. I work for Riptide Auction House now. I hope you don't think I have an agenda. I didn't know who you were. I wasn't here for you."

"I didn't think that, Allison," he assures me and steps closer, towering over me, the stretch of his sweater over his chest fairly magnificent. "Why'd you leave publishing?" he asks. "You seem to love books. An auction house doesn't exactly resemble publishing."

"Books and treasures, one and the same."

"Are they?"

"More than you might think. And as for how it happened, I was in a weird place when I walked into a coffee shop at the same time as the founder of Riptide. We hit it off, and she offered me a job. I took it rather spontaneously, which really isn't me. I'm not spontaneous."

"I wonder if you're not more spontaneous than you might think," he observes. "Do you regret your decision?"

"My mother says regrets are for sinking ships," I say, and the statement punches at me pretty darn hard. She never once thought of herself as a sinking ship, and yet that is how I've felt about myself these past few weeks. "I like to think I'm not that."

"Wise words from a beautiful lady."

My cheeks heat with a compliment from this man of all men. "Thank you, and you must be freezing." I motion to the side street. "I'm right over there. You don't have to—"

"No," he says. "I don't, but I want to. I'm coming with you."

His insistence pleases me.

We head in that direction, and I dig the keys out of my purse to my ancient college car, a Nissan Altima that's seen better days, not sure why my mother kept the thing, but glad for it now. I don't actually have another car and with good reason. Parking is expensive in New York City, and traffic is hell.

"This is me," I say, stopping at the driver's door and click the locks before turning to face him. "Thank you for walking me." I slide out of his jacket and offer it back to him.

He accepts it and slips it on, but he doesn't make any effort to leave. He's studying me again, a bit intensely actually. "Why were you at the party tonight?" he asks.

"I'm here in Nashville for a few months, until January actually. Tyler needs help with his charity auction. I'm going to fill in for the other Allison." I know then that I've made my decision. I'm taking the job.

"You're going to work for Tyler," he says, and there's an odd vibe of disapproval to his tone.

"Yes. I agreed to work for Tyler."

"What about Riptide?" he asks.

"I'm forging a partnership between Hawk Legal and Riptide and, in the meantime, helping a good cause. The auction is for charity." I frown. "I actually don't even know what it is yet or which Hawk client chose the charity. I'm passionate about helping a good cause. I can't believe I didn't ask for details but it's your chosen organization, right?"

"Drive Sober and Safely. Yes. It's my charity. And I'm sure you'll do an amazing job. Goodnight, Allison." He steps back from me, turns, and walks away. It's as if I've turned a switch from on to off, and I don't know why.

CHAPTER TEN

I arrive at my parents' place in the old Nashville neighborhood of Germantown at ten o'clock.

It's late for my mom and stepdad, who are early to bed and earlier to rise, but with the garage on the east side of the house, I easily slip inside and kill the engine without disturbing them. The walk to the pool house where I've been staying the past three months is down a short, dark path I know well. I didn't grow up in this house, but I spent my later teen years here, and a few friends and I adored the pool house. It was our hideaway. Sneaking to it in the dark was a skill I mastered oh so well. Doing so felt naughty but really quite nice since that was the extent of my bad girl years.

Truly, I had no idea what naughty was back then. I wish sometimes that I could return to that age of innocence, but then again, I'm not convinced I wouldn't make the same mistakes all over again.

Reaching the door easily, I unlock it, and once I'm inside the house, I turn on the lights and kick off my shoes, leaving them by the door.

Inhaling on a familiar scent, I realize, with a mixed reaction of hot and cold, that I can smell Dash's cologne on my clothes.

I left him back at the museum, but he's still with me in all kinds of ways. I'm coordinating an auction for his chosen charity, for his legal counsel. I will see him again. I'm thrilled by the prospect but also fretful. I'm confused about this man. I'm confused about a lot of things in my life right now.

Suddenly parched, I walk to the fridge, grab a bottle of water and then sit down at the kitchen bar that serves as my table. The pool house is tiny, the air doesn't work, but thankfully the cooler weather has delivered me some relief on that end. Not that tiny really matters to me. I live and rent in Manhattan where tiny apartments rule. I rent, but right before my mother's illness, I'd been considering buying a place. I'd thought it represented stability and independence, but buying a home wouldn't have made me feel any more stable when my mother was fighting for her life. Nothing will ever make me feel stable again, not even her remission. I'll always fear the next cancer scan.

Always.

How am I ever going to go back to New York and leave her here?

This brings me to Mark's offer to move her there. She won't go, of course. She and my stepdad have a life here, a good one, too. She's a nurse. He's an established fire chief. They both enjoy their work. The hardest part of my mother's illness for both of them, it seemed, was not being able to fix the problem themselves. They felt helpless. So did I.

I blink myself back into focus and the here and now. I worry that Mark is going to think I took this job with Tyler Hawk as a setup for me to stay here. And maybe, subconsciously, that's exactly what I did. Riptide is a future though, a dream job, that I am blessed to have. But I only have one mother and my savings is taking a beating.

My mind races and an idea hits me, a really good idea that's a win-win for everyone involved. I quickly dial Mark, "Ms. Wright," he greets, answering on the first ring. "It's late. I expect the party went well and you have good news to share?"

I glance at the clock and cringe. It's after eleven in New York. "Hi. Sorry. I didn't even think about the time difference. But yes, I'm calling about the party. I met Tyler Hawk. I have an idea how to make this auction he's holding good for us all."

"An idea," he repeats dryly. "Do please, tell me about this *idea*."

"First, I want to just remind you that Hawk Legal represents a huge chunk of country royalty, among other genres of talent, all of whom are the perfect clientele for Riptide. But the country music world especially, because it's rather removed from the New York City scene."

"All right," he says. "You have my attention. Keep going."

"The auction is this December. Tyler's coordinator for the event took an emergency leave, much like I was forced to do. Hawk Legal is committed to a charity auction and to its donors. They have to move forward."

"Which rules us out," he comments. "We don't operate that quickly. It compromises the auction numbers."

"Understood, but I don't think this has to knock us out," I say. "I'm here for a few months, and I can handle their auction—they have to pay me of course, not you— but Riptide could sponsor the event as well. It's great press with a high-profile clientele. On top of all of this," I say, talking really fast, trying to get it all out before he says no, "I told Tyler Hawk, I'd have the right to seize and exploit all opportunities for Riptide, of which I plan to create many. So there. That's the idea."

"How much will this sponsorship cost me?"

"How much are you willing to pay?" I counter.

"Get me a price. Then I'll let you know."

"Okay," I say. "Yes, I can do that."

"Are you working for him or me, Ms. Wright?"

"You," I say quickly. "Or well, I guess both of you, but I'm going to turn this into a Riptide win. I'm going to come back and make you glad you kept me on."

"Big words, Ms. Wright. Big words. All talk and no action makes me displeased."

"It makes me just as displeased."

"Doubtful, but let's see what you can do. Get me more details. Goodnight, Ms. Wright." He pauses and adds, "If you act in fear, so will she." With that warning, he hangs up.

I'm left to digest his words. Of course, the *she* he references is my mother. And his words match the words spoken to me by my mother's doctor.

Mark Compton just read me and my motives like a book and in turn, he gave me advice, not a walking ticket. But then, his mother is sick, too. He understands what some cannot. I'm torn between two worlds, but this auction feels like solid ground, and even more so, a purpose.

Feeling motivated, I'm ready to educate myself and head in, firing hot. I key in my password on my MacBook and pull up Hawk Legal, clicking on the "About Us" button. The first thing I scan for is Allison. There's nothing about her on the site, but then again, there is nothing about anyone who is not an attorney. There's, of course, the founding family's story with Tyler Hawk in a featured position on the webpage. He's thirty-four, a graduate of Yale, and he's worked his entire career with the firm. He represents some of the biggest athletes, musicians, and actors on planet Earth. The interesting thing is that his client list does not seem to include Dash Black. Maybe one of his parents represents Dash.

That brings me to my interest in Dash Black and how easily that happened.

WHAT IF I NEVER

I google his name. He has a Wikipedia page, which informs me that he's thirty-six, and an ex-FBI agent turned writer. I had no idea. I'm shocked that he was an FBI agent considering his father is—and I knew this—Nathan Black, a famous author of a dystopian series that has sold millions upon millions of copies worldwide. There are comic books for his series as well, also written by him. I'm really surprised there hasn't been a movie yet, but I've heard it's been on and off several times. He wasn't with our publishing house, but it's a small industry. I wonder how he dealt with Dash nabbing a movie deal before he did? I mean, Nathan is known to be difficult. An asshole, actually, which oh God, what if Dash thought I was talking about his father when I said I'd edited an author who was just that: an asshole? I draw in a breath and let it out. His father has had the same editor for his entire career. He won't think that.

Relieved by this realization, I move on.

Dash's mother was Alice Black. She's deceased, the cause of death was an aneurysm. God, how horrible and unexpected. I pull up her photo and find that she was beautiful and only forty-nine when she died. She was also the founder of the Alice Home Shopping Network, *the* ultimate home shopping network. Five years ago, I think, scanning the date. Which was almost exactly when Dash's first book hit the shelves. Just the idea of how the two events must have played against each other for him undoes me. I tab back to the Wikipedia page. Dash had a younger brother, who is also deceased. He died a sophomore in college in a car accident. Unreal. Dash Black has known tragedy and pain, which sadly, is probably what makes him such a good writer. He funnels his emotions into his words, which is a lesson I need to learn in concept, at least. I'm not a writer, but I will funnel my emotions into this auction.

And as a bonus, maybe I'll find Allison. This job, and helping other people, is exactly what the doctor ordered.

I reach in my purse and pull out the necklace that I had to carry in a velvet bag to fit in my purse. The box it came in is on the table and I open it, settling the necklace back on top of the velvet. The truly unique, and stunning, star-shaped diamonds wink and twinkle like real stars in a night sky. It's gorgeous, and I wonder if, in its beauty, the sender believed he and Allison would find happiness?

I could have told him the answer. I've learned from first-hand experience.

No, diamonds and gifts do *not* bring happiness, nor do they substitute for love. And they absolutely do not erase the sins of betrayal.

CHAPTER ELEVEN

I work myself into a nervous wreck over the weekend.

A part of me decides that Tyler Hawk was just in the moment Friday night. I could arrive to Hawk Legal's offices on Monday morning and have no job at all. That thought lends itself to an even bigger bucket of nerves on the morning of my first day of work. I mean, the man didn't even tell me what time to report, but I improvise. According to the website, the day starts at eight in the morning.

I arrive at seven forty-five, stepping off the elevator with so many jitters I'm fairly certain they've formed a puddle at my feet. Katie, the receptionist, is already behind her desk, looking youthful and pretty in a light blue dress, her brown hair flowing softly around her shoulders. She pops to her feet at the sight of me, and instead of that air of privilege she's offered me in the past, she smiles a greeting. Apparently, Tyler Hawk wasn't just talking. I'm expected.

"I see you've been lured to the dark side," she teases, holding up a finger as she snags the phone receiver, and presses it to her ear. Punching a button before she speaks to whoever she's called. "Vivienne, you are summoned. Come cover for me, sweetie."

With that, she sets the receiver back in place, rounds the desk to join me, and gives me a once-over before announcing, "You look fabulous. I love what you're wearing today," she adds of my simple, but I hope elegant black dress. "Armani, right?"

"It is," I agree. "And thank you."

"Of course. I'm a label whore and Armani is so very Hawk Legal chic, which is a perfect choice. Everyone here is oh so stylish and it's by demand. Our clientele can roll out of bed, come in here wearing cut-out jeans and a shirt with a stain on it, but we have to look like we're going to church, or we're beneath them. Okay, we're beneath some of them no matter what, but you can't let that get to you. Bottom line," she says as she does a mock fluff of her hair and offers up her best snobby voice, "you look fabulous, darlin'."

I decide right then she's not a snob, but more guarded, by necessity of the job. My nerves break into a laugh. I like her. She's adorable and sweet. "Thank you, darlin'," I reply with my own best snobby voice, not about to tell her my dress is a secondhand find from a little Manhattan shop a friend at Riptide told me about. It would have cost me seven hundred dollars in a box store. I got it for ninety-three-fifty plus tax.

Right then, a pretty Asian woman appears on the opposite side of the desk and waves at me. "I'm Vivienne, but call me Vivi. Only my mother calls me Vivienne." She points at Katie. "And her, to irritate me."

Katie grins and nods. "It works."

Vivi rolls her eyes at Katie and speaks to me. "I work in accounting right around the corner and cover for Katie here and there. In return, she gives me hell."

"Yep," Katie agrees. "I really do."

"Nice to meet you, Vivi," I say, smiling at the pair.

Vivi tilts her head to study me and then glances at Katie. "You're right," she declares. "She looks like her and just as stylish, too."

Confused, I eye Katie who explains, "She means you look like the other Allison. You could be sisters."

I blink, surprised. I look like the other Allison? I'm speechless, and I can't help but think of the necklace I received for a woman with the same name who I'm told resembles me. It's one coincidence on top of another. It's almost too much. I'm not sure what to do with that information, but for now, Katie motions for me to follow her, and I tuck it away for later review.

Soon we're in a hallway, and it's a short walk to our right before she pauses at a doorway. "This will be your office," she says. "Allison's office." She gives me a sideways look. "Funny how it's been Allison's office times two."

It's borderline strange, I think, entering the indicated space to find a desk, a small round conference table, and a sitting area with a bookshelf on either side of the corner behind it. "It's a wonderful office," I say. "It smells good. Like—"

"Vanilla and honey," she says. "She had some candle she always burned."

"And the smell still lingers. You're sure Allison won't mind me using her office?"

Her lips purse. "We're not sure when she'll be back. It'll be fine. If she really does show back up, we'll move you." She motions to the desk. "If you want to put your purse and briefcase down, I'll show you around."

They'll move me if needed? Hmmm. Okay. That sounds very temporary, but then I *am* temporary, I remind myself. I'm here to fill a short gap and obviously, Allison knew someone had to help in her time away. I try not to think about how my being here might affect my role at Riptide. Allison might be doing the same about her departure and time away from here. This is her job. I have to respect that as fact.

For now, I hurry to my desk, and open the drawer to the left, hoping for a spot big enough for my oversized purse. My gaze catches on a red envelope and curiosity has me vowing to inspect it later. For now, the drawer is too small and my purse too big.

"This," Katie announces, stepping across from me and indicating a folder in the center of the desk, "has everything inside you will need to get started. Allison handed it to me the day she left. It should have the names of donors and so on."

I shut the drawer and she taps the MacBook sitting next to the file. "This is also for your use. You can take it home and treat it as your own. Natalie from HR will stop by to see you in about an hour. She had a meeting planned this morning and you were unexpected." She motions me to the door again.

"What is Allison's role here?" I ask, joining Katie in the hallway again.

"Charity liaison," she says, motioning me to the left, and we start walking. "She coordinates all things charity oriented. That job really expanded when we launched the annual auction. Last year was a really over-the-top fancy event but kind of thrown together last minute. She was very high-profile with our clients and a big part of building our public image."

I want to ask if she knew Allison well, or knows how to reach her, but Katie pauses at a door with her hand on the knob. "This is the restaurant and coffee bar," and already she's opening the door and urging me inside.

I pass through the entryway to a full-blown café, complete with a large seating area of cute little tables, a full coffee bar, and an area where a chef is making what smells like waffles and omelets.

"Everything here is free, so enjoy," she informs me. "Unfortunately, I hate to run off and leave you, but Vivi has a meeting. She can't cover me much longer. Grab a coffee or whatever you want. I'll check on you the minute I can."

"No problem. I'm resourceful. Thanks so much, Katie."

"Of course," she says. "Welcome. I'm so glad he finally gave in and hired someone. It's been weeks, and Vivi and I have been trying to handle the auction. But the good news is that I can answer a lot of questions you might have after you look at the file. Vivi and I have been stressing over this, but we'll both help you in any way we can. See you soon." With that, she rushes away, leaving me to wonder about Allison and the hunt for someone to fill her shoes. Was Tyler holding out for her return, or was he really looking for a replacement, and I just happened to show up at the right time?

CHAPTER TWELVE

Pondering the likelihood that I just happened to show up at the right time and at the right place as unlikely, but possible, I remind myself that's exactly how I got the job at Riptide. Dismissing my weird vibe about this job and the other Allison, at least for now, I walk to the coffee bar and order a latte, a cinnamon mocha that is a house specialty, apparently. A few minutes later, I'm sipping a truly delicious drink when I settle behind my desk. I open the drawer and pull out the red envelope. Inside I find two airline tickets to Italy, with dates that have passed. There's a note that reads: *We need this.* That's all. There's no signature. There was no signature on the card with the necklace, either. Maybe this explains where Allison is right now. Maybe she went to Italy. She wouldn't need the paper tickets. And yet, the dates for the travel are mid-August. It's October 11th today and everyone seems to speak of Allison's departure as more recent. And besides, would she really leave the auction in limbo for a trip with a lover?

I guess some people might, right? I'm just not one of those people. Yes, I left the museum without notice, but the truth is, my job there wasn't something that required a special knowledge of art or collectibles. It was just something to keep me from focusing on my mother's mortality. And the fact that my role wasn't huge is exactly why my supervisor easily let me go for the Hawk Legal job, with nothing more than a Saturday morning good luck email. Even so, I emailed her back an offer to help on the side. She declined. And that was for a job that was not a big deal. The auction isn't just about Hawk Legal. It's about a charity event to help other people.

There's a shift in the air, and I look up to find Tyler Hawk standing in the doorway. I inhale slightly, taken aback by just how good-looking my new boss actually is, not sure why I haven't truly acknowledged that fact until now. He's tall and handsome personified, in a dark blue suit fitted to his athletic body. There is no question that Tyler Hawk screams power, money, and demand.

And I'm not sure how long he's been standing there, watching me. Too long, I decide. "Hi," I say, sliding the tickets back into the envelope, and shoving it under the folder. "I'm here, but you know that, right?" I cringe with the stupid rambling, trying to tell myself that most people find it more charming than stupid, but he's staring at me with hooded eyes, and somehow, I don't think Tyler Hawk is one of those people.

"I see you found the coffee bar," he comments. "I hope we're up to Riptide standards?"

"Oh yes," I assure him quickly. "The restaurant, the office, it's all wonderful." I settle my hand on the file. "I'm about to dig into Allison's work. Is there anything I should know?"

"Read the file, and then we'll talk," he replies.

"Am I allowed to contact the clients and introduce myself?"

He walks into the office, toward me, and I push to my feet. We end up face to face with the desk between us. Well, as face to face as we can be with him towering over me. "Are you going to pitch them Riptide?" he asks softly, a challenge in his words, his blue eyes, so unlike Dash's in their sharpness, their darkness, steady on my face, watching my reaction—looking for a reason to send me packing.

I could bristle at the question, but I don't. Instead, I say, "I understand that any high-profile client represents money for your firm. I wouldn't do anything to jeopardize your business. And while I also understand that you fear my loyalty is with Riptide, not Hawk Legal, I can assure you that I'm motivated to build allies, not enemies. And—" I hesitate to get too personal.

He seizes on my hesitation. "And what, Ms. Wright?"

I could hold back, the way I could have bristled at his last question, and perhaps I should, but he already knows about my mother. And in some way, this right now is my interview, the one we bypassed, and I have to respect his need to trust me. "I need this right now. The fact that this is a charity event motivates me. It gives me a purpose that doesn't include worrying about my mother."

His eyes narrow. "She's in remission, though, correct?"

"She is," I confirm, "but cancer is forever a part of her life. When it's time for me to leave, you'll probably be pushing me out of the door. It's hard to leave her behind." I've now taken this a little too far, and I add, "I wouldn't use your client list to pitch Riptide. If a mutually beneficial opportunity comes up, I'll talk to you about it."

His lips quirk ever so slightly before he says, "Mutually beneficial. I do like how that sounds." I read what I think is a hint of suggestion in that comment, but I can't be sure before he adds, "It's Dash Black's charity we're covering this year."

He's studying me again, looking for a reaction, and I school my features and pray he doesn't find one. "He told me," I say. "And I'm frankly relieved the charity is not a cancer organization. As much as that subject touches my heart, I'd be fearful cancer has cut me too deeply and too recently for me to be professional right now."

Seconds tick by that stretch eternally before he says, "Check in with me before you leave tonight." He says nothing more. He just turns and, in a blink, he's gone and gone before he gives me the go-ahead to call clients. Gone before I can ask him if he called Riptide. Did he even check my references?

Surely he did. Or he will.

CHAPTER THIRTEEN

I'd like to think that love is priceless, but I've learned that when the very concept of love is subjective, so is the cost. In the case of an auction and a possession desired, which is to some the definition of love, value is created in dollars and usually an element of emotion. There is often an emotional component to bidding, but the monetary value supports the price tag. This is exactly why establishing a baseline starting bid as high as possible is critical. Sought after possessions are like sought after companions: the harder to get, the bigger the payoff in satisfaction, or at least that's how we hope it turns out. To become sought after, a person, or an item, establishes value in some way, shape, or form. Maybe that is just in who they are as a person, or how they look, or who they know.

Or who their father is.

I grimace and shove aside that thought.

Bottom line, it's lunchtime, and I've established a basic fact: the auction has no established value.

None.

Not a penny.

I've found an Excel spreadsheet that Allison created, listing out each donated item for the auction. The list is small, and while a few items appear alluring from an auction standpoint, nothing has been assessed. We can't establish a starting bid if we don't know where we need the bid to end. The good news is that there is an extensive prospect list with well-known sports and entertainment personalities, as well as an array of high-profile business people. It's not a list I'm uncomfortable with. After working in publishing and at Riptide I've been exposed to money and power. The calls and contacts I can handle, but I can't create time. And I need time or manpower, or really both, but I'll settle for one or the other. I need to speak to Tyler about that and the Riptide sponsorship, though I'm not sure there is enough here yet to even entice Mark to align himself with the endgame.

I stand up and sit back down. I don't even know where Tyler's office is located. I grab my phone and punch the operator button. Katie answers immediately. "Hi, Allison. What can I help with?"

"How do I reach Tyler?"

"He just left for a meeting," she says, "but he's in the offices on the other side of the elevators. Those are his private offices. The partners are all on the upper level. He's a bit of an isolationist."

"And his parents?"

"His father is upset with the partners. His mother is rarely in the office anymore. She started another business, and don't ask me what. I have no idea. That's just the rumor I heard."

Somehow Tyler being an isolationist doesn't really surprise me.

"And just an FYI," she adds, "he's extension eleven on the panel. There should be a phone list somewhere in or on your desk."

"Okay. I'll find it. Thanks. Can you leave him a message to call me?"

"Of course. Can I help?"

"Not right now, but thank you. I do appreciate everything."

"I'll check in later," she promises. "I really will. It's been nuts today. Has HR been by?"

"Not yet."

"I'll nudge her. And I have a visitor. Gotta run."

WHAT IF I NEVER

We disconnect, and I decide the best thing I can do right now is to get organized and fully acclimated to everything I can. For now, I start by putting a call into Millie Roberts, the head of the charity association, and setting up a meeting for the next day. After that, I call the event venue and set yet another meeting for the next day. From there, I start the tedious process of researching auction prices on the items we do have confirmed. A few things are potential hot ticket items and I email photos and notes to Casey Reid, our expert at Riptide. If the prices are high enough, I'm going to try to strike a bargain between Tyler and Mark.

My stomach rumbles, and I cannot ignore it. I decide to head to the restaurant to grab a quick bite. Still eager to get my work done, I haul the MacBook along for what is now a late lunch, considering it's after one. Once I'm in the restaurant, I end up with an egg salad croissant sandwich that looks amazing, an iced sugar cookie, and more coffee. Obviously, I can't do this kind of eating every day, or I won't fit into my clothes. I grab a small table for two beside a window that overlooks the city, open my MacBook, and begin researching a vase—yes, a vase—while eating one of the best sandwiches I've ever had in a company restaurant. Amazing.

I've just stuffed the last large bite in my mouth when a pair of muscular legs appear on the opposite side of the table. In this place, where everyone is someone, my visitor is obviously someone *important*. I grab my napkin, cover my mouth and try to swallow without making a fool of myself, but the sandwich is dry, and it won't go down.

I'm all but choking when I glance up to find the one and only Dash Black standing above me.

CHAPTER FOURTEEN

My eyes go wide at the sight of the sexy bestselling author, and his eyes light with amusement at the whole show I just put on. I'm still performing, because that bite of sandwich just won't go down.

I turn away from him, forcing myself to chew and swallow quickly, and grabbing my coffee to sip before I clear my throat and face him again, with a less than brilliant greeting of, "Hi." And Lord, help me, the man is sin and sex, in black jeans and a snug black T-shirt, and a matching blazer paired with boots.

"Hi," he says, his eyes still dancing because, of course, I've entertained him. At least I repaid him for all the entertainment he's given me with his books, I decide dryly. "You okay?" he asks.

"Other than embarrassing myself, yes, just fine. It was an incredible sandwich, which I'm sure you guessed since I was stuffing it in my face."

"I would, too," he says. "The egg salad is one of my favorites." He motions to the chair. "Can I sit?"

He wants to sit? "With me?" Lord, help me, that just came out of my mouth.

"Yes, Allison," he laughs. "With you."

"Oh," I say, "well yes, yes, of course."

He slides into the seat across from me and eyes my cookie. I pull it between us. "You can have half, but not all of it. It was the last one, and I need to know if it's as good as it looks."

"It is," he assures me. "Which I know because I grab one every time I'm here. I'd normally fight you for it, but since it's your first day I'll let you have it."

"You sure?"

"Completely," he assures me. "Enjoy it."

I will, I think, but not while he's watching me. "How often are you here?" I ask as he's sounding like he's here so much he might as well work here.

"It depends on what negotiations I have going on at the time," he says, shifting the topic. "Millie Roberts called me and told me you set up a meeting with her."

"I see," I say, sitting up taller at the knowledge that the charity head reported back on my actions almost immediately. "Is that why you're here? Did I overstep?"

"Not at all," he says. "I'm glad to see some attention being put on the event. I was starting to think my check was going to be the only one they get this year."

I relax with that response and quickly say, "Definitely not. I'm on this, but I have to be honest, Allison hadn't done much to prepare. She must have left quickly."

"That's what I hear," he says. "I get the impression Tyler gambled on her coming back sooner than later. Can you pull it together, or do I need to prepare Millie for a cancellation?"

I hold up a hand. "No, no. We won't cancel. I'm a little concerned about the timeline, but I'm resourceful. I'll find a way to make this go well."

He studies me for several beats and surprises me with, "Why are you here? Why are you doing this?"

I blink at the unexpected question. "I—well, the auction and—"

"I mean in Nashville. Riptide is in New York City."

My fingers curl into my palms on the table and I wet my lips, a bite in my chest with the direction we're traveling, but it's unavoidable. I value honesty and I try to offer it where I can and where it matters. I think it does now. "My mother had cancer."

Realization washes over his handsome face and his expression softens. "Had?"

66

"She's in remission," I explain.

"You don't seem relieved," he assesses quite perceptively, seeing more than I've intended.

Unbidden, my eyes burn and my lashes lower. *Damn it.* I quickly blink away the sensation, I hope, and look at him, but I can't seem to find a fluff answer. Not on this topic. "What does remission even mean?"

"More time," he promises me.

"How much?" I ask, and I want him to answer, I want him to use the magic of his words to offer me the world.

"Do any of us ever really know how much time we have left?"

Wise words.

His words, I know from reading up on him, come from experience, from losing his own mother.

And because of this, that simple statement slides inside me and grabs hold of me in a way none other have in a very long time. "No one has put it in that perspective for me. I think they're all too afraid of saying the wrong thing."

"All we can do is live—"

"—like tomorrow is our last day?"

"Exactly," he agrees.

"And that pretty much sums up why I'm here and not in New York, working the dream job many would kill for right now."

"Because you're afraid to live?" he challenges.

"That's a bold statement from a man who barely knows me."

"I'm simply stating what I understand."

My eyes narrow. "From personal experience?"

"Yes," he readily confirms. "From experience." But he offers nothing more, making it clear he doesn't intend to share more. "At some point," he adds, "you have to move forward. You'll have to decide if you want to go back home."

"I'm pretty sure *this* is home. New York is the place I live."

"But Riptide is holding your job for you?"

"They are," I confirm. "Generously so."

I steel myself for him to push for more, perhaps beyond my comfort zone, even more so than now, but he seems to read me and changes the subject. "That tells me we're lucky to have you on this auction. What can I do to help?"

"Nothing yet," I say, and because I want to know more about this man, I add, "but you obviously chose the charity for a reason. It means something to you, and maybe I can pick your brain at some point about how to do it justice."

"Anything and anytime," he agrees and while he offers me nothing personal, no look into the pain that guided his advice, his words are warm, intimate even, I think. His eyes even more so. "Why don't you take my number?" he suggests. "You can call me when you need me."

He wants me to take his number. Dash Black wants me to take his number, and somehow despite the flutter in my belly, I play it cool. I remind myself that he's just a man. A ridiculously talented man, but just a man. "All right," I agree, pulling my phone from my pocket. "I'm ready."

He dictates, and I plug in the number and then text him: *This is Allison Wright.* When his phone pings, I say, "That was me."

"Perfect. Now I know how to reach you, and you know how to reach me."

I'm suddenly caught in the magnetic pull of his eyes, his presence, or maybe it's something else, something that is me and him, not just him, and I'm too afraid of where that leads me to admit that fully. I'm vulnerable right now, and I know it. I can feel how much this man could affect me, and that means good and bad.

There's a shift in the air, an energy that breaks our connection, and instinctively, we both look for the source. That's when I realize the blonde woman he'd been with at the elevator that first day we met, is walking toward us. Oh God. What a fool I am. I look down and reach for my coffee, needing to occupy myself with something, anything but this man and his woman.

"Allison," he says softly, willing me to look at him, his attention on me when it should be on her.

I steel myself for the impact and school my features, I hope, to unaffected. "Yes?" I ask, meeting his stare, which still feels intimate, and I am confused, so very confused by this man.

"I want you to meet my agent," he says. "This charity means a lot to her as well. She'll be helpful as we move forward."

We.

As *we* move forward.

This is not a man who uses words without intent. He chose them, used them, wanted me to understand them. Us. We. What is this?

The woman stops beside us. "There you are, Dash," she says. "I've been looking for you. And why are you always eating?"

The jest simply confirms a comfortable, personal relationship that does nothing to make this moment any easier for me.

Dash stands, and I follow him to his feet, both of us angling toward the woman. I can see her fully now, up close and personal, and the conclusion is as expected. She's gorgeous, her skin pale perfection, her eyes remarkably light blue, almost the same shade as Dash's. "Bella," he says. "Meet Allison, the woman I told you about."

"Right," she concludes "The woman from Riptide." She glances over at me. "Welcome, Allison."

"Allison," Dash says next, motioning to the other woman. "This is Bella. My agent and," he looks at me, "*my sister.*"

His sister? Did he just say his sister?

He did.

He said sister.

I try not to gape, but I look at her and then him, and damn it, there is relief flooding my body in a ridiculous wave, I'm fairly certain is all over my face. And oh yes, the mischief is back in Dash's eyes, as he adds, "She's a bitch, but only to me. She'll be a good person to know around here."

"Asshole," Bella snaps. "I just got you double on your contract." She shoves his arm and eyes me. "He's never grateful. *Ever.* And I'd tell you more—all the gossip he doesn't want me to tell—but sadly, considering I'd enjoy that, I can't right now. I have to steal Dash for a conference call with his publisher, but I'll find you tomorrow. I want to chat about the charity auction. I really appreciate you swooping in to save us." She motions to Dash. "Come." She turns and starts walking away, quite obviously leaving him to say his goodbye to me on his own.

Dash shifts his body toward mine. "You thought she was my girlfriend," he accuses softly.

"I mean, well—it's not my place to think anything."

"Why not?"

I blink at him, tongue-tied and finally just say, "I have no idea how to answer that."

He smiles, and damn, it's a sexy smile. "You have my number. Call me after your meeting tomorrow."

It's both a question and a command, and oddly, considering I'm not exactly great at taking commands, both sit well with me. He turns and walks away, all swagger and hot man, and there is no denying that I'm melting for him, right here in the Hawk Legal café.

LISA RENEE JONES

CHAPTER FIFTEEN

I sit down at my desk and do the only thing a girl can do when she's trapped in a small office with a cookie after getting hot and bothered by a man like Dash Black. I stuff a big bite of the cookie in my mouth. It's at that moment, that a bosomy, fiftyish redhead in a black dress and heels walks into my office. Because of course, why would I shut my door before stuffing my face?

"Best damn cookie in the city," she approves, closing the space between me and her to sit in front of me. "I'm Natalie Jolie from Human Resources—no relation to the movie star because I'm just not that lucky in life."

At this point, I've thankfully swallowed without choking and I say, "Hi, Natalie Jolie, no relation to the movie star. I'm not that lucky either, or you wouldn't have caught me with a cookie in my mouth."

"You're luckier than me. I couldn't get one today. They sell out by lunchtime every day, and I've been in meetings. You obviously wowed the boss. I found out about you at seven this morning."

"I think it's more about the right time and place for both of us. He needs help with the auction, and I'm here for a few months before going back to New York."

"Yeah well, I heard your story, and you sounded too good to be true. Reminded me of the last man I dated. I wanted to check you out and check you out fast. So I called Riptide."

"I would have given you my boss's direct number, but I never got the chance. Tyler hired me and told me to show up. Then he walked away."

She laughs. "Sounds like Tyler. The man's a bull in a china shop, but somehow, he never breaks anything. This time is no exception. I talked to Crystal Smith."

Crystal being the operations manager at Riptide.

"She wants you back at work," she continues, "but she told me that she and the entire team at Riptide support your need to be here right now." She clears her throat. "I know about your mother."

"I told Tyler. It's not a secret. She's in remission. I just—to be frank—I'm not ready to leave her."

"My mother's a bitch, and I'd still feel the same way. I get it. And I'm going to tell you the truth, honey, I haven't done your paperwork. Tyler told me about it this morning, no warning at all."

"No worries," I say. "I'm committed to the auction."

"Good. Allison leaving like she did has been a bit of hell. Fair warning, people are going to confuse you two, and I'm sure she dropped the ball on a few things that were promised to people."

"What do I need to say if they ask questions?"

"Tell them she had a family emergency and had to take a leave of absence. I don't want them dragging you down that rabbit hole of questions, and that's not fair to you. 'Family emergency' should keep them from asking for more detail. I don't think she's coming back, but Tyler does, so we do what the boss wants. We wait on her."

I'm dying to ask more questions, but I stick to, "Can I reach her if I have specific questions?"

"She won't call me back, but maybe if you call and say you're doing her job, she will." She grimaces. "No, it's not fair to use you that way."

"I don't mind. It would help me to chat with her."

"Let me think about it. I don't want Tyler doing his oh so formal, sharp-toned, 'Ms. Jolie,' routine on me anytime soon." She stiffens her spine and imitates his deep voice. "That means I'm in trouble."

"I've experienced that version of scolding already," I laugh.

"I'm sure you have," she says and moves on. "I'll email you the paperwork if you can shoot me your address. You have a company email as well, but I haven't even put the order into tech yet to set it up."

I grab a sticky note and write down my email. "Here you go," I say, handing it to her.

"Great. Oh, and a couple more things. Riptide confirmed your salary. We matched it." She reaches into her pocket and sets a business card on my desk, flipping it over. "That's the address and the code to get into the house. There's a new air conditioner being put in. It will be done tomorrow. You can move in as early as tomorrow night."

I blink. "House?"

"The house." She studies me, searching my face. "You don't know about the house?"

"No. Sorry. What house?"

"Tyler owns a house not far from here, with a cellar filled with rare and collectible wines. He can't get it insured if it's unoccupied. Allison lived there as part of her salary. I can't believe he didn't tell you this."

I'm stunned by this offer, which is quite generous. "No. I had no idea."

"This situation, as you can see, is why I believe she won't be back. She moved out. Tyler thought that since you actually live in New York, this might be a win-win for you and him. You live there. He holds onto his insurance. You can think about it, but I need to know soon."

"Why don't you live there?" I ask. "Or someone else?"

"It was never offered to me or someone else. Just Allison. I'm not sure how she ended up there. I just know that Tyler wants the house occupied, but he also wants it available if Allison comes back."

My head is spinning, but I try to think logically. "I'm a little concerned about the wine. Am I responsible for it? Not that I think anything will happen, but what if the house is robbed while I'm there?"

"He has insurance. Think about it. You don't have to accept."

"No. No. I'll do it. I'll take the offer. Honestly, I'm in my mother's pool house right now. I need to start small, give her some space. It will make leaving easier. It's actually a perfect situation, but I do have to be back to work at Riptide right after New Year's."

"If she's not back by then, I think it will be time for Tyler to accept that she's not returning. Watch for the email." She stands and heads for the door.

I stand and call out to her. "What if Allison comes back?"

She pauses in the doorway and glances back at me. "It's yours until you leave. I already put that in your paperwork. You look like her, by the way," she adds.

This comment yet again takes me off guard, and I blanch. But just that quickly, she is gone, and before I can remind her to get me Allison's phone number. I've now taken over Allison's office, her job, and her house. She lived in Tyler's house. Did he send her that necklace? No, of course not. He wouldn't send her a necklace to the office when he knew she was gone. Unless it was never supposed to go to the office?

Suddenly I'm eager to get to my new house, Allison's house. Maybe I'll find out where she is when I get there.

CHAPTER SIXTEEN

My mother calls me mid-afternoon to check-in. "How's the job, honey bear?"

"It's good," I say. "I like what I'm doing. I like working to help a good cause."

"See, I always thought you could be a nurse."

I laugh. "Except the part where I don't like blood, Mom. Or needles."

"Right. True. You do scream when you see a needle."

"When I was a kid," I remind her indignantly.

"Really? I thought you still did that."

I laugh again. "All right. Someone has her smart mouth back."

"I'm back, honey. I don't know why you can't see that."

"I do," I assure her. "I do."

"Good, then you'll be excited to know that I'm enjoying life again which is why Barry and I are going to take a little trip to Texas to see his brother."

I drop the pen in my hand. "What? Are you up for that?"

"Honey," she says her tone a soft, stern note. "This is me telling you that I'm okay. You need to be okay, too. You can go back to New York."

"In January," I say. "After the holidays and the auction I'm coordinating for my new job. But as a bonus, I'm being given free housing. I'll give you two some space, but I'll still be nearby."

"Oh. Well, that's good, but where is it? Is it safe? Do you know the neighborhood?"

I smile. "Now who's being too protective?" I tease. "Yes. It's my boss's house and I assure you, Tyler Hawk would not own anything that wasn't up to his reputation."

Barry calls her in the background and then she says, "Gotta go. We have a flight to catch, but be careful. Be *very* careful, honey."

I'm focused on her, not me. "Wait. What? *Today?* You're leaving today?"

"Yes, today. I wasn't giving you time to talk me out of this."

"How long are you going to be gone?"

"We're not sure yet," she says. "There's a Garth Brooks concert in four days. We're going to that and—"

"Should you be around that many people?" I challenge.

"You need to stop," she chides. "I'm healthy and I do not want to be treated like I'm on my last leg. I'm not. Now go do your job. Send me photos of the house. I love you."

Guilt stabs at me with the warning. She's right. I have to stop, which is why I quickly say, "I love you, too, and Mom, have fun."

"I will," she promises and hangs up.

I pick up the card Natalie gave me and eye the address. Things happen for a reason. People come together at the time when they are needed. I do believe Tyler Hawk needs me right now, but when I think about Allison, and the plane tickets, the necklace, and the home I'm taking over, I can't help but wonder if she needs me, too.

But does she need me to fill in for her or find her?

That question nags at me and I'm not sure why.

CHAPTER SEVENTEEN

"Are you leaving soon?"

At the sound of Katie's voice, I glance up from my MacBook, and the HR paperwork I'm filling out, to find her in the doorway. "I won't be much longer. Any word from Tyler?"

"I left a message with his assistant Debbie earlier and on his phone. I don't think he's here."

I think about the limited timeline for this auction and dare to ask, "Is there a way to reach him outside of the office? A cellphone maybe?"

"His office is across the hall. You could try and talk to Debbie, but she's probably gone already."

"Okay, thank you. I'll try to catch him or her on my way out. Thank you, Katie."

"Tomorrow I can dive in and help you a bit," she says. "Today was just nuts. There was a big client on the upper level who had paparazzi insanity here at the building."

"Thank you for the offer. No pressure on that. And as for today, I had no idea anything was going on," I say, "I've been in my own world, trying to get a grip on this auction."

"Be glad you didn't. Truly when the press gets involved, it's always just ridiculous around here." She shifts the topic. "You want to have lunch tomorrow?"

"I have a meeting with the charity off-site tomorrow so I probably can't, but how about coffee in the morning? I can come in a little early and we can chat."

"I'd love that," she says. "That way once I sit down at the reception desk, I'll already know what you need from me for the day."

"Research," I say. "Easy really, but tedious."

"So are those phones, so I should be a master researcher. I'll head out and see you soon. Goodnight, Allison, and welcome."

"Goodnight, and thank you for making me feel welcome."

She smiles and exits the office. I quickly return to my work and finish my paperwork, shooting it back to Natalie. I'm official now. Who would have ever thought a few months ago that I'd be here now? Not me, that's for sure. But the opportunity has become compelling in all kinds of ways.

Ready to head home, I load up my briefcase with the auction information to work on at my mom's place. I then hurry toward the elevator, where I spy the glass doors opposite the main lobby, doors that I now know house Tyler's office. I wonder why he's there and not upstairs with the partners. *An isolationist*, I think again. And while I know why I've become that person, why I left a career, and chose to leave most of the people in my life behind with it, I can't help but wonder what created that in Tyler. Because something did.

The lobby lights are on and I decide to push forward and try to talk to him. I enter the reception area to find an empty desk that I assume belongs to Tyler's assistant. Boldly, I cut right down a hallway that leads to an office. Nerves light me up, but I keep on keeping on. I remind myself that Tyler will be eager to talk to me when he knows I have challenges with the auction. He needs me right now, but I remind myself there is no denying that I need this job, too, and not for money, but for my sanity.

Reaching the office door, I pause just outside the room and knock before leaning in. He's not at his desk. Damn, maybe he's not here at all.

A sudden tingling sensation washes over me and I whirl around to find Tyler standing in front of me, towering over me, so very close. There's a pulse of power to this man that is a bit unnerving. As is the way he stares down at me with hooded eyes.

"Can I help you, Ms. Wright?"

"Allison," I say and I have no idea what comes over me, but I add, "and if you can't bring yourself to say her name, just call me Allie. Lots of people do."

His eyes narrow, the angles of his handsome face darkening to what might be anger, but he's just too damn reserved to know. I immediately regret my comment, and since I can't take it back, I quickly add, "Nothing has been done on the auction. It's a concept, not an actualized event. I can change that, but time is not my friend, nor our friend. I need manpower. I need help, and at least one extra person."

He studies me again and does so with such intensity that I think he's assessing my very character in this very moment. I expect questions, I expect rejection. Instead, all he says is, "Consider it done. You'll have help tomorrow." He steps around me and enters his office.

I rotate with the intent to follow him inside his office, but as soon as I've done so, I find he's stopped as well, and he's now in front of me again. "Something else, Ms. Wright?"

Again with the Ms. Wright, I think, and I wonder if he's trying to present a line between me and him. Why? Because he does so with everyone or because he didn't do so with the other Allison?

"I'm going to stay in the house," I announce. "Thank you. It's a good way for me to be close to my mother without suffocating her."

"It seems we've met at the right time," he replies, and then he seems to read between the lines, to sense something in me that has him asking, "What do you want to ask me?"

"Why did she leave?"

His lips press together and he cuts his stare, almost as if counting down the beats to control before he turns away from me and walks into the office. He then rounds his desk and sits down behind it. I'm still in the hallway, just beyond the office, and I'm not sure if this is a dismissal or an invitation, but I choose the latter, boldly following his path but pausing on this side of the desk.

Forcing confidence, I sit down in the chair in front of him.

"You don't know how to take no for an answer, do you?"

"I wasn't aware you gave me an answer at all," I state, not sure why I need to know about Allison the way I do, but it's not about the necklace.

"She left for personal reasons, Ms. Wright," he replies. "And not everyone is the open book you are about your personal affairs."

I feel those words with a sharp pang, but I reject them as well. There was a time when he would have been right when I was indeed an open book, but I am far from that place now. But rather than say so, which would, in fact, make me an open book, I find myself challenging him instead. "Would you have hired me without knowing my motivation to take the job?"

"No," he says, leaning closer. "I would not have hired you without knowing your motivation for taking the job. What else, Ms. Wright?"

"Do I know your motivation for hiring me for the job?"

He leans back in his seat. "I need the auction to be a success. Isn't that obvious?"

It should be, but it's not. "I don't think it is," I say.

He doesn't deny my statement. Instead, he asks, "Does my motivation matter?"

"Maybe," I say, "and you answered my question. I do *not* know your motivation. Why do I feel like I'm part of a story and I'm the only one who doesn't know the secrets written on the pages?"

"When you look for something that isn't there, you create something that is."

"And yet, when you don't look closely at what's around you, sometimes you miss what is right in front of your face."

"Sounds like one experience you had is dictating this experience," he counters.

He's probably not wrong. "Hopefully that's true and my gut feeling doesn't become a problem because I've decided I want to do this. I really want to do this job."

He studies me a long moment, seconds ticking by, his blue eyes unreadable, before he says, "Goodnight, Allie."

Goodnight, Allie.

He's used my name and it feels like an answer, but it also becomes a question. I'm just not sure what the question is just yet.

Nevertheless, I'm dismissed, which is fine. I've gotten what I wanted and said what I had to say. I stand and walk toward the door, half expecting him to stop me, but he doesn't. I leave the office but I don't leave Tyler behind. I'm still thinking about him, and Allison, when I climb into my car and drive away from Hawk Legal, at least for tonight.

I think about the reasons I need to know about Allison so badly and I decide I feel a connection to her. She had a dream job at Hawk Legal and yet, she walked away. We are connected in that way, and if she doesn't come back to her established life, I wonder if I will either. And I'm not sure if that is good or bad. And I can't help but feel that I really am part of a story, and I'm the only one who doesn't know where the next page leads.

Everyone except maybe Allison.

CHAPTER EIGHTEEN

I drive to the address on the card, to the house I'll be staying in for the next few months, to the house where Allison lived. It's in the heart of the Belle Meade neighborhood, an area that's a cool mix of old money and new money, but there's also a section of more affordable, moderate homes, but I'm eager to get a clear picture. I assume I'll be in the more moderate area, of course, but turns out, I've assumed wrong. The address leads me to the old money area, and soon, I'm sitting in front of a home that could be on a dream board to motivate me to keep working. It's aglow in outdoor lighting, white with two steeped rooftops divided by a stairwell to the door. The grounds are immaculate and expansive. This house is more than a perk of the job. It's a luxury bonus. It's not a normal offer.

And Allison left it behind. That feels decisive. It doesn't feel like she's coming back.

I think of Tyler's reaction to my questions about her and decide that this house, and his evasiveness, scream of a personal relationship. Then again, he offered me the house as well. I'm not sure why I pushed him the way I did. It's none of my business why Allison did what she did or why he is using me to fill in for her rather than replacing her.

I draw a breath and admit what I wish was not true.

Nothing about what happened in that office, nothing about me pushing Tyler for his motivations, was about Tyler. I've known men who have agendas that were not what they seem. The truth is that Tyler reminds me of those men. That's why I pushed him like I did tonight, inappropriately so, I fear. He hired me too easily. He offered me this house too easily.

He does have an agenda and it's not what it seems.

But then I do as well, and it's not really what it seems, either. It's not about my mother, not completely, not if I'm honest with myself. It's about what happened back in New York.

CHAPTER NINETEEN

You can tell someone not to judge a book by its cover, but they do it anyway.

It's true of humans as well. People judge us first with their eyes, then with their minds. I have no doubt that if I really do resemble Allison, people look at me and see her. Oddly, some part of me is okay with that idea, which tells me that I'm still living through an identity crisis that started some time back. Truly, I could blame that fact on my father—or my ex, Brandon—and people who knew my stories, would agree.

Or I could be brave and claim that fame myself.

I mostly choose the latter.

Eager to separate myself from a past that obviously still haunts me and stand out on my own, I arrive to work the next day quite early and do so in my favorite black Chanel skirt. The same skirt I'd worn to the party, but this time with a matching black blouse, with a red belt for a pop of color. With a piping hot thermal mug filled with Oh Fudge! coffee from my favorite brand, Bones Coffee, I waste no time getting to work. I'm deep into an inventory list, right up until the moment I hear, "Good morning, boss lady," about a half-hour later.

I glance up to find Katie standing in the doorway, looking adorable in a pink dress and holding two cups of coffee. "I brought the coffee date to you," she informs me.

"Morning to you, too," I say. "And aren't you the best? Coffee is the way to my heart."

She crosses the room and sets a cup in front of me. "It's a skinny cinnamon churro latte with whipped cream. One of my favorites."

"Sounds wonderful," I say. "Thank you. I didn't know the coffee bar was already open." I sip and the warm, wonderful, sweet beverage touches my tongue, my eyes lighting as I say, "I approve."

She smiles her pleasure, and says, "Oh good. I thought you would. Anyone who doesn't like this cup of coffee is just not right, you know?"

I laugh. "Yes," I agree conspiratorially. "There is something not right about someone who doesn't like coffee. Of course, the non-coffee lovers probably say that about us, too."

She waves that off. "Oh pooh on them. They don't know what they're talking about," she grins before she adds, "and the coffee bar just opened."

"Good to know," I say, eyeing the clock for reference and then asking, "and what's with the boss lady? What in the world did I do to earn that nickname?"

"Debbie called me at ten last night to tell me that one of the girls from accounting is covering the front desk. I'm all yours until the auction is over."

I'm stunned with just how quickly Tyler has worked, and how much support this shows for my efforts. It's actually quite shocking after I'd laid in bed last night thinking that I'd pushed him too hard and too far. I'd worried I'd end up without a job today. Worry that some might say is unreasonable, considering I have a job in New York. Nevertheless, there is no denying my relief.

"That's excellent news," I say. "Let's get started." And with that, I dive into training my new employee with a zeal befitting a drowning woman, who just got thrown a life vest.

Once I've finished going over my plans with Katie and sent her off to work in an office down the hall, I pause for a moment with an admission. I'm embracing this job and living the other Allison's life as if it were my own. I'm not sure what that says about where my head is right now, but I'll analyze myself and my reasoning a bit more later, alone in the house where she once lived and probably will again. Maybe. I don't know much about her or even myself right now.

I dive back into my work and end up losing track of time. I blink and it's time to go to my meeting. I grab my purse and briefcase, pull on the short, light trenchcoat I bought for the in-between seasons, and exit my office.

I round the reception desk and enter the lobby to find Tyler and Dash standing together, Tyler regal in an expensive fitted suit, and Dash oozing cool style and hotness in jeans, a blue sweater, and a matching blazer. The two men are in deep conversation, and while their body language is not tense, there's an energy about them I wouldn't call friendly. But then, this doesn't really surprise me for a number of reasons, including the exchange I witnessed between them at the party. Not to mention there couldn't be two men more alike and at the same time, so different.

And yet, here they stand, together, in my path.

I hesitate, not certain I should dare interrupt, but also not sure how I can walk past them and not speak at all. I can't, I decide. I just have to casually wave and say something smart and snappy.

Drawing a deep breath, and steeling my spine for an overload of testosterone and intensity, I walk toward them. Tyler is angled toward me and when his gaze lifts in my direction, the weight of his attention settling on me, the impact is forceful. But when Dash shifts his position, when Dash brings me into view, and his eyes are on me, *it's fire*. I feel his assessment in a heavy, warm way that refuses to set me free. Not that I really want to be free from Dash Black one little bit, which is actually a dangerous thought. The kind that will get me tripping over reasonable thought and falling right into trouble.

I halt within a circle of the two men, and say, "Hi," with a little, ridiculously goofy wave. Good grief, I'm really special in all the wrong ways with these two men. "I don't want to interrupt," I say quickly. "I'm headed to my meeting with the charity head. I'll update you both on how it goes."

Tyler's attention sharpens, a hardness in his stare now, that despite his indecipherable expression, ticks like anger. "Come and see me when you get back."

He doesn't know I've been talking to Dash, I realize, and I can assume that's a problem for him. I'm not sure why though, considering this is Dash's charity choice, but it's the only logical answer to his reaction.

"I will," I promise. "I won't be back until late, though. I have an afternoon meeting with the venue, so I'll grab lunch and head that way." I don't ask if that's okay. That's one thing Queen Compton taught me. Never, ever, give someone high on power, more power. Claim your space, she'd instructed, and live in it.

She was good for me. And now she's sick, too, and I haven't seen her. I need to go see her.

"I'll be here," Tyler states, pulling me back into the moment. "Just make sure you are as well, Ms. Wright."

We're back to Ms. Wright. That doesn't seem good. But as smart-mouthed as I was to him last night, respect matters. What is done in private shouldn't always be done in public. Therefore, I simply say, "Absolutely," before I shift my attention to meet Dash's keen stare, the look in his eyes telling me he's not pleased, and that's not about me, but rather Tyler. But I'm also not sure if that's about the present exchange or if I walked into something I should not have. Whatever the case, it's time for me to leave.

WHAT IF I NEVER

"I'll update you," I assure Tyler again, offering a small nod and then parting the circle to rush to the elevator, willing myself not to stumble over my feet and fall down. I can see how that would go. Dash would help me. Tyler would watch in disdain.

Fortunately, I make it to the elevator without trips, twists, or falls. It even opens as I arrive, as if it were waiting on me. Luck is with me, for sure, thank goodness. I step inside and let out a breath of relief and too soon. It's right then that the strap to my bag breaks and it crashes to the ground. I panic, no longer thinking about the two men who are now out of sight, but rather the company MacBook that has slammed to the floor.

Urgently, I squat to retrieve it, and as I do, a pair of familiar jean-clad legs step into my view. I blink and Dash Black is squatting in front of me.

CHAPTER TWENTY

I've turned international and *New York Times* bestselling author Dash Black into an elevator squatter. I'm mortified.

The doors shut and I reach for the MacBook at the same time he reaches for it. Our hands collide, the results starting a sizzling dart up my arm that expands across my chest, and through my body. "I'm embarrassed right now," is all I manage to say.

"Don't be," he says. "You're human and really quite adorable."

"Adorable," I repeat, mortified all over again. Adorable is cute, and cute is not what a woman wants to be to a man. Suddenly all the more awkward, I reach for my bag, shoving a folder back inside, thankful the paperwork didn't come out of it.

Eager to regain my dignity, I pop to my feet and Dash follows, straightening to his full height, easily juggling the MacBook as he opens it and tests the keyboard. "It's alive," he says, turning to the screen to face me.

"Oh, thank God," I gush. "It's not mine. It belongs to Hawk Legal." I hold up my bag, the strap dangling. "How is this even possible? But I'm glad it happened here, not in my meeting with Millie."

"True," he says, his eyes lighting and his eyebrow wiggling as he adds, "I wouldn't have been there to save the day. And no harm, no foul," he adds, taking the bag from me and sliding the computer inside. "The computer isn't broken, and more importantly, neither are you."

It's an innocent statement, but it hits me rather profoundly in how not true it is. I *am* broken. I've been running from that for a while and I have this sense that all that running stops here. I'm just not sure I'm ready.

"Lower level okay?" he asks, breaking me out of my little self-evaluating reverie, his fingers hovering over the elevator's panel.

"Oh my gosh," I say with a little laugh. "We're not even moving. Yes, lower level, please. I'm headed to the garage."

He punches the button and sets us in motion and then he's facing me again. Unbidden, my eyes collide with his and the air expands between us and there is a ping in my chest, an awareness of Dash that I've never experienced with another man.

My lips are dry and I wet them and say, "You really do keep saving me. First in the elevator the other day, then with your jacket, and now, well, in the elevator again."

"Always happy to help a damsel in distress. Any time, Allison." He says my name like silk and sultry nights, and there is a zip in the air between us, or there is for me. Maybe not for him. Maybe I'm just—I don't know what I am to him. Perhaps just a girl, just an adorable, cute girl, aka the girl a guy never wants to date, who keeps awkwardly, accidentally, stepping right smack into his path.

"Allie," I say softly. "You can call me Allie."

"Allie," he repeats, and my name on this man's tongue is an intimate suggestion. "Everything okay with you and Tyler?" he asks.

"He's not going to drive me away mid-auction, if that's what you're afraid of. I'm committed and I want to do this. And Tyler is not my first Tyler. I work for Riptide. Mark Compton, and even his mother, are both what I would call earthquakes—scattering people into nervous frenzies—when they walk into the room. Queen

Compton does this quite loudly while Mark, much like Tyler, does it quietly."

"Tyler officially has a new nickname. Earthquake. And it's fitting."

The doors ding and open. Dash is quick to hold them open, motioning me forward. I exit, and just outside, I pause and wait on him. "I can take my bag," I offer.

"I'm in the garage, too. I'll ride down with you and walk you to your car." There's an insistence in his voice, an absoluteness.

I'm charmed, but I also remind myself that he's just being a gentleman. "Because you're afraid I'll drop everything again."

"The bag broke," he teases, "and then jumped right out of your arms. Why would I be worried?"

I laugh. "Yes. Stupid bag, but I also love it. I hope it can be repaired."

"Never trust what has already failed you," he says, a shift to his mood that is far more serious now.

I'm suddenly not sure we're talking about the bag anymore and neither of us are moving. "Sounds like experience talking again," I comment.

"It is," he assures me, something dark in his expression, but there's no time to press for more.

We quickly go from the lobby to the garage elevator, and then the actual garage. We exit and he motions to the rows of cars. "Where are you parked?" he asks, and whatever I just thought I saw in him seems to be gone. Or maybe it never existed.

I indicate left, and hit the button to ping the car as we start walking in that direction.

Once we're there, he opens my door and then sets my bag in the back for me, "I'd say good luck with your meeting," he offers, "but you won't need it. Millie's excited to get the event going. And after talking to me about your background, and my first impression, she's excited about you. You still haven't asked me about that."

"About what?"

"My first impression of you." His voice is low, warm, and there seems to be a hint of flirtation to his tone.

My heart flutters and I quickly say, "I still don't want to know. And I'm getting in the car before you tell me anyway." And I do. I climb into the car, set the MacBook on the passenger seat, and when I would look up at Dash, he's squatting beside me. "Let me know when you're ready, Allie." With no further explanation, his lips curve and he stands back up, shutting my door.

Let him know when I'm ready?

My head is spinning with those words that I don't understand.

I watch him walk away, and then he's gone, but he's made sure I will think about him. But will I be ready when I see him again?

CHAPTER TWENTY-ONE

The charity Drive Sober and Safely is run from a small office space next to a Starbucks. It doesn't get much better than that.

I arrive to the meeting just in time, and I'm instantly greeted by a warm smile and a handshake from Millie Roberts, the charity's president. Millie appears to be thirty-something, quite stylish in a cream-colored tailored dress, with a mass of red curls spiraling to her shoulders.

We quickly move from the lobby to her office, sitting at a small, round conference table, and her eagerness and relief over my involvement all but vibrates from her. "We're really counting on this event for next year's funding. Dash told me about your experience and position at Riptide. It's such a relief to have you involved."

"I'm glad I can help and motivate," I say. "Honestly, it's almost as if it was meant to be. I'm here for just the right amount of time to get this done. And I'm passionate about making a difference. Tell me what I need to know."

"Absolutely," she says. "We're lucky to have you." She then launches into a great deal of information about who they are and what they do, which helps me to help her. She finishes with, "This is personal to me. My sister died in a car accident. A drunk driver hit her head-on. She was coming over a hill. She never saw it coming. So tell me, please. What can I do for you?"

My heart squeezes and I, in turn, squeeze her hand. "I won't say I'm sorry. I know you hear that all the time, but my mother just recovered from cancer. That's why

I'm here. In some way, I hope my fear of losing her helps me help the cause."

Her eyes soften. "I do believe it will and I'm so thankful that she recovered."

"Me, too," I say, "but I don't really feel like she has, and she needs me to see her as whole again. This project is going to help me do that." I swallow the lump in my throat and say, "The biggest challenge right now is the fact that not much has been done, and time is crucial. If you can call your reliable donors and ask for support, that would help."

"I have some high-profile donors," she says. "Of course, we do, but I feel like they might open their wallets for you, with your Riptide association."

"I don't have a problem calling them," I say, "and frankly, it could be good for Riptide to make that connection, but I need to know what you know about each of them first. Would you have time soon to go over that with me? Maybe we can do coffee tomorrow for just that purpose? There's a little bookshop a few blocks down that has the best cupcakes ever."

"Oh my God, yes. Cupcakes and Books. Such a simple name and such a sweet place. Can you do late afternoon, like three o'clock?"

"It's a date," I say. "Three o'clock."

***

A few minutes later, I'm outside, in what is turning into a rather chilly day. I huddle into my jacket, and with lots of time before my meeting, I head toward one of my favorite places in the neighborhood: Cupcakes and Books. Only a short walk later, I enter the double wood and glass doors with bells chiming. I really love those bells—they remind me of home.

Nashville really is home. New York never became that to me.

With a smile, my eyes devour the rows of books, while my nose delights at the scent of cupcakes and coffee. Back in the day, when I'd dreamed of being an editor, I'd come here often. One of my favorite things had been to cozy up at a table with coffee, cupcakes, and my work. I'd break to wander around the book aisles and try to resist buying everything in sight.

Eager to feel that nostalgia to the fullest extent, today I will lunch on cupcakes, books, and coffee. I cut right, toward the bakery area, passing under the arched doorway, only to stop dead in my tracks at what I discover, my heart thundering in my chest.

Dash Black is here and he's sitting at my favorite nook of a corner table.

CHAPTER TWENTY-TWO

Dash's MacBook is open in front of him. The best cupcake in the house, the chocolate on white, is sitting next to him. Beside the cupcake is a steaming cup of coffee in one of the large oval mugs that come in a variety of colors with just the right weight to the hand. His mug is white. I prefer the red. I ask for the red, as silly as that may sound to some, but it's part of the experience of being here for me. His blazer is hanging on his chair, his navy sweater fitted snugly to what is most definitely now confirmed to be a perfect chest, the kind only achieved with hard work and good genetics.

And good Lord, I'm just standing here staring at him.

Like a fangirl stalker.

Appalled at myself, I back out of the bakery and quickly rush away, cutting down one of my favorite book aisles, and Lord help me yet again, I stop right in front of the Dash Black section. What would I be like if I really *was* stalking the man? I draw in a breath and will my heart to calm down.

"Why'd you run away?"

At the sound of Dash's voice, I whirl around to find him standing right in front of me, so damn tall and perfect, so stylish, in a masculine perfection kind of way, that it's really quite overwhelming. *He's* overwhelming and I'm not sure if that's good or bad right about now.

"Hi," I say because apparently, that's the only word I know right now. I've never been a pro at the whole man meets woman thing, as proven by my romantic history, but it's just getting worse. So much worse.

"Why'd you run away, Allie?" he asks.

"I didn't run away."

He arches a brow and I hold up my hands and quickly add, "Okay. I saw you, but I didn't want to intrude on your private space or creative time. If there's one thing I can appreciate, it's the need for quiet to concentrate on a book."

He props a shoulder on the divider between two bookshelves. "You weren't interrupting."

"I wanted to respect your space." I motion to the shelf to my right. "Somehow I ended up right next to your books." I reach for a title and manage to grab the one I edited. "The whipped cream was hilarious, by the way." It's a reference to a scene where Ghost is about to assassinate someone and they shoot whipped cream in his face. It's about the only thing that ever stopped the deadly killer and Dash executed Ghost's reaction to perfection.

"That really happened," he says. "Not to Ghost, but to me."

"You're kidding." I'm smiling now and thrilled to have a little glimpse into his writing world. "It happened to you?"

"Yeah," he confirms. "I went to arrest a woman and she sprayed me with whipped cream. I reacted about like Ghost. It was a 'what the fuck?' kind of moment."

I laugh. "Definitely not what anyone would expect. And Ghost just licked the whipped cream and kept moving. Did you?"

Now he laughs. "No. Most definitely *not*. I was not as agile on my feet as Ghost. She got away and I looked foolish. But that's the fun part of writing him. He can be everything I'm not."

I'm charmed by his ability to laugh at himself, probably more so because I've worked with enough authors to know that many cannot. Especially those in the big league, as Dash most certainly is in his career.

"It was perfect," I say. "It really was. And so many of the reviews talked about that scene. It made Ghost human. That's where your talent is. You have a Dexter thing going on. You make us root for someone we probably shouldn't root for, and as a former editor and reader, I respect that skill." I hold my hands up again. "And I'm not just saying that. Believe me, I've had books I edited I didn't truly love. And I certainly did ramble on about loving them."

"Did you say you didn't love them?"

"Not to the author, and that's not out of a lack of courage. Editing isn't always about the books you like as an editor. Sometimes it's about books that will speak to other people, like a different item on the dinner menu."

He grimaces. "I don't think anybody is going to like the book I'm working on now."

"Said every author while writing their current work."

"No," he says. "I'm not normally this off when I'm writing." He scrubs his jaw and then studies me. "I never let anyone read my work while I'm writing, but maybe you can do it? Just tell me what you think is off."

"I'd be very intimidated to do that. And besides, I don't think you should change your process. If you don't let people read, don't start now." The seriousness of my advice is overshadowed by a loud grumble from my stomach.

Heat rushes to my cheeks and Dash laughs, motioning toward the bakery. "Sounds like you need a cupcake. Want to have it with me?"

"I would *love* to have a cupcake with you and a coffee in one of those mugs you have on your table. I love those mugs and everything about this place. I used to come here when I was in college to study."

"I found it when I moved to the neighborhood a few years ago," he says. "I've actually written a good part of

several books sitting at the table I'm saving for us now."
He motions me forward. "Let's go get you a cupcake and
coffee," he adds and there is warmth in his eyes, and a
warmth between us that is as intriguing as the man.

I don't know what this is between me and Dash
Black, perhaps nothing but friendship, but whatever it
is, cupcakes and him are too much to resist. Perhaps too
much for my own good, but I can't seem to care right
now. Dash Black intrigues me, he excites me, and I
haven't felt those things in a very long time.

CHAPTER TWENTY-THREE

Dash and I enter the bakery side by side to be greeted by Jackson Summer, the owner of the establishment. Jackson is fifty-something, a tall, distinguished-looking Black man with a neatly trimmed beard, and a friendly smile. His voice and eyes are warm as they land on me. "There's my girl," he greets, pulling me into a full-on bear hug. "How you been, babe?"

Jackson calls everyone babe, including men, but somehow it works for him and makes us all feel like his special guests.

"Good," I say. "It feels good to be back here. It's been a while."

"Yeah, it has," he says, motioning to Dash. "You his editor or something?"

"More like he's my cupcake companion for now," I say. "Your cupcakes are yummy. Cupcakes and his books together are the best. I'm a lucky girl."

"I'm working on getting her to read the piece of shit I'm writing right now," Dash says grumpily. "It just won't come together."

Jackson offers a knowing look and leans in close to me with a conspiratorial, not-so-quiet whisper, "He thinks they're all shit. I've never heard him say a book was good until after it releases. Even then," he scratches his jaw, "I'm not sure he's ever said his books are good."

"That's not true," Dash argues. "I'm just trying to do Ghost justice."

Jackson winks at me and pats Dash's arm. "I love this guy. Ghost is as real as you and me to him. The way he frets, it's almost as if he's afraid Ghost is going to shoot him if he doesn't write the book as he'd want it." He glances at me. "You'd never know he's a superstar, now would you?" He doesn't wait for my reply, adding, "Black and white cupcake with a cinnamon dolce latte in a red cup?"

I pep up. "Yes, please."

"Don't tell me you're doing that thing you do and skipping lunch to eat a cupcake?"

"It's a trade-off," I say. "And the cupcakes are worth it. So is the coffee."

He scowls at me over his nose. "I'm bringing you a sandwich, too. On the house." He hurries away.

"I think we're both in trouble," Dash laughs, doing a little head lean toward the table.

"I do believe we are," I say, as the two of us claim our seats and I slide out of my coat.

It's a small space and I'm right across from him, his computer between us.

He shuts the lid and sets it aside.

"See now," I chide, "you're not going to make your word count with your computer shut."

"How did it go with Millie?"

"Excellent," I say. "I like her. I want to help. She asked me to call some of the donors that have helped them out in the past. She thinks my connection to Riptide will help. I'm actually meeting her tomorrow to go through the list."

"I'll help," he says. "I can split the list up with you."

"You don't have to do that, Dash."

"I want this to go well, and you've been thrown into this with a limited amount of time to spare."

"Well, that's true," I say, "but I'm not in panic mode. Katie is mine full time until the event is over. I have some help at Riptide. It's all going to work out. And who knows, maybe the real Allison will show up and we can finish this together."

"You think Allison is coming back?"

"You don't?" I ask.

"I don't really know. I barely know Allison, but from what my sister told me, she was here one day and gone the next. I'm surprised Tyler would let her come back."

"Katie seems to think he was holding off on hiring for her return. It's just lucky that our paths crossed when they did. It's a little strange. You know I'm moving into the house she was living in?"

He arches a brow. "You're moving into her house? How does that work?"

"I guess it's a place Tyler owns and it has to be occupied to have insurance to cover the wine cellar. So when she left, she really left. She moved out."

"And now you're moving in," he states and it's not a question. There's a sense of disapproval in his tone, a shuttering of his features.

"Don't say it like that," I push back.

"I don't think I said much of anything."

"You didn't have to," I say. "It's in your eyes." I lean in closer. "It's not like Tyler is living there."

"I didn't say anything, Allison."

Allison again. Not Allie. He's unhappy and I'm confused. Illogically, I feel like I need to explain myself. I lean in closer. "My mom wants me to act like her cancer never existed. This is the best way for me to give her space and not leave town. I still have rent in New York City. This lets me leave her pool house with no expense. And as a bonus, I have this charity event to keep me busy and out of her business and my own fear. It's all kind of perfect." With that, I realize that I've bared my soul to this man more than any other person in a very long time, including the man I was engaged to. I don't know what I'm doing. He probably thinks I'm a lunatic. I ease back into my chair. "Don't judge me," I say, and it's rather defensive. God, I'm losing it.

His eyes—those crystal, intelligent blue eyes—study me for several long beats before he says, "I'm not judging you." He leans in closer. "I'm glad you're here, *Allie*."

CHAPTER TWENTY-FOUR

I've never been to one of those striking ocean cities where you stare out at water of brilliant blues and greens, all the while wondering if there is another magical world beneath that beauty. But I suspect it's a lot like looking into Dash Black's eyes.

For long seconds, I'm just spellbound, lost in his gaze, awash in the richness of his presence, aware of him in ways I wasn't sure I would ever be capable of with a man again. But I also admire him. His ease with himself, his air of confidence, of knowing who and what he is, and I envy that in him. I'm more a small little fish in the ocean he owns, swimming here and there, trying to find my own little pond. I'm not sure why I'm so lost, maybe because of my mother, or maybe it's deeper, about me, but there is no denying, I am right now.

"I'm glad to be here," I say softly and once again drive home where my heart is right now. "I meant it when I said, it feels meant to be, like I'm at the right time and the right place."

A ham and cheese croissant and a soda are set in front of me and I glance up to find Jackson's wife standing beside and above me. I beam and pop to my feet. "Adrianna!" I greet her, giving her a big hug. "So good to see you." I give her boots, sweater, and jeans a once over—all worn with style to die for—and add, "You're as gorgeous as ever." Which is true. Adrianna is tall, which means she doesn't have short legs like me, with striking model-worthy cheekbones, long full hair, and the most beautiful skin.

"Says the gorgeous girl herself," she replies, "and thank you. I'm so happy you're here. Your mom hasn't been in forever. We have to lure her back to the sweet spot. Should I send her cupcakes?"

There's a pinch in my chest at the mention of my mother, but I push past it and say, "She'd love that, but she's off on a vacation with my stepfather right now. When she gets back, I'll bring her in."

"Excellent," she approves. "She and I need to catch up." She waves at Dash.

"Hi, Adrianna," he says warmly.

"Write that damn book," she orders him, and then to me, she points at the table. "Eat. You're skinny. I remember you having more meat on your bones. You have room to grow, I promise honey. I'll bring your coffee and cupcake here in just a few minutes." She starts to turn and I catch her arm. "I distracted Dash. I made his coffee get cold. Can you bring him another on me?"

She glances at him and then me. "It's on the house." She winks and rushes away.

I settle back down into my seat and say, "Write the damn book. I'll eat in silence."

"Read it and tell me what's wrong."

"No," I say. "That's a mistake. Follow your process. Why break it for me?"

"How many people could I ask, that have the skills and knowledge of the book, to be able to do this for me?"

I lean forward. "You know how to write a book. I can't tell you that. If it's not magic, go back to the beginning and start there. You'll figure out what's wrong." I pick up my fork and cut a bite of the sandwich, "Have you tried these? They're so good."

"I just had one," he says, but he's preoccupied with what I've told him. "Maybe I will reread it."

"When's your deadline?"

"Three months. I have time. If I get my shit together."

I motion to the computer. "Read."

His cellphone rings and he snags it from his pocket. "My agent," he says. "Otherwise known as my sister. She does it all these days. I'll be right back." He stands and walks away, but the earthy wonderful scent of him lingers.

Oh how easily I'm affected by everything about him. I'm in trouble with Dash if I'm not careful. And I'm not foolish enough to pretend I'm not a little vulnerable right now. Which is how I got in trouble once before. Timing matters. This is also why I'd like to eat my food while he's gone and not watching me make a mess. Turns out I have plenty of time. I finish off my scrumptious croissant just as he returns.

"Sorry about that," he says. "She likes to yell. *A lot.*"

"Isn't that what sisters are for?"

"I suppose it is," he says. "Do you have siblings?"

"I do not," I say. "But I've seen how you sibling teams roll. Does she represent your father as well?"

"We're half-siblings. He's not her father and they don't get along. So, no. She doesn't represent my father." There's a sharpness to his tone at this reply that I don't take offensively at all. It's not about me. It does tell a story, that it would be inappropriate for me to ask for now. "Is your father here?" he asks.

"No," I say, and I can almost feel myself clam up, a little as he did. "New York. He lives in New York."

His eyes register my reaction and he says, "I'll leave that alone. Tell me something I don't know about you, Allie."

There's something about this man saying my name that does funny things to my belly. "I love country music, chocolate, books, coffee, cupcakes, and high heels."

His lips curve. "Good choices. I too like country music, chocolate, books, coffee, cupcakes, and high heels. Just not on me."

I laugh and there is this easy comfort between us that I really don't know that I've ever experienced with a man, that defies how attracted I am to him. "I don't think that would suit the assassin-writing author image."

He smiles and it's truly a charming smile. It's right then that Jackson reappears with two coffees and sets them on the table. One of his staff slides a cupcake next to me and takes the cold coffee sitting next to Dash. "You two enjoy," he says, smiling his goodbye and departing.

"In case you didn't hear, I told them to bring you more coffee," I say. "I interrupted your caffeine fix and you're writing today." I glance at my watch. "But you don't have me much longer. I have to go by the venue. I want to know what the event will look like while I'm setting it all up."

He sips his coffee. "They do make a damn good coffee," he says.

I follow his lead and sip mine as well. "God, I've missed these. There are some perks to being in town for the next few months."

"There are definite perks," he says, his voice warm, almost flirtatious, but I can't really read him. "Why do you like the red mugs?" he asks.

"I have no idea. I just like the red. I have to have the red. It's silly, I know, but that's just how I roll."

"It's not silly," he says, his eyes warm with a mix of friendliness and amusement. "It's adorable. You're adorable."

Adorable again.

I'm adorable.

I'm that girl he doesn't want to date.

WHAT IF I NEVER

Who am I kidding? He's told me twice now how he really feels about me and it's not what I'd secretly hoped for.

CHAPTER TWENTY-FIVE

Dash's eyebrow inches up. "You don't like being adorable," he says, no question. He read me like I read his books, all too easily.

"It's not that," I say.

"I think it is."

"Puppies are adorable. And kitty cats. And this cupcake." I point to my plate. "It's really cute. I also think the flowers on this red cup are adorable as well, which is part of the reason I love the red mug."

He smiles a charming smile and says, "Now you sound like me reading the reviews on my first book, picking at words and making bad out of good. What would you want me to call you?"

"No description, remember? We talked about this. I don't want to know what you think of me." I pick up my fork and take a bite. I mean, why do I care how I look eating in front of Dash? I'm the adorable, sweet girl you're friends with but don't date.

"Okay," he reasons. "Let's try this another way. When I say a woman is adorable, what does that woman, any woman, think?"

I hesitate, but we're past anything romantic so there's no reason I can't be straight-up with him. "When I was growing up, my best friend was gorgeous, blonde, Swedish. Everyone called her beautiful. I was cute, which is basically adorable."

"And what if I told you you're both?"

"I'd say good save and eat your cupcake, but thank you for trying."

His eyes are alight with a smile, but his cellphone rings again and he grimaces. "That's going to be my sister again." He grabs it from the table and says, "Yes. My sister." His eyes meet mine. "And for the record, I never say anything I don't mean. More on that later." He doesn't give me time to reply. He answers the call with, "Have I told you how much you irritate the hell out of me?"

He's teasing, of course. It's in his voice. He and his sister are close, able to tease each other in a way that only siblings can tease each other. I take another bite of my cupcake while they chat. I'm not sure what all is said, but my cupcake is gone by the time he starts to wrap up with, "Good. Then we're even." He listens a moment. "I'm not moving the deadline up. Don't ask again. And yes, I'll come by later." He hangs up.

My brows lift. "Was that about the book you're struggling with?"

"Yes. Hollywood wants the manuscript. They're considering a Ghost TV show and they want all they can get from me, but giving them the book too soon doesn't serve them or me well." He scrubs his jaw. "And now you know why I want you to read it for me."

"First, the TV show is exciting. Congratulations. And second, now I know why you *think* you need me to read it. You're feeling pressure that isn't normally there. You have to remove yourself from that pressure, not add more by having someone, me, critique your work. Your writing is always magnificent." I lean in a little closer, a smile on my lips as I add, "And for the record, I never say anything I don't mean. I hate liars and fakes. I'm not that." I ease back and sip my coffee. "And with that brilliant advice, and it *is* brilliant advice, I probably need to go." I scoot my chair out slightly. "I'm going to take Katie and the team back a box of cupcakes. Katie's really eager to help with this auction." I stand up. "I'll be right back."

I hurry to the counter and Adrianna greets me. "It really is good to see you."

"And you," I say. "This feels like home. And I'm recruiting you some new customers. Can I get a mixed dozen sent to Hawk Legal to Katie and the team from me?"

"Of course. Today?"

"Yes, please."

"You got it. I'll have them there in an hour," she says, and then gives me a coy look. "Interesting to see you with Dash."

"I'm working on a charity auction he's involved with. In fact, I might want to contract you guys for cupcakes."

"We'd love that. Just let us know. I thought you were working in New York?"

"I am, but this is in partnership with the company I work for there, so it's perfect. A little at-home holiday time."

"Good. Good." She eyes something over my shoulder—Dash, I assume—and says, "He's an interesting guy. Kind of famous, and so very good-looking. Don't you think?"

Seeing where she's going with this, I hold up my hands, "We're *friends*. That's all."

"That's not how he looks at you, darlin', or the way you look at him."

"I don't know what you're talking about," I say, and I don't. At least not where Dash is concerned but she's hooked me with that tease and now I'm curious. I ease closer and whisper, "How does he look at me?"

"Like you're a cupcake he wants to lick." She grins. "Cupcakes on the way. And they're on Dash. He said to put whatever you want on his tab." Her grin widens and she walks away.

117

LISA RENEE JONES

CHAPTER TWENTY-SIX

My heart thunders in my chest. Adrianna thinks Dash looks at me like I'm a cupcake he wants to lick? No. That's ridiculous. Isn't it?

I turn to face the seating area and find Dash watching me. I wave like a silly school girl.

Shoot me now, I'm *an idiot*.

His response is the slow curve of his sexy mouth into one of those perfect smiles of his. Probably because I'm just so *adorable* and not in a good way.

I draw in a calming breath that is not really calming at all. Not when I'm walking toward the table and Dash isn't even pretending to look away. He watches my every step and when I slide into the seat, I nervously fill the space with conversation. "I got Katie two cupcakes and me ten."

He laughs. "I might have to demand at least two for me."

"Hmmm," I contemplate. "Maybe one. Two really is a little demanding."

"I can be *very* demanding," he replies, his eyes alight with what reads like flirtatious mischief, but once again I dismiss such an idea. He's just playing around.

"You won't be at the office to claim your one little cupcake."

"Two," he rebuts.

"One and I had them delivered, so you'll have to come to the office to claim your order. Actually, I think you paid for my order, which was quite kind of you. I owe you cupcakes." My voice softens. "Thank you for everything." I sigh. "But alas, on that note, I should go." I glance at the time on my watch. "Yes. Definitely."

He slides his computer inside the black leather bag on the chair.

"What are you doing?" I ask, pushing to my feet at the same time he stands up and pulls his bag to his shoulder.

"Going with you." He rounds the table and grabs my coat.

"Why are you going with me?" I ask, now worried that he believes me destined to mishandle the auction.

"Because I *want* to go with you, Allie," he says, his voice low and velvety while his blue eyes glint with a hint of green in the overhead lights.

I dare to step closer to him, lowering my voice to ask, "Why?"

"When something matters to you, you act like it."

"You know I'll do a good job, right?" I ask and not defensively. Not at all. His name is attached to the auction and I know how mishandled it's been thus far.

"I do know. Me being involved is actually a reflection of my trust in you, Allie." He holds open my coat.

"Thank you," I say, before I slide inside it, and turn to face him. "But I don't understand that answer. You weren't involved. Now I'm involved and you want to take time from your writing to go look at the venue?"

"You're holding my cupcake ransom, cupcake. Remember?"

I laugh. "Cupcake?"

"Yep. It's pretty adorable, right?"

"No. No, my new nickname is not cupcake and it is not adorable."

"All right then, *beautiful*," he says and that velvety quality to his voice is back. "Let's get to that meeting."

My cheeks heat with his obvious reference to my name preferences. "I'm never going to live down the whole adorable thing, am I?"

He retrieves my bag from the back of my chair. "Eventually," he promises with a wink. "But in the meantime, I'll have some fun with it."

He indicates my bag. "I see you got a new one."

"An old friend," I say of the well-worn Coach bag. "It works as a purse and a briefcase since I still haven't taken my broken bag to the store to get it repaired." I take it from him. "It doesn't match your shoes."

He laughs and motions to the door and I give into the inevitable. I'm going to be spending time with Dash Black. Somehow, I can't be sorry about this realization but I warn myself to be careful.

Dash Black could be trouble.

The kind I won't handle any better than the last time I found trouble, and almost married him.

LISA RENEE JONES

LISA RENEE JONES

LISA RENEE JONES

CHAPTER TWENTY-SEVEN

The moment Dash and I exit the bookstore, the wind whistles with a wicked cold front moving across the city, and the promise that winter is arriving.

I shiver and huddle into my coat. "It was so much warmer yesterday and even this morning. How are you not cold? You have no coat on. And how is this Nashville? I don't remember it being like this."

"I read there was some sort of weather phenomenon going on," he replies. "And it's not going away any time soon." He indicates right. "We're headed this way."

We fall into step together and I say, "Well then you might need to actually wear a coat."

"Nah," he says. "I've spent some time in hellish cold climates. This is nothing."

When he was in the FBI, I assume, which clearly, from his whipped cream story, was a big part of how he created the incredible character of Ghost. I'm eager to know this man and his creative process, but I'm sure he gets those types of questions incessantly. Instead, I wonder about him, just him, and all there is to know about the man, not the author. "Are you from Nashville?" I ask.

"Boston," he replies with an exaggerated accent and a smile. "And now you know how I know bitter cold."

"You hide that accent well," I laugh. "I would never have guessed. But then again, I've never been to Boston either. I know the East Coast though. New York is the hottest and the coldest I've ever been in my life."

"But you want to go back?" he asks as we halt at an intersection.

"I don't know," I say, and I can't believe how easily being indecisive on this topic comes to me. "I should. I really should be eager to get back." I hug myself against the wind, or maybe, the storm of confusion that is my life right now, eagerly changing the topic. "What do you think about the venue?"

"I'm more interested in what you think," he replies, glancing down at me. "Your opinion will either validate what I think or prove me wrong."

I'm fairly certain that means he doesn't like it, and I wonder why in the world Hawk Legal chose his charity and didn't want him more involved. Or maybe he simply had deadlines and didn't have the time to be involved when this event originated, but he and Tyler just have such a tense vibe with each other it's hard not to read into anything involving the two of them.

The light turns and we walk another block to the venue. It is, indeed, a big, modern, fancy hotel. A few minutes later, Dash and I are standing in a very basic event room with a woman named Evelyn, the pretty blonde event coordinator who can't stop batting her lashes at Dash. For his part, he either doesn't notice, or he's immune to such attention. I mean he's famous and good-looking. He probably gets a lot of attention from everyone and often.

As for the event room, I'm not impressed. "Do you have vault services?" I ask.

Evelyn blinks and forces her gaze from Dash to me. "No, but you can hire private transport and security." Her cellphone buzzes in her hand and she glances at the screen. "I have to run up front," she says. "I'll swing back here in a few." She offers Dash her card. "If I miss you, my cellphone is on the card."

She doesn't offer me a card. She simply turns on her heels and starts walking. I watch her exit the room and when I glance back toward Dash, he's not watching her. He's watching me.

He steps closer to me, almost intimately so, and hands me the card, "What do you think, cupcake?"

His silly nickname for me is actually rather charming, but I resist a smile that will surely encourage him to continue the game. "Well, buttercup," I say, sticking the card in my purse. "I think it's impersonal and it doesn't feel special. We want people to feel that they're attending something highly exclusive and unique. And we have to have a vault on site."

"Exactly my thoughts," he concurs. "What if we had the event at Riptide? I know it's New York City, but it's certainly attention-grabbing."

"Unfortunately, Riptide can't accommodate the timeline needed," I say, "but we don't need fancy and elite to make this auction special. Intimate and exclusive could work just as well."

"Have you seen the rooftop at the Hawk Legal offices?"

"I haven't seen it but I'd say my primary concern is a need for a vault service."

"Tyler has a vault with lockboxes he uses for valuables and contracts."

"Oh. Well, that's unexpected."

"From what my sister tells me when you're dealing with their kind of clientele, there are times when those people want to protect assets and do so off the books."

The remark makes it clear that he doesn't see himself as one of those people. I like this about Dash. There's a lot I like about Dash. "Okay, so we have the event at Hawk Legal. I like it. But I'm sure Tyler won't like losing the money he put down at this venue."

"I doubt he'll lose it," he replies. "Hawk Legal is nothing if not powerful and resourceful."

My cellphone rings and I snake it from my purse to find an unfamiliar local number. Concerned for my mother, I quickly answer with, "Allison Wright."

"Ms. Wright."

At the sound of Tyler's sharp tone I stiffen and meet Dash's gaze as I reply with, "Mr. Hawk," I say, not pushing the name issue, not when I can hear the displeasure in his voice.

"When will you be returning to the office?" he queries. "We need to talk and set a few boundaries before I head to a meeting."

My heart races with the inference that I've done something wrong. "I'm at the venue now," I state. "I'll head that way."

"I'll be waiting." He hangs up. No goodbye. No other words.

Frowning, I shove my phone back inside my purse.

"Problem?" Dash asks, but his intelligent blue eyes say he already suspects what's going on.

With that in mind, I don't even consider mincing words. "I'm pretty sure you're the problem. I could tell that Tyler was pissed that I'd talked to you about what I had going on before I talked to him. He said he needs me back at the office to *set boundaries*."

His jaw sharpens. "I would agree with Tyler. You *do* need to set boundaries. Yours, not his."

"Easier done when I'm educated on what I'm dealing with," I say, continuing down my direct path. "There's a notable tension between you and Tyler," I dare. "I'm not asking what it's about. That's not my business, but I do need to know how to navigate it."

"Tyler and I have an understanding that works for us," he says tightly. "I've drawn my line in the sand. Make sure you draw that line for yourself. Make sure he knows you don't need this job because he does need

126

you." When I would reply, he steps closer to me, really close, so close I can feel the heat of his body, and I seem to have lost not just my thought, but the use of my vocabulary.

I hold my breath anticipating whatever is coming.

But seconds tick by, and he says nothing. He's just looking at me, staring at me, and then, "Let's get you back," and I can all but feel a wall slam between us, but I'm not sure why. He steps back and motions me toward the door.

I feel like I should say something, defuse the tension with some brilliant joke that I just can't come up with. Forced to accept the awkwardness, I start walking.

We exit into the hallway and head for the lobby, and his pace is quick, our path through the hotel quick with it. Once we're outside, the wind, fiercer than earlier, pounces on us but he doesn't react. He is truly more stone than man right now and I don't understand how the easy laughter between us transformed and became as chilled as the weather. Stealing a peek at him, I search for a sign of the former, but there is nothing to find but hard lines and obstacles.

We are winding down on our path to the Hawk building, and I fear our goodbye to be as cold as this walk. At this point, we're a few feet from the Hawk entryway, when unexpectantly, Dash catches my arm and pulls me behind one of two towering statues of guitars. His hand that so quickly scorches me with his touch, is just suddenly gone, and now presses above my head. But he is close again, so very close, the earthy, wonderfully male scent of him, teases my senses. Every part of me is aware of this man.

"You're vulnerable right now, Allie," he says roughly, "a lamb in a lion's cage. Go back home before you end up hurt."

I blanch, shocked at what I can only call a dismissal and one that I do not expect. "What? I—I don't understand. You said Tyler needs me. You said we'd work together, not that I need you to do that, but I'm—I'm just very confused right now."

There is a flicker in his eyes I cannot read, and even as I try, his lashes lower, seconds ticking by, dark shadows flirting across his expression before he says, "Go home," and when he meets my stare, whatever I'd thought I'd seen before, is wiped away. "Before you get hurt," he adds.

"By Tyler or by you, Dash?" I challenge.

He captures my waist under my jacket, his touch branding me, and pulls me flush against him, all of my softness molded to his hard body. A hot fire burns in my belly as his warm breath fans my face. His gaze lingers on mine and then drops to my mouth. I think—I think he's thinking of kissing me and I can barely breathe. I *want* him to kiss me like I have never wanted to be kissed before and that need, that *absolute need*, expands in my belly.

Seconds tick by and neither of us move, speak—we barely breathe. I don't know what he's thinking, what he's feeling. I don't know if it's anger, lust, regret, but I do believe I crave any and all of it with this man. But then Dash breaks the moment before anything can be realized, at least for me.

"Go back to New York, Allison," he orders, and with that he releases me, and then he leaves. He walks away.

I collapse against the statue, trying to catch my breath, confused, so very confused. And Lord help me, I can still feel his hands on my body, still feel the warmth from where our bodies had melded together. He accused me of being vulnerable, and I can't argue that point. He's not wrong. I've had that very thought myself. I *am* vulnerable, and it's not the first time I've found myself feeling as such, but I'm also stronger than I was before. I'm here, and it feels like part of my journey and my growth.

And I'm not leaving my mother, or Nashville, until I'm ready to.

CHAPTER TWENTY-EIGHT

By the time I'm inside the Hawk Legal building I've admitted to myself that I not only feel judged by Dash, I was judged unworthy. At least I think that's what happened. I'm honestly not all that sure. And I'm not sure how any of this impacts my job. It's Dash's choice of charity this year and I'm the head of that project. Or I was. Maybe I'm not anymore.

Stepping into the elevator car, I jab angrily at the button for my floor, not sure why I'm so upset. I barely know Dash. He has no idea what I can and cannot do and I have another job waiting for me at Riptide.

I am *not* a lamb in a lion's cage.

Been there, done that, will never do it again.

Dash Black is wrong. And an asshole.

I might not know what I'm doing with my life right now, but I'm not lost. I was wrong about that. I mean, not really. I certainly don't need to be found. I'm simply keeping doors open and options plentiful which means that I need to click with Tyler and Hawk Legal.

The elevator arrives at my destination, and I face facts. I might not be able to leave my mother and go back to New York City. That means a job with Hawk Legal long-term could work for me, even if the other Allison does come back. With this in mind, I turn right and head toward Tyler's offices, entering the receptionist area to find the desk empty again. I hook a path down the hallway and make a beeline for Tyler's office.

His door stands open and I knock on the frame but he doesn't answer. Peeking inside the room, I find him absent. Sighing, I turn around and decide to walk down the hallway to my right. I end up in a media room

131

complete with leather chairs and TVs lining the walls. Tyler is standing in the center of the space watching a golf game. I'm struck instantly by how he all but punches a room with power, just by being in it.

At present, Eddie V., the hottest golfer on the scene, is center stage—so hot that I know him and I don't know golf. The next Tiger Woods, he's being called.

"Is he a client?" I ask, stepping into the room and joining Tyler.

"He is," he replies, glancing over at me for the first time since I entered the room. "And it won't matter if he wins or loses, I have to be ready to game his position."

"I don't think I realized your team operated like agents to the extent you obviously do," I comment, interested in this side of the Hawk Legal business, as publishing has set me up to be comfortable in these types of relationship dynamics.

"And I don't think you realize that you work for me, not Dash Black," he replies, turning to face me, thus I turn to face him. "Do I or do I not *own* you for the next three months?"

He *owns me.*

Those words and the force of his blue eyes, scream of dominance and demand, that hits about a dozen personal triggers me, and therefore borders outside the lines of professional and becomes personal.

I fight the urge to push back and push back hard, but I'm not sure that would be about him, and this moment, or me and those that I've known before him. For this reason, I choose to discreetly share my view on his role versus my own role here at Hawk Legal.

"I know that I work for you, Tyler, but I need direction."

His eyes glint with what I believe to be amusement, and to my surprise, what I believe to be just a hint of respect, but his reply is no less demanding. "And I'll be happy to give you all the direction you need, Ms. Wright. Me, *not him.*"

This is where I should probably tell Tyler that Dash told me to go back to New York, but somehow that doesn't seem a vote for me to keep my job. Maybe Dash is testing me. Maybe he just wants to know I won't buckle and run. No. No, I'm not going to run or tell Tyler about my confrontation with Dash.

"I expect to know what's going on," he adds.

To which I say, "All right then. The venue is a fail. I think we should ask for a refund. It's cold and plain, and cold and plain doesn't do justice to the Hawk Legal name. And it lacks a vault system. Dash suggested we hold it on the rooftop here and use your vaults. In my opinion, an exclusive intimate event works."

"I'd rather hear your opinion," he says, in a clear rebuff of all things Dash Black. "Have you seen the rooftop?"

"I haven't yet. No."

"Then get back to me when you make the same suggestion. What else?"

"Can we use the vaults here?"

"Yes."

"We'll need armed guards on hand," I add.

"Make it happen. What else?"

"We need a few high-profile auction items and we need them quickly. I'm working on donations but if you can get me a few items to tease the event that would help."

"You'll get what you need," he says simply.

I don't know what that means but he's proven to be a man of his word. "How much are we going to charge Riptide to sponsor the event?"

"What do you suggest I should charge them?"

"I suggest we should pay them to authenticate the items. I believe I can get them to discount that service if they're the official sponsors at no charge. That's a win for both parties."

He just looks at me, his stare hard and flat, unreadable. Unbidden, it rattles me, and I am forced to recognize how much I actually want to please this man. But I'm not sure that need is really as much about Tyler and it is a broader view of my life, and the men I've encountered along my way. Powerful and demanding men. Men like Tyler. It's a problem for me and I know it.

And because I'm suffocating in my own head, I choose to do exactly his bidding. I take the bait of the silence and end it myself. "Do we have a deal?" I press.

"Yes, Ms. Wright," he says, his voice transforming to a softer tone, his eyes sharper now on my face. "We have a deal. What else?"

It's the third time he's asked that, but I hesitate with where I want to go which is to Allison, again. I want to know about the house, and what happens if I move in and she comes back. I want to ask who would send her a necklace. I want to ask so many things, but bringing up Allison when he's still chewing on Dash doesn't seem smart. Instead, I say, "Thank you for taking my need for help seriously. I like Katie and I think she'll be helpful."

The crowd on the television feed blows up with excitement over something his client has done but his focus stays on me. "I've emailed you a budget for the event that I expect you to manage and a schedule of events you'll be attending."

"I'll look it all over right away," I say. "I need to call the clients of the firm and ask for donations. Am I allowed to do so?"

"I've already introduced you to the firm by email. The attorneys are talking to their clients. They'll connect you. At that point, yes, you may talk to the clients."

"Time matters," I argue. "And your attorneys are busy with other things."

"Everyone here has clients who need tax write-offs," he assures me, effectively tying my hands on communication. "You will have that need," he says, "my voice on the matter, and the party, on the side of progress."

I'd argue that I need all those things and a voice of my own, but I obviously need to earn his trust. Therefore, I simply say, "What else do you need from me?"

That's when he sideswipes me. "I trust you've accepted the offer to live in my rental house?"

"Yes, about that," I say and seize my window of opportunity he's now presented, "what if Allison returns?"

I expect him to tell me I have a contract. Instead, he simply says, "We'll deal with that when the time comes."

"Does she know I'm staying in the house?"

There's a tic to his jaw and something sharp in his eyes that's there and gone in a blink of a moment. Not for the first time, I wonder if Allison is personal to him. "Are you staying in the house or not, Ms. Wright?"

"It's a generous offer," I reply. "Thank you. I packed to move in tonight."

"Good. There's wine in the cellar. The only bottles off-limits are in the vault." His cellphone rings and he snakes it from his pocket, glances at the caller ID, and then me, "I need to take this. Keep me informed and remember who you *work for*." His lips twitch with the obvious reference to our "own" versus "work for" exchange. He heads for the door and I turn to watch him exit the room, but he pauses and looks back at me. "There are many things I need, Ms. Wright. I have yet to determine if I need them from you specifically."

I blanch, not sure he's actually talking about the job. I mean he *is* talking about the job, but that little smile gives me the distinct impression he wants me to wonder.

He disappears out of the room.

CHAPTER TWENTY-NINE

After discarding my coat and bags in my office, I head for the office Katie's presently using as her own. I find her sitting behind her desk, finger deep in the icing on top of a cupcake. She grins when she sees me and licks the icing from her finger. I laugh and she says, "This is the best icing I've ever had. Thank you for the cupcakes."

"I'm glad you like them. And I love that icing, so much."

"We should order these for the auction," she suggests.

"My thought as well," I say, "and on that note, how about showing me the rooftop, please? I'm thinking of using it for the auction."

"What happened to the hotel?"

"It's very cold and average."

"Hmmm. Yes. I couldn't agree more." She takes a bite of her cupcake, gives me a thumbs-up, and then reluctantly leaves her sweet treat for later.

A few minutes later, we're inside a spacious rectangular room lined with windows that allow for a stunning view of downtown Nashville. There are cozy seating areas speckled throughout the space, a high-end restaurant-worthy bar, and a food service area. Televisions are strategically located near seating areas.

"This is really quite perfect," I approve. "Do you know where the vaults are located?"

"On this floor," she says. "Just down the hall. But how do we get out of the hotel reservations? Didn't we put down a deposit?"

"I assume we did," I concur, "but if I can make this happen, I want to. We need this to be more intimate, more exclusive." I step to the window, staring out at the bright colored lights marking the dark night, and one could say New York City has a bigger, better skyline. But not everyone. Maybe not me.

Katie steps to my side. "It's an addictive city, don't you think?"

"It is," I agree, glancing over at her. "Are you from Nashville?"

"Texas," she says. "I went to school in Knoxville but I fell in love with Nashville. When I graduated two years ago, I landed here."

"And Allison was here then?"

"She started after me but she was a favorite quickly."

"Favorite?"

"Of Tyler's," she explains. "She had it made. That's why I'm shocked that she left us like she did and really truly, kind of high and dry for this auction. I mean, she had it made here. We all knew it. She knew it, too."

"What do you mean? She knew?"

"She just *knew*. It's hard to explain."

"She worked closely with Tyler, almost more his assistant than his assistant is."

Interesting, I think, but there's no proof they were involved. I don't ask about that, either. I just don't know Katie well enough to know how that would travel through the office.

"One day she was here," Katie adds, "and the next, she wasn't, but she was acting weird the week before she left, withdrawn, and edgy when that just wasn't her. Clearly, she had something personal going on."

Considering the necklace delivery, Katie is probably exactly right on that. "Maybe it was man trouble," I comment, fishing for a name.

"Maybe. She went on a week-long trip to some tropical island with a rich guy right before she quit. That's what was so weird about all of this. She was only back a week and then she was gone."

"Maybe her rich man proposed and she took time off to get married."

"There was no ring and she wouldn't tell me his name. I think he must have been married."

Married, I repeat in my head. Considering Allison's sudden departure, and weird behavior, that sounds rather ominous.

And considering what I know of my father's wining and dining of his mistresses with expensive gifts and fancy trips, the necklace definitely falls into form. Unfortunately, my mother not only found out about those gifts, but one of the other women told her he used those lavish gifts to take the sting out of the other woman, whoever she was at the time, being *the other woman*. This all comes together and reminds me of a book I once edited. The mistress ended up dead. I don't like where my head is going right now.

"I do believe I like my version of the story better," I reply, glancing over at Katie with a growing urgency to erase the silence between me and the other Allison. "Do you happen to have Allison's phone number?"

"I do," she says. "I left her a message earlier today just to talk about the auction, but it went to her voicemail. She hasn't called me back and I really don't know if she will. We were more casual work friends than real friends." She indicates her phone. "I'll text you her number. Then you'll have mine and hers."

"Great," I say. "Thank you." I give her my number and she pings my phone with a text.

Katie glances at her watch. "Shit. I have to do reception relief. I've got to run." She races for the door.

My finger itches to dial Allison, but I wait until Katie exits the room, and I'm alone. After which, I punch the link to the number and wait for it to ring. The call goes straight to voicemail.

This is Allison. I'm not available right now but you know the drill. Leave a number. Or don't, and text me.

Her voice is sweet and young and a little familiar, which is odd. There's a beep and I say, "Hi Allison. This is also Allison. I'm filling in for you at Hawk Legal. I'd really like to talk to you about the auction. Please call me if you can." I leave my number and hang up.

Drawing a breath, I glance around the room, with low lighting, and empty seating, with an eerie feeling of emptiness and unease, I can't quite really explain. My gaze returns to my phone and I type out a text message to Allison that says basically the same thing as my message. I'm horrible at listening to voice messages. Maybe she is as well. Once the message is sent, my gaze goes to the horizon where hues of orange and yellow are like watercolors melding into the quickly darkening skyline. A bit like Allison's life is melded with mine. I'm living her life, not mine, which is probably, most likely, not a good thing, but I'm here, I'm not leaving. And as of lately, I've become an expert worrier and I'm using those skills on her now.

I tell myself that she packed her things and left the house I'm about to live in. She made an active decision to leave her job and her home. She's fine.

And yet, unease inside me squeezes a little harder and I can't help but feel something is not right with her departure and therefore my arrival in her place.

CHAPTER THIRTY

Me and Katie work late that night.

For reasons I can't explain I dread going to my new temporary home, the one the other Allison left behind. As for Katie, I don't know what her excuse for refusing to leave is, but it's nearly seven when I push her out of the door for the evening. It's nearly eight when I finally leave the dimly lit, ghost town of an office, and mostly because I'm feeling a creepy vibe right about now. I walk through the lobby, rubbing my neck with the tingling sensation there. Once I'm in the parking garage, I make sure my keys are in my hand, and I all but run to my car. Truly, I can't climb inside fast enough and get the doors locked. As I'm pulling onto the street, I laugh at myself. This is what a fiction editor does. She sees a murder mystery everywhere she looks, as I did earlier, talking to Katie about Allison.

I'm driving myself nuts.

Dismissing the creepy feeling, on the way to my new home, which is *her* old home, I continue my stall tactics by swinging by the grocery store where I shop like the single person who doesn't cook that I am. I buy Lean Cuisines, low-fat cherry yogurt, coffee, creamer, Splenda, and not much else. I'm exciting like that. I pull up to the garage and guess at the password on the security panel being the same as the door. Sure enough, it is.

Once I'm safely sealed inside the garage, I leave my things behind and head for the door.

I pause there with butterflies in my belly and a hint of that creepy feeling I'd had back at the office.

Drawing a deep breath, I key in the code and open the door. I enter through a mudroom that leads to an open concept kitchen and a living room with a fireplace. Wood beams line the ceiling giving it a cozy feeling. The kitchen is a beautiful teal blue with an impressively modern and quite spacious island. Just this area of the house alone is bigger than my entire apartment back in New York City. The house is pretty incredible. My discomfort evaporates.

Eager now to get settled, I hurry back into the garage and retrieve my bags, making several trips. Once my groceries are put away in the fancy stainless steel fridge, I'm relieved to find a coffee pot which means I won't go without my morning fix. I didn't even consider not having one when I bought groceries. Turns out, the kitchen is fully stocked which supports Tyler having a "tenant" for insurance reasons, I guess.

Leaving my personal things in the kitchen, I survey the rest of the house which includes a small library, a balcony overlooking a pool, a gym which, considering my bad eating habits lately, really excites me, several bedrooms, and finally a master. The en suite bathroom is magnificent, complete with a fancy half egg-shaped tub and a walk-in closet with so much space I could sleep in it. Fortunately, considering I'd forgotten the need for such things, the linen closet is stocked. I feel spoiled and out of my element, but I remind myself that New York City is about living compact. This is Nashville. Everything is bigger in Nashville.

A few minutes later, my feet are in my Ugg slippers, my Lean Cuisine is microwaving, and I am now noticing the door off the main room I haven't explored. This must lead to the wine vault. I open the door, flip on a light and find a long set of stairs. Hurrying downstairs, I find an incredible room lined with bottles of wine, with a fancy shiny wood table in the center of the shelving. Just beyond this space, is the vault. It's strange that Tyler keeps this here. I don't understand it, but I guess it's not my business.

Per Tyler, I'm allowed to drink whatever wine I like. With this in mind, I surf the many shelves to find a red blend that I suspect is ridiculously expensive. I'm tempted, I really am, but I slide it back into place. No matter what Tyler said about drinking whatever I want, I feel weird about it. The microwave buzzer goes off to indicate my TV dinner is ready and I head upstairs. A few minutes later, I'm at the island with my meal and my MacBook. I intend to do my work. Instead, I google "Dash Black dating."

It's a mistake.

He was notably in a relationship with a gorgeous blonde model who probably never eats cupcakes. God, what was I thinking? He's not into *me*. I don't know what that was going on between us, but I assume it has something to do with his charity and public image. I really should have opened the bottle of wine. Instead, I stuff a bite of food in my mouth. Once my dinner is in my belly, apparently being upset over Dash doesn't hurt my appetite, I pull the necklace from my briefcase and set it on the counter next to me. Flipping open the lid, I stare down at the sparkling jewels, wondering if this could be a gift from Tyler. I mean he gave her this house. Of course, he gave it to me, too, and there's nothing between me and Tyler. And why would Tyler have the necklace delivered to the very office they both worked at?

No. I don't think Tyler sent the necklace, but I'm speculating.

I google Allison and try to find her social profiles, but come up dry. I'd say that was odd but sometimes people are hard to find. Probably because I hate social media, therefore I'm not that savvy with the search. Truly the only reason I have accounts is for work reasons. Even then, I rely on our dedicated social media person at Riptide for most things.

I'm just not sure what to do with it now. Maybe I could ask Tyler to put it in the vault and watch his reaction when he sees it? Not yet, I think. This is Allison's private matter. I'll give her time to call me back.

Glancing from the necklace and around the cozy room, I find it hard to believe Allison left all of this.

It's almost as if she was running away and not necessarily out of fear. If I'm honest with myself, there are things in New York I'd like to run from.

It would be so easy just to stay here in Nashville.

The question is: would I regret it?

And will Allison regret leaving all this behind?

And where will either of us be in the aftermath of our regret?

CHAPTER THIRTY-ONE

Models with long legs and perfect bodies, who date famous authors probably eat fruit. Or they don't eat at all. Cupcakes make for a good breakfast for us humans who have to go to work early. I say this at the wee hour of seven AM, as I sit behind my desk and take a bite of my cupcake. And because I'm me, and things go this way for me, Tyler—looking oh so arrogantly good-looking in a blue pinstriped suit—chooses that moment to appear in the doorway.

I quickly sip my home-brewed coffee and try to swallow as delicately as possible, but the entire process doesn't go well. I'm two for two on this eating around hot men thing and I don't believe I'll try for three for three. It takes a moment or ten and Tyler just stands there, watching my struggle. Funny thing is how judged I feel while the same situation with Dash felt—different. It was different.

"Morning," I finally say.

"Good morning, Ms. Wright," he replies, thankfully ignoring my struggle. "I trust you settled into the house well?"

"I did. It's a beautiful house. I feel spoiled. Thank you." I stand up.

"Quid pro quo," he says. "It helps me and it helps you. Did you look at our lounge area?"

"I did. It's beautiful and perfect. I'd love to hold the event there, but how much will that cost you with the hotel?"

"Nothing. Tell them we want a refund. If they don't cooperate, tell me. Then I assure you, they will."

Of this, I have no doubt. "I'll do that this morning."

"What is your plan to intake auction donations?"

"I'm meeting with the head of the charity again today for that very reason. Obviously, we plan to have Hawk Legal's clients become the biggest source of donations, but if they bid on items and win, that counts as a donation as well. That means I need items for them to want to bid on. I'm going to call her prior donors myself, but first, we're going to go over what I need to know about each before I do so. I'd like to do the same with someone here on a list of clients."

"Email me a list," he states. "Don't call anyone I don't approve first. You should have my number in your phone, but check your email. I sent it anyway. We're holding a birthday event for a client Friday night at my house. I suggest you attend and figure people out yourself. You might find at least one noteworthy surprise."

He says nothing more. He just disappears into the hallway, leaving me and my cupcake to wonder what an event at Tyler Hawk's house will be like. I think of him catching me eating a cupcake and decide there is one certain word: uncomfortable. And of course, my next thought is to wonder if Dash Black will be there. Just as I wonder if he will be at my meeting with Millie this afternoon. He knows about it, but he also told me to quit. Okay, technically he told me to go home. Same thing. Isn't it? I really should tell Tyler about this little Dash situation but it might well be the end for me. I could call Dash and try to talk things out, but somehow that doesn't feel right either.

I'll just go to the meeting with Millie and carry on.

Good or bad, that's my plan.

CHAPTER THIRTY-TWO

My meeting time with Millie arrives with me a bundle of nerves that all come down to my hope and fear that Dash might attend.

So much so that as I walk to the meeting, the cold day doesn't even compute. Instead, all the ways this meeting could go badly consume me. My rambling mind goes a little like this:

Dash told me to go back to New York.

Asshole.

Dash is supposed to be at this meeting.

Asshole.

Dash may have told Millie there's no need to meet me at the bookstore for those reasons.

Or Dash could just show up and tell me to go home all over again.

Please don't be an asshole, Dash.

I enter the bakery side of the bookstore, and my fear that Dash might have instructed Millie to cold-shoulder me ends quickly. Millie, looking quite beautiful in a black dress that contrasts with her red curls, greets me with a hug and a smile. "Thank God you're involved in this," she proclaims. "I really feel better about things."

"Hopefully Dash does as well," I say, feeling her out for any input he might have offered or any blow that might be to follow. If it's coming, just hit me with it now.

"Dash is wonderful," she says. "Truly committed to our cause and now that we have you on board, I feel good about meeting and exceeding our fundraising goals."

That's it. That's all she says about Dash. Obviously, he hasn't talked to her at all and she moves on to the topic of Allison. "I really liked Allison, but she seemed distracted. I really wasn't surprised to hear she left."

"She's on leave," I say. "I do think she'll be back."

"Please tell me that doesn't mean you won't be here to the finish line."

"I will. Even if I have to finish up as a part of Riptide's team, rather than that of Hawk Legal. This is going to be grand," I promise. "Which reminds me. I need to call my boss about the sponsorship, and we need coffee, don't you think?"

"Yes, indeed," she agrees.

After that, the meeting is productive. Mark is on board with the free sponsorship in trade for helping with the valuation of the auction items, and Millie has a great list of prospective donors. And while for the most part, I'm fully engrossed in the meeting, I can't help a few hopeful peeks at the table where Dash was working yesterday. He simply never shows up.

It's disappointing, more so than I truly expected it to be.

CHAPTER THIRTY-THREE

That evening me and my Lean Cuisine are keeping each other company at my new kitchen island. I shoot a quick email to Tyler detailing how I'd like to handle the Riptide sponsorship, as well as the list of clients Allison kept as auction prospects.

He replies almost immediately: I'm headed out of town for the remainder of the week. We'll discuss everything when I return, after I see how you handle my clients at the party.

The email stings of distrust. No, I amend, not distrust. *Control.*

A familiar quality I've come to know well.

My cellphone rings where it sits on the counter next to me, my mother's number on caller ID. "Hey, Mom," I greet. "Are you headed home?"

"We're going to Vegas first. Remember the Garth Brooks Concert?"

"You said Texas, not Vegas."

"I meant Vegas. I guess I subconsciously thought you'd freak out if you knew we were going to both."

The idea of Vegas punches me in the chest one moment but in the next, I feel joy. My mother loves Garth, and she's alive and living a happy life. It's then that I realize that freedom is both a right and a choice.

That sounds crazy, I know, but too often so many of us are guilty of being chained by our own fears, worries, inhibitions, and of course, self-esteem issues. I know I'm guilty of all of these things, my fear of losing my mother has become not only my own chains but my mother's.

"You're not saying anything," she says. "You're freaking out, aren't you?"

"I'm not freaking out. I'm jealous. I love Garth, too. You should have invited me."

"Then I couldn't make-out with your stepfather when the romantic songs come on."

"Oh, good Lord, Mother. My ears. The images in my head."

"Oh, whatever, silly girl. How's the new job?"

I'm smiling when I say, "It's good," and let her off the hook for everything about this conversation. We then chat a bit about the auction. "I really think it's a good cause. They need me and I need this. I'm *supposed* to be here right now, doing this."

"I do believe you are," she agrees. "How about brunch next Sunday? I want to hear more about it. Maybe I can help. I'll make those waffles you love."

"I'd love that mom. See you then."

When we disconnect, I feel more at peace with her recovery than I have since her illness rocked our worlds. She is free of that monster, I tell myself.

And so am I.

Later, when I lay in bed alone, I don't fret about her safety. Instead, I think of Dash, remembering his hands on my body. And I wonder if he will be at Tyler's party, but I decide he won't be. The two men do not get along. Of that, I am certain.

CHAPTER THIRTY-FOUR

On the evening of the party, I leave work much later than planned, but do so with the knowledge that, thanks to Millie's list, I've secured a few hot ticket auction items, sure to entice bidders to attend. I'm actually starting to feel like I can pull this off as a big win for the charity and in the end, Riptide will see this as a win for them as well.

But I'm really pushing it on time.

It's six when I step in the door to the house and immediately head for the bedroom.

After fretting much of this week about what to wear tonight, I change my mind again tonight at least three times. I end up in a belted burgundy dress with a pleated skirt and a V-neck. It's simple but classy, and it feels like the right choice. It's also expensive, a Chanel label, and one of my high-end thrift store finds, I most love. With a little black Burberry bag at my hip, I head to the garage and climb in my car. It doesn't start. I try again. And again and again, before I accept the inevitable. The car is old, so old it was my car in college, and it's barely been used in years. Why my mother kept it, I don't know, but it was convenient to have it here until it wasn't.

I don't have time to deal with this now.

My cellphone rings and I glance down to find Tyler on my caller ID. Great, fabulous. Wonderful. I answer with, "Hi," my definitive way to prove I'm intelligent and on the ball.

"Where are you, Ms. Wright? I'd have assumed you'd want to be here early, not after the guests have arrived."

"I would have been but Milton Ryder, the CEO of Ryder Electronics, called me as I was walking out the door. He donated a comic book to the auction worth a pretty penny. But I'm dressed and ready to go. I'm about to call an Uber now."

"Where is your car?"

"Apparently it's ready for the graveyard. It's my old college car my mother refused to let go."

"I'll send a driver. Be ready." He disconnects.

I scowl at the phone. I guess any discussion on the topic is over.

With a sigh, I hurry to the front of the house where I wait for the car, which arrives with remarkable quickness. I'm then driven to a nearby location. The high-end ritzy side of Belle Meade, where we enter through a security panel-controlled gate and follow a round drive. The center of the grounds, which are quite expansive, sports a round waterfall, while the house itself is modern looking with several levels, almost like two rectangles stacked unevenly.

I'd expected Tyler's home to be stunning. I wasn't wrong.

Nor am I surprised to find a valet parking cars. The driver pulls me to the door, and the valet attends to my exit. Soon, I'm walking several levels of steps to the double frosted-glass front doors. I'm greeted by a doorman who opens the door for me and invites me inside. My coat is taken from me and I wonder who the party is for since Tyler didn't tell me and I didn't know if I was allowed to discuss it elsewhere. Not when everything could be a test.

I ease into the room where the floors are dark wood and the room is all clean lines, with the fireplace as the modern centerpiece. The furniture is brown, rich, masculine leather. I'd expect nothing less from Tyler Hawk. The kitchen island is a brown and cream combo of my dreams with fancy designer lights hanging low. But the most impactful part of the room is the double doors opened to a spectacular pool area while at least fifty people inside and out mingle about.

It's a stunning home.

I accept a glass of champagne, which I sip, just in time to have Tyler appear in front of me.

He's in a suit, of course, because he's Tyler. He probably sleeps just like he is right in this moment. Or naked. Not that I want to find out. Tyler might be the kind of powerful man I've been drawn to in the past, but never again. Of that, I firmly vow.

His blue eyes narrow on me, almost as if he can hear my thoughts, and then slide up and down my body. The blatant inspection that follows heats my cheeks and ends with a burning look of approval and command. "Come with me."

He turns and starts walking.

I quickly keep pace, praying I don't spill the drink I should have declined. Our destination is the center of a group of people near the fireplace, and Tyler easily parts the crowd. I join him and suck in a breath, as I find myself standing directly across from, the one, and only, Dash Black.

LISA RENEE JONES

CHAPTER THIRTY-FIVE

My heart is racing.

Tyler is talking to the group, *about me*, I think, but I can't process what he's saying. Not really. Not when Dash is standing right in front of me looking like sin and seduction in jeans, a sweater, and a sleek black jacket he's paired with boots. And when my eyes meet his eyes, he's looking at me, too.

I expect to find anger or contempt in his stare at my presence, but that's not what I find at all. There's an instant, intense punch of awareness between us that steals my breath and quakes the ground beneath my feet. In my mind, we're back at that guitar statue, and his hands are on my body. Heat rushes over my skin.

"Meet Allison," Tyler says, jolting me back to the group. "She's heading up our new annual charity auction this year." And then he's introducing me to people, and I'm shaking hands with one man, then another, then a woman.

The woman, Susie, fifty-something, in a red dress, with light brown hair, eyes Dash. "The charity is your choice this year, correct?" She grins at Tyler. "See? I really read your emails."

"Nice to hear," Tyler replies, "though I doubt that's true. You're too busy directing mega film projects to read my emails. I suggest you heard about the auction here tonight."

"It is my charity choice," Dash replies, and there's no missing his cool confidence, and comfort in himself, something that contrasts Tyler's wicked arrogance.

"Allie works for the world-class auction house Riptide in New York," Dash adds, saying what Tyler has not. "We won't have her for long, but I have a feeling she'll leave a lasting impression."

I'm instantly unsure how to take the comment. Is he complimenting me or reminding me that I don't belong here?

My eyes meet his again, and that punch is still there, but there is something else, something I cannot read, nor do I have time to contemplate. Susie answers with, "I have a few items from movie sets I can donate. Do you have a card, Allison?"

"I do," I say, reaching in my purse and handing her a Riptide card. "You can email, text, or call. And thank you for any donations."

"Of course," she replies. "Anything for Dash." She turns to face him. "Let's talk about your next project. The one you can do with me."

Dash holds up his hands and says, "Let me get through the one I'm writing now first. Call Bella. She knows more than I know, or so she thinks."

"She's always been the brains in your operation," Tyler says dryly.

"There's a reason why she's my agent," Dash replies, a lift to his lips that isn't quite a smile nor is it a smirk.

The two men stare at each other, a crackle in the air between them, that's hard to miss, as if they've spoken beyond the obvious words, and nothing pleasant.

Susie though, appearing oblivious to this interaction, be it by choice or ignorance, quickly chimes in with, "We all know who has the creativity in the group," Susie interjects, "and it's not me." She eyes Dash again. "That's why I need to partner with people like you."

Tyler's lips thin. "I need to check on the guest of honor," he says, glancing down at me with a piercing stare as he adds, "Meet people, Ms. Wright, and remember what we talked about." With that command,

and the reminder that I work for him, not Dash, he fades out of the circle.

Dash arches a brow at me.

And for reasons I can't explain I react defensively, my arms folding in front of me.

"Why don't you, me, and Bella have lunch?" Susie asks Dash, unconcerned about Tyler's absence.

Dash is saved a reply as a good-looking man with sandy brown hair joins our little circle. Susie lights up at his appearance. "The best stuntman in the business," she says. "Good to see you, Joe."

Dash uses Joe's presence as an opportunity to step closer to me, catching my elbow heat igniting with the touch. "Why don't we go outside and talk?" he asks softly, urging me to walk with him.

And I do because frankly, I'm unable to think clearly when he's touching me. Really truly, I'm quite angry with him and me, that he can snub me and still impact me this much, this easily. Which is exactly why, the minute we step outside and he pulls me into a corner of the patio rather than melding us with the crowd, I round on him with demand. "Why are you even here? You and Tyler clearly don't like each other."

"For you, Allie," he answers softly, his voice butter soft and silky, but I refused to be seduced. "I came for you."

My chin lifts in defiance. "Because you wanted to tell me to go home again?"

"I'm not going to tell you to go home again." His hand not so discreetly settles at my waist, a hot branding that weakens my knees. "I think we can make this auction successful together."

"But you said—"

"And I was wrong," he admits, the confession taking me off guard. "I don't want you to get hurt."

"I don't need you to protect me."

"I know that, too," he says. "If I made it seem as if that wasn't the case, I'm sorry."

My lips part in surprise and for good reason. A second apology drives home sincerity. And most men, or rather, the men I know who are as powerful as Dash Black, never apologize, at least not and mean it. Further unraveling my resistance to his charms this night, he adds, "But I also can't seem to help myself."

"I don't know what that means," I reply, breathless and I'm not sure why aside from the fact that he affects me in ways no other man ever has. And I barely know him.

"I don't either," he says, and it feels like a confession, that only adds to my confusion. "But we'll figure it out."

"There you are, Dash. I swear I need a drink and a friendly audience."

At the sound of Bella's voice, Dash's hand falls away, but not before he promises, "We'll talk later."

There's an implication in those words, that "later" means, *much* later, when we're alone, or at least I think there is. I'm not sure of anything ever with this man. I'm not even sure I'm over being angry with him and I'm pretty sure I should run from him.

But right then I admit, really admit, what I've tried to deny. I've been running a lot lately. And I'm also so damn tired of running away.

CHAPTER THIRTY-SIX

In unison, Dash and I turn to greet Bella. She's stunning in a black dress, with a flare at the bottom, her blonde hair flowing over her shoulders. Her blue eyes are so strikingly similar to Dash's, it's remarkable.

"Why are his parties always so stiff and uncomfortable?" Bella asks softly.

"Because he's stiff and uncomfortable," Dash replies, echoing my thoughts.

"No comment," she replies, giving me a wink. "I'll let you form your own opinions without mine, Allison."

"Allie," I say. "Call me Allie."

"Allie," she says, seemingly delighted at the offer. "How's the auction going?"

"Good," I say. "I scored a couple of big items this week and I feel like tonight will help move things along."

"I emailed my clients and asked for donations. I'll have some 'scores' for you soon."

"Thank you," I say. "I really appreciate that."

It's right then that Susie finds us again. "Just the two people I want to see together."

Of course, there are three of us, but she sees only money and success, which means Dash and Bella. But Bella proves her match, brilliantly avoiding the lunch commitment. Her finesse is inspiring but we're also joined by yet another guest, and our hiding place in the corner becomes Grand Central Station.

Later, much later, after I've met too many people to count, and with Bella or Dash by my side at all times, it seems, I've received a great many auction donation commitments.

At present, Dash is chatting with the stuntman, while Bella and I are standing by the cake display, eating birthday cake for some up-and-coming TV writer that I have yet to meet, and I share my observation of her party skills. "You're so smooth I think I need you to be my life agent."

"I'll be your life agent if you'll be mine. You're pretty smooth, too. The auction has had a good night."

"*If* everyone who promised donations comes through."

"They will. They all need the tax write-offs. And substance abuse is a real issue in our industry and our youth in general. It's easy to sell the connection, but it's a real one. Oh jeez," she murmurs, lifting a discreet finger toward Dash.

I glance up to find Susie by his side again.

Bella scowls. "So much for smooth. I need to go and save him." She sets her cake on the little round table we're standing at and heads in that direction.

I'm smiling as I watch her rescue Dash, but as my gaze shifts to the door of the house, my smile flatlines. I now know the "surprise" Tyler spoke of when telling me about the party and most likely the reason he hired me at all. My father, the Super Bowl champ quarterback, is headed in my direction. The world spins under my feet. I told him I never wanted to see him again, and now, he's here, and the swell of emotions in my chest, tells me I'm not going to handle this well.

Fortunately, his fans are many, and he's cornered by a group of men. I quickly step away from the table and head the only way that appears to be safe—down a garden path. I've made it several feet, dim lights around the path guiding me around a corner when someone catches my hand.

I whirl around to find Dash, holding onto me. "Dash," I whisper, swallowing hard.

He walks me to him, aligning our legs, and I let him. "What just happened?"

"Nothing, I just—"

"What just happened?" he presses gently.

"You'll think you were right about me being weak."

To my shock, he pulls me closer, and his fingers tangle in my hair. "I said vulnerable. Vulnerable is not weak. But make no mistake, *I am* weak when it comes to you, Allie."

"What does that even mean, Dash?" I whisper barely able to breathe with his touch.

"It means, I tried to stay away, I tried so damn hard, but I couldn't do it. I *can't stop* thinking about you. I can't stop *wanting* you."

On some remote level, I know that we're close to the other guests, to the crowd, and I know I should stop this now. I catch his hands near my waist as if this will halt the assault on my senses, but it does nothing except stir hunger in me, a hunger I am helpless to fight.

"We shouldn't be doing this," I manage weakly.

"Why do you think I've stayed away?" His fingers slide into my hair and he tilts my gaze, my mouth, to his. "If you don't tell me to stop now, Allie, I'm going to kiss you."

It's exactly what I've wanted since I met Dash and yet, I'm terrified right now. Terrified by how easily I believe this man could not only own me, but hurt me. And I try to fight what I need, too. I try so hard, but what I say is, "Don't," followed by, "Don't stop."

His mouth closes down on mine, his tongue pressing past my teeth in a sultry stroke that seduces every part of me. And just that easily, my arms circle his neck, and more than a year of recoiling into myself and licking my wounds, of protecting myself from being hurt again, evaporates as if the reasons I chose to do so never existed. Every part of me is done denying what I want. And what I want is Dash Black.

His hand molds me closer, a possessive touch that on some level, I know is dangerous. *He* is dangerous. His ability to affect me, to hurt me, *is dangerous,* but I can't seem to care. Voices sound nearby and I want them to just go away, and leave us alone, but it's too late to save the moment. Dash tears his mouth from mine and does so purposefully. "Let's get out of here," he says, catching my hand, his voice low and sounds as frustrated as I feel.

My reaction is an instant mental, *yes, please. Let's get out of here.* But Dash tugs me in the wrong direction, toward the voices, not away, forcing me to dig in my heels. "I can't go back out there."

The voices are just around the corner now, and I quickly explain. "Rob Wright is my father. And he's—"

"Here," he supplies. "Yes. I saw him." And he reads my rather obvious lead and adds, "But you don't want to see him."

"No," I admit feeling no guilt at my words. Not after what my father put me through. "No, I do *not* want to see him."

He studies me, searches my face, and when I think he might question why, he doesn't. "Come with me." And then he's leading down the path again, but this time, away from the party and I go willingly. Every step that places distance between me and my father, allows me to breathe just a little easier. And every step, somehow, brings me closer to Dash.

Our escape leads us to a side gate exit in a shadowed corner of the garden. "Where is your car?" Dash asks.

"Tyler sent a driver. I need to call for a ride." I reach for my purse to grab my phone.

He catches it and my hand. "I drove," he says. "Come with me, Allie."

It's a question filled with promise that I will not end this night alone, nor will he.

Come with me, Allie.

Simple words, but when spoken by this man, on this night, are not simple at all. And while my first reaction is another, *yes, please,* there is a voice of reason and self-preservation that has me saying, "I think you're dangerous, Dash Black."

His hand settles on my hip. "More than is good for you, baby, but tonight, I say, why don't you find out for yourself?" With the challenge, his hand slides to my lower back, fingers splaying there as he adds, "You need to know that I won't take you to Tyler's house. If you leave with me, you go *with me,* Allie."

There's a hint of something sharp in his tone, that I cannot name—jealousy, I decide. He's jealous of Tyler. This sexy, talented, confident man is jealous. And as proof of just how fucked up I am, this pleases me. It pleases me to near excess. "With you," I whisper.

His eyes warm, telling me, this pleases *him.*

He lifts my hand he still holds to his lips and kisses it, and somehow, it's the sexiest thing ever. "Stay here. I'll pull around and get you."

And then he's walking away, all confidence and swagger, leaving me alone to talk myself out of this. I wonder if he knows this, that time breeds regret and second thoughts.

But it doesn't matter his motivation, not on this.

I just want out of this place. And I want out *with him.*

CHAPTER THIRTY-SEVEN

My coat is inside Tyler's house, but I don't have any intention of going back in that house to get it.

Instead, I wait on Dash to pull his car around and do so as I hug myself against the chilly night and the even chillier reality of my relationship with my father. I cannot believe he showed up here. I don't know what Tyler's role was in sideswiping me, but I do know that my father intended just that—to sideswipe me. And it worked. I cannot get out of here quickly enough, but I also don't even know what car Dash drives.

I'm contemplating the need to exit the garden and walk out toward the driveway where I might risk a run-in with my father when the gate opens and Dash is standing there.

"Come on, baby," he says, catching my hand and pulling me through the gate, my belly fluttering with the endearment.

But when I think we will finally escape this party, and my father, Dash has no such idea. At least, not yet. He halts, just outside the garden, his hands catching my waist. "Ready to back out?"

My fingers curl on the hard, warm wall of his chest. "Why?" I challenge. "Because I'm a lamb and you're a lion?"

"Yes," he says softly.

I have no idea why his simple answer triggers me, but it's most likely about my father, but then again, I'm not sure I want to allow Dash that out, either. The second thoughts I wasn't having are now clear and present. I twist away from him, but when I would start walking, he catches me, rotating me back into him. His fingers splay on my lower back, our bodies molded snuggly together. "Where are you going?"

"I don't have it in me to play head games, Dash. My father is all about games. Tyler is no different. I can't take that from you, too."

"I don't play games."

"I'm having a hard time believing that right now. Just—I'll call an Uber."

"No, you will *not* call an Uber. If you really want to go back to Tyler's house—"

"My house," I amend. "I don't live in Tyler's house any more than any tenant does a rental property. And that house is the last place I want to be right now." My cellphone rings and I pull it from my purse to find Tyler's number on my caller ID. Anger jabs at me. He did this. He arranged for my father to be a *surprise* tonight. I hit decline.

Dash, who has obviously seen my caller ID, arches a brow.

I answer that non-question with a non-answer. "Can we please go now?"

His eyes glint intensely through the darkness, a second that becomes three before he captures my hand and starts walking.

Our destination turns out to be a sporty black BMW at the side of the house, out of the view of the front door, and parked under a willow tree. Dash is opening the passenger door for me and eager for the escape, I slide into the seat, sleek leather hugging my body. Dash shuts me inside, seals my fate for this evening, which will end with him. I think, on some level, this night, me going home with him, was always where we were going to land. I've just hooked my seatbelt and Dash is already sliding in beside me, man and machine, both fiercely masculine. He revs the engine and glances over at me. "My place."

It's not a question, but yet, it is a question. "Your place," I repeat.

His lips curve, satisfaction filling his handsome face, before he sets us in motion, driving us away from Tyler's house and toward his own.

CHAPTER THIRTY-EIGHT

Dash pulls us onto the highway, heading back toward downtown, and turns up the radio as Jason Aldean's "Girl Like You" begins to play. I smile at him and the radio choice. He smiles back and that push and pull of me staying behind or going has passed. I'm going with him. I'm all in on this night and so is he. The words of the song fill the air.

The night's moving fast but we ain't taking it slower
You hit me harder than a drink does
You're gonna take me all the way up
Something about you baby, got me going crazy

I sink back into my seat, the attraction between me and Dash charging the air, the earthy, masculine scent of him all around me, and I am swimming in the vast ocean of this man. He catches my hand and the heat between us is downright visceral, the looks we share heated, intimate. We've just entered downtown, anticipation and tension building, when a siren whirls behind us. Dash eyes his speed and then glances at me. "And I'm speeding." He glances over at me. "Obviously, I'm in a hurry to get you to my place."

And I'm in a hurry to get there, I think, as he pulls us over and then rolls down his window. An officer shows up at the door. "Sorry about that, officer. I do believe I was speeding."

"Well, sir," the officer replies, "I'll let you off if you let me just take a gander at this here car of yours. She is a beauty."

I'm kind of appalled at this reply, but Dash laughs a low rumble of laughter. "You can drive it if you want, Jack."

That's when I realize he knows Dash. "And wreck it?" Jack asks. "*Hell no. I just want to gander. And it's official, the M4 special edition Kith is a stunner.*"

Dash glances over at me. "Give me a minute, cupcake. I'll be right back."

I smile and nod, starting to actually like the "cupcake" nickname. Dash opens the door and steps outside and I can hear him talking to Jack. "Come by this weekend," Dash tells him. "You can drive it."

"No, man. I don't need to do that."

"It's cool," Dash says. "I don't mind at all. Just text me first to make sure I'm there."

They talk another minute or so, and Dash climbs back inside. "Sorry about that."

"No ticket?"

"No ticket," he says. "Jack's a good guy. He actually gave me a ticket when I first moved to Nashville and I took it on the chin. We ran into each other at a restaurant a few months later and we've been friends ever since."

I like this about Dash, the way he seems to get along with everyone. Well, except Tyler, of course. "So, he never intended to give you a ticket tonight?" I ask.

"No. He knew I'd custom ordered the car and was dying to see it. He had no idea I had company tonight."

Me. I'm the company, I think. Oh, how life changes in a blink of an eye. One minute he's saving me in an elevator and the next I'm going home with him. "I thought I smelled the scent of fresh leather."

"Two weeks old," he says. "And I love this thing."

"It's a beautiful car."

"Not as beautiful as you. And most certainly not as adorable." He winks and sets us in motion again, while butterflies flutter about in my belly, both from his charm and my nerves.

WHAT IF I NEVER

Nerves that barely have time to take flight as in only a few short blocks we arrive at our destination, which turns out to be a fancy high-rise in The Gulch neighborhood—where food, entertainment, and living are walkable and upscale.

"If you're hungry, there's a great late-night restaurant in the building," Dash says, pulling the M4 to the front door of the building and glancing over at me. "I'll come around and get you." He exits the BMW and the nerves that jolt through me deliver doubts. Suddenly, I wonder how many women the doorman has seen in a moment just like this one, headed up to Dash's apartment, ordering takeout. What am I doing right now? What am I thinking?

It doesn't matter, I remind myself. The past, the future, isn't a part of the present, the right now. This is one night, just one night for me, with him. For once in my life, I want to give myself permission, to just live in the moment and do something for me.

I reach for my door and already Dash is there, opening it for me, and helping me to my feet, his hand settling on my hip, fingers flexing against my skin. He surprises me by walking me to him and leaning in close. "I have a rule, Allie."

The night is cold, while his breath is warm on my cheek, his touch hot on my body, I inch back and look at him. "A rule?"

"I never bring women to my apartment. *Ever*. And yet, here you are."

My breath hitches with this surprising confession, but I am suddenly emboldened on this night, eager for the freedom of not looking forward, but only living here and now. "Because you invited me." I push to my toes, and now I'm the one leaning in close, my lips at his ear. "Last chance to change your mind."

171

His hand presses to my lower back, molding me close. "I want you, Allie, on my tongue, naked and on top of me, beneath me, beside me, and any which way I can convince you to let me *fuck you*."

I suck in a breath at his bold words, words no man has ever spoken to me, and apparently, this generally good girl likes just how naughty he is because my body reacts of its own accord. My sex clenches and my nipples pucker. Dash Black wants to fuck me in as many ways as I'll let him fuck me. And I want him to fuck me every single way he can possibly fuck me.

He eases back and stares down at me. "What do you want, cupcake?"

As Adrianna might say, to lick him all over, but what I say is, "To go upstairs."

His lips curve and his eyes darken. "I'll demand you be more precise about that request upstairs," he promises.

Feeling brave and bold, I decide maybe games aren't so bad at all, and I respond with, "You can certainly try."

Sexy laughter rumbles from deep in his perfect chest, and his arm slides around my shoulders. "Come with me, my little kitten. I promise not to hurt you. Well, maybe I will, but you'll like it, I promise."

He turns us toward the door, tossing his keys at a young, redheaded man by the door. "Drive her slow and easy, Bobby, or I'll find you and claim your firstborn."

Bobby laughs and heads toward the car, while Dash leads me inside his building, and I'm no longer thinking about my father's stunt tonight. I'm thinking about being alone with Dash Black. And just how good he can hurt me.

CHAPTER THIRTY-NINE

Dash leads me through the lobby toward the elevator, lifting a hand at a tall Black man in an official-looking jacket where he stands behind the security desk. "Howdy there, Brian," Dash calls out, and I can't help but laugh at the "howdy" that is so not Dash Black at all, but it's over-the-top Nashville. I also can't help but notice the surprised look Brian casts in my direction. Maybe Dash really doesn't bring women to his place, a possibility that pleases me perhaps more than it should, but I set aside my overthinking. Tonight is about tonight. Just tonight. I'll deal with tomorrow.

I think this, and I mean it, but then he kind of sideswipes me yet again.

We enter the elevator and I watch as he punches in a code before he pushes the penthouse button. I'm taken off guard by this elite location and I don't know why—he's highly successful—he deserves to live on that floor. Just like my father and just like my ex. I can't pull back the comparison and I hate myself for it. I hate that I'm here with Dash, and those two men, who are nothing like him, managed to push their way into this elevator car. Dash catches my hips and eases me in close, our legs intimately aligned. "What's wrong, cupcake?"

And of course, once again, Dash has read me like a book, and I chide myself for being incapable of keeping my emotions between the covers. "Nothing is wrong," I say, not playing coy, not at all. There's nothing wrong. Or nothing logically wrong. Nothing worthy of my feelings, that's for certain. Certainly nothing worthy of speaking aloud.

His eyes, those intelligent eyes that miss nothing, narrow on me. "Try again."

It's a gentle nudge, but a nudge, that leads me to just say what is on my mind. "It's really nothing. I just reacted to you being in the penthouse."

"And that's a problem for you why?"

"It's not a problem. I mean come on, Dash. You're rich, powerful, successful, and good-looking. What more could a girl want?"

"That's not an answer. Why is that a *problem* for you, Allie?"

"It's not," I assure him. "How you handle those things is what matters."

"And how do I handle them?"

"I don't know how you handle anything, Dash. Not really. How can I know that?" Then because I've been honest with Dash because I need things that are honest in my life, I continue, and I say what I once would not have. "But I'm here," I add, "and I wouldn't be if I thought you let money and success make you forget that you're just a man, and men, and women, are human. That means they're capable of mistakes."

I must hit a nerve for him now because his jaw hardens, his expression with it, and there is something in the depths of his stare, something I cannot, no matter how hard I try, name. "More flawed than you might think, Allie," he says.

The ghost of a painful past lurks beneath those words, and I realize then that our connection is all about just that: pain. I find that I want to know what has hurt this man, but I know that I may never know anything beyond where our naked bodies take us this one night. This night though is ours. I press my hand to his jaw and speak the words that in every part of me, I want to believe. And I want him to believe them, too. "We're all flawed, Dash. And inside those flaws is everything that makes us stronger."

"And vulnerable," he adds softly.

"A very famous writer once told me that being vulnerable is not weakness."

He catches my hand and brings it to his lips. "It's only weak if you allow that vulnerability to control you."

Considering he's confessed to a weakness for me, I'm not sure how to take this comment, but I read between the lines. He's telling me that he needs to be in control. Before I can digest what that might truly mean, the elevator halts with our arrival. And the door opens to the penthouse floor.

CHAPTER FORTY

Dash captures my hand with his bigger hand and guides me to the door. We step into the hallway together and walk to the only door on the floor. It's actually two grand double wood doors and Dash uses a code on a panel to clear our path. Once the apartment is opened, he motions me forward. All my bravado about being present and in the moment, boldly going where the night leads me, plunges down a steep hill. But the most unexpected thing happens. I draw a deep breath that vibrates with nerves, and look at Dash. His eyes meet mine, and there's a warm invitation there that somehow makes me smile. And then he smiles and it's this easy wonderful feeling between us that has me entering his apartment more than a little eager to see where his brilliance lives.

I step inside to find what is nothing short of an architectural masterpiece.

The ceilings are a half-moon shape with steel rails across them and an epic view of downtown as the centerpiece from everywhere you look. "Who designed this?" I ask, as Dash steps to my side, while I turn to admire the open kitchen to the rear of a dark cream-colored couch and chairs.

"Apparently some crazy famous architect contracted by the original owner. I just inherited that owner's good taste. How about a drink?"

"Yes, please," I say, thinking a drink will help check my nerves. "But it won't take much to get me drunk, so just a very little bit of whatever you suggest."

"I have wine, whiskey, and the leftovers of a batch of lemon drops my sister made last weekend."

I love that he's so close to his sister, I really do, and of course, that he was with her last weekend, not some other woman. Or maybe he did both, at different times. I don't want to think about it. "Will Bella mind?"

"She'll make more," he says. "She lives right around the corner and is always dropping by to cook. I'll grab the drinks." He motions to the apartment. "Look around if you want."

He heads into the kitchen and while I'd love to look around more, for now, I'm drawn to the window view, and I ease in closer for the full effect. The city lights sparkle in the darkness, drawing me in, hypnotizing me. I stare out at the city I grew up in and love so very much. I'm not sure how I left. I'm not sure how I'll leave again. Dash turns on a country music station, and the room is filled with Lady A's "What If I Never Get Over You."

It's supposed to hurt, it's a broken heart

I touch the window just as the chorus continues with:

What if I never get over you

I didn't have that issue with Brandon. I was over him the minute I knew the kind of man he truly was, which was probably because on some level I already knew. And because I wasn't really in love. I think I always knew that as well. I'd wanted to come home after it all blew up, but it had felt like I was running away. I didn't realize then, what I do now—there are ways to run that have nothing to do with location. Curling into oneself is isolation. And isolation is its own form of running.

"Do you have a view in New York?" Dash asks, rejoining me.

"Of a wall," I laugh, glancing over at him. "I make good money, but a box-sized place in the right building, with no view, is still high-end for me." That's when I realize he's holding a carafe and two glasses by the stems.

WHAT IF I NEVER

"Let me take the glasses," I offer, and he allows me to scoop them up but then, for a moment, that stretches miles it seems. we just stare at each other, heat radiating between us.

"We make a good team," he says softly.

Team.

I try not to read into those words, as if they represent something with longevity, a partnership that lasts. Nothing about tonight is about anything but tonight. "Yes," I say softly, and he lifts his chin behind my back, indicating a direction.

To *his* bedroom, I know.

LISA RENEE JONES

CHAPTER FORTY-ONE

I'd like to say that my bravado is like a fine wine, exploding with various flavors and tastes. But it's more like a cheap wine that hurts so bad going down, you might as well drink it as a shot. I did that once in college. I shared an entire bottle of cheap wine with a friend. I threw up the next day. As Dash and I walk toward his bedroom, I've got the bad wine bravado going on.

I enter the bedroom first, stepping inside his private space, his room, and I find the designer ceiling flows through the entire apartment, as do the views. There's a king-sized bed, with a built-in dark wooden bookshelf and headboard, and a fireplace on the opposite wall of the footboard.

Beyond the bed, is a step-up to a seating area facing the window and a fireplace that is built into the windows. I wonder if that's actually safe because it's easier than wondering what comes next.

"It's cold in here," Dash says. "Let's go to the couch by the fireplace and I'll power it up."

Relief at this location suggestion is instant, and now instead of the safety of the fireplace, I wonder if he knows the bed, *his bed*, is a whole lot more intimidating than the couch. His bed actually intimidates me more than his résumé of success. I think it comes back to just what I said in the elevator, how he handles his success which appears to be as if it's no success at all.

We pass the bed, with a few vivid images of him naked and on top of me, or vice versa, do a seedy number in my head. Meanwhile, we reach the couch and I primly sit down, knees together and everything. He sits, too, but not so properly. His knee presses to mine, heat in the connection, so much heat that I feel in every part of my body.

Mostly because I need something to do with my hands, I slide my purse off my body, and set it on the couch while he hits a remote and the possibly dangerous fireplace flares to life. With another button, the room fills with country music again. This time it's Jimmie Allen's "Best Shot." I can't even decipher the words at this point. I'm just not capable.

Dash fills our glasses with his sister's lemon drop creation. I reach for mine and lift it to my lips, sipping, but my nerves just won't let go of me and I don't know why. I want this. I want him. I deserve this. It's about me for once, and I haven't done anything for me in a very long time. I down the drink, vodka and sweetness burning and soothing my throat, while the rush to my head is instant.

"Considering I barely drink that was probably not smart." I set my glass down and glance over at him. "No more. Not a good idea at all. I'm not a big drinker so I hope you don't think—"

"I don't," he says, catching my leg just under my skirt and angling me toward him. "Why are you so nervous?"

"It's that obvious?"

"Yes, cupcake, it's obvious."

"Cupcake," I laugh. "It's a silly nickname."

"You don't like it?"

"No. I mean, yes. I—I guess I somehow do."

He strokes my hair behind my ear, tenderness in the touch I don't expect, and the sensations that follow tingle through my entire body. That's how affected I am by Dash, one touch and I'm alive, so very alive in a way I haven't been in a long time.

"I'm glad you do," he says, "because I want you to like everything, Allie. I don't want you to be nervous."

"It's not you. It's your fireplace. I think the window is going to crack."

He laughs. "Is that right?"

"Yes. Okay, no. I'm sure your fancy architect knew what he was doing. It's not the fireplace. It's me." I swallow hard and confess, "It's been a while, Dash."

"How long?"

I can't bring myself to say just how long. A year. More. I might be frozen down there. "I just needed some me time," I say. "I'm a little rusty, but I didn't forget—"

"No," he smiles. "No, I'm sure you didn't forget, but don't worry. I'll take care of you."

The emotions that statement stirs in me that reach beyond sex, open a Pandora's box of baggage for me. I don't need to be taken care of. I don't *want* to be taken care of. And I don't want to be in the headspace where he just took me. With the warm lethargy of vodka in my system and the courage that "no wanting" so many things just created, I lean into him. He doesn't make me take it from there. His hand slides under my hair to my neck and his lips lower, lingering a hot breath from a touch.

"God, woman," he murmurs, and then he's kissing me, really kissing me, his tongue sliding against mine, seductive in every possible way, and I cannot contain a soft moan.

The next thing I know he's pulled me onto his lap and I'm straddling him, unhooking my belt. By the time I've tossed it away, he's dragging my mouth to his mouth, and when his fingers tangle roughly, erotically, in my hair, he demands the attention my nerves had moments before. I'm no longer consumed by it, but rather him. I pant into his mouth, aroused beyond belief. Something about this man, this night, and the way he touches me grants me the freedom to be what I want to be and take what I want to take. I sink into his kisses, drink him in, and now *my fingers* are diving into the soft strands of *his* light brown hair, and not gently. *Give what I get,* I think. That is something I've never really lived, but I am now. His teeth scrape my lips and then he catches the zipper at the front of my dress and drags it down. With this dress that's all it takes to get me all but naked, only two small pieces of lace and my thigh highs between us.

He eases back and studies me, just looks at me, with dark, intense, unreadable eyes. He drags my dress down my arms, over my back, and then catches my hands with the material, holding my hands behind my back. His eyes meet mine, a challenge in their depths, a question in that challenge.

And just like that, I know I was right about his message in the elevator. His version of taking care of me is taking control. Plain and simple, he wants me to give him what I have given no one, at least not in bed. He wants complete control.

CHAPTER FORTY-TWO

I'm there, on top of him, in the power position, but I don't have the power at all, not with my hands behind my back. If anyone knew my past, they'd expect me to push back, to demand my freedom, but the interesting thing about me and Dash is that while I don't own the control right now, I don't feel *out of control.*

For the first time in my life, I realize the difference.

Seconds tick by, and he studies me, almost as if he expects my objection. I even wonder if some part of him wants that from me—but that tug of attraction between us is all-consuming, the real source of power. He tangles his fingers in my hair and tilts my gaze to his. "I'm not a forever kind of guy, Allie. You need to know that."

Okay, there it is.

Suddenly, I know why I'm on top of him with my hands bound by his. This isn't *just* about control. It's about his ability to read me, his fear that while he might say vulnerable is not weak, he isn't sure he believes it. It's in that moment that I become aware of the song on the radio. Carly Pearce and Lee Brice's, "I Hope You're Happy Now." The words fill me up and expand and tell a story that speaks to me.

I'm a wreck, I'm a mess
And I ain't got nothing left

And I was, I really was a mess, but I'm *not* anymore. I'm finding my way to a new me, and tonight is all about just that. Finding me through him, but not *because* of him. I'm actually a little angry that he can't even see that in me and with that anger my nerves evaporate. "I'm not looking for a husband, Dash. Forever *isn't* real, but *this,* what we're doing now, is. So kiss me and get naked already or let me get up and leave."

A look of surprise flickers over his face and he drags me to him, our bodies snug, our lips close. His fingers are still in my hair, a pull to his grip that should hurt, but it only hurts *so good.*

"I don't know what to think about you, Allison Wright," he declares.

"Thinking is not what I want right now."

His lips curve slightly and then his mouth is slanting over my mouth, his tongue stroking deep and slow. I moan with the taste of him, sweet with the lemon drop and wild with need. He moans with me, telling me he, too, is in the moment, affected by me, and the very idea that I can do this to Dash Black is empowering. He wants control, and he's claimed that control, but I have my own as well. Our tongues battle and it's a wicked battle at that. I don't hold back. I always hold back, but not tonight. Tonight, I give myself permission to just be here, really here, really in the moment. And I am. I'm right here with him, demanding as much as I give.

Almost as if he's responded to what's in my head, he tears his mouth from mine, our lips lingering there for several hard beats. He unhooks the front clasp of my bra, and then he drags it down my shoulders, he tears away the dress binding my arms. My nipples pucker with the contrast of the cold air and his hot inspection that follows, raking over my naked breasts. Tension builds between us and I do what anyone would do right in this moment.

I reach for him, but he catches my wrists. "Not yet."

"I want to touch you," I whisper.

His answer is that he rotates me, moving with me, laying me down on the couch, yanking his shirt over his head and tossing it away. Before I can fully appreciate just how perfect his muscles truly are, he's dragging my panties down my hips and tossing them. Then his big body is settling on top of me, his hips spreading my legs. And when I would touch him, he catches my hands, pinning them over my head, his earthy scent and the feel of him on top of me, in control, demanding my submission without words, is both heady and addictive.

I'm more turned on than I have ever been in my life.

He leans in, his lips on my neck, the breath a warm caress on the delicate skin, and I swear he draws in a breath, breathing me in as I am him. I arch into his body, murmuring his name, "Dash." And it's a plea to touch him, God, how I need to touch him.

His answer once again is to deny me my wish.

He lifts off of me, my sex clenching with how much I need him to come back. He catches my hips and turns me over, pulling me to my knees. Now he really does have control. I'm exposed and vulnerable, with my backside in the air, with him behind me. He smacks my ass, just enough to get my attention, and I arch my back, gasping with the surprise contact. His hands stroke up my body, over my breasts, and then back to my backside, where he smacks me again.

No one has ever done anything like this to me, and I can't think of anything but what comes next. I mean I've had demands, but they were the wrong kind of demands, ones that stirred dread, not arousal. Anger, not desire.

Dash caresses my backside and spreads me wider, his fingers sliding into the wet heat of my body, teasing me, arousing me. My God, I'm going to come. The bloom of orgasm is there and as if he knows, as if he's tormenting me, he's suddenly gone again. I want to cry out with my body's protest. The only relief I find is the sound of a condom wrapper tearing, and the promise that he will soon return, that he will finally be inside me.

And then he's there, his hands on my hips, the thick ridge of his erection pressed against the wet heat of my body.

"I'm going to fuck you now, Allie."

Yes, please, I think, only to pant with the feel of his cock stroking the seam of my body, up and down, back and forth, teasing my swollen, aching flesh. "Dash," I groan, impatient now, done with the teasing.

He laughs low and sexy, and then he thrusts inside me. Now, my groan has morphed into a moan and he moans with me, shifting inside me, settling deeper. Already he thrusts again, hard and fast, and yes, thank you, he's done teasing me. He pumps over and over, and when neither of us can get enough, he folds himself around me, covering my breasts with his hands. And while I welcome his touch, I still cannot touch him and I just can't take it.

That need to touch him drives an illogical action. I reach for his hand on my breast as if I can actually hold my weight and his with one hand. I fail miserably, forced to catch myself on my elbows. Dash responds, rolling with me, pulling us to our sides, him behind me, his powerful leg catching my leg. His hand reaching around me, cups my face, his mouth stretches to my mouth. My mouth stretches to his mouth. A new intimacy stretches between us.

In the midst of that kiss, in the way his body cradles mine, in the sway of our bodies, there's a slow, sultry passion erupting between us. The room fills with the music, our soft pants, the burn of desire. Too soon, I'm on the edge, not ready for this to end but I'm so *there*, in that sweet spot, there's no turning back. His hand is on my breast, and my hand is on his when he thrusts into me, and my sex spasms around the thick pump of his cock. I jerk with the impact and tremble all over. Dash's entire body seems to hug mine as he pumps one more time and quakes, his body jerking right along with mine.

The world is nothing but pleasure, and time stands still. I lose the ability to be anywhere but in the moment. And when I come back to the present, it's with the heavy stated feeling of complete satisfaction and the wonderful weight of Dash draped over me. Dash strokes my hair from my face and kisses my neck. "You okay?"

I laugh. "Okay? Ah, yeah. I'm pretty okay right now. Are *you* okay?"

"I'm fucking wonderful," he says. "Let's eat and do that again."

LISA RENEE JONES

CHAPTER FORTY-THREE

Let's eat and do that again.

Just that easily Dash wipes away any chance of the dreaded after-sex awkwardness.

That is until he kisses my neck and then he's standing, pulling on the pants I never saw him take off, and I'm sitting on the edge of the couch, *naked*. I stand up and reach for my dress where it lies on the floor, all balled up. He reaches for it as well and then we're both standing there with me naked and him not. His lips curve. "I object to you getting dressed. I like you better naked."

It's my turn to object. "I'm *not* hanging out naked, Dash."

"Why not?"

"Dash," I plead, tugging on my dress.

He folds me close, scrunching it between us. "I'll get you a shirt. It's more comfortable than the dress and easier to take off. Don't move," he orders, his lips curving at his obvious play on all the times he just ordered me around. "I'll be right back."

"Still bossing me around?"

"You're still naked so I still get to boss you around."

"When do I get to boss *you* around?"

"Probably never, but we'll negotiate." He winks. "Naked."

I'm smiling when he kisses me, and says, "I don't trust you not to get dressed." He catches my hand and starts walking toward a doorway I assume leads to both the bathroom and the closet, and I'm no longer thinking of me being naked. Not when he's half-naked, his jeans slung low over a muscular backside, and he doesn't have on underwear. I decide right then that I am not leaving until I've properly touched him all over.

For now, we enter what turns out to be a hallway leading to the bathroom, with not one, but two closets, one on either side of the walkway. Dash pulls me into the one to our right which appears to be his shirt room. Dash grabs a T-shirt from a hanger and tugs the dress I've forgotten I'm holding from my arms.

Now I'm naked again, not that I wasn't before when I only had my dress in my hands. Dash catches my hip, his eyes warm as they slide over my body and back to my face. "You're beautiful, Allie, and what's crazy is that I don't think you know it." His voice is low, raspy, affected.

And I'm affected. Because it's him giving me the compliment. And because he's hit a sore spot for me.

I don't see myself as beautiful. I've tried, I really have, but confidence runs much like a choppy winding river. A trait I inherited from my mother, compliments of my father. "Thank you," I say softly, and it's interesting to me that I'm touching him now, my hand on his chest, fingers curling in the springy hair there, and he's letting me. Obviously, his need for control has been sated, whatever his trigger for such things, flipped the other direction. At least for now.

"Just telling the truth, baby," he says. "And holy hell, you need to put this shirt on or we are not going to get around to eating." He slides it over my head and I shove my arms into the sleeves as it falls to my knees.

He gives me a once over again and grins. "You look adorable, cupcake."

"Adorable again?"

He drags me to him and squeezes my now T-shirt-covered backside, and says, "Your ass is definitely adorable. And so is the way you're blushing. Little miss 'thinking is not what I want from you right now.'"

"You were testing me," I accuse.

He plays coy. "Was I?"

"Yes," I say firmly. "You were."

"And you weren't testing me?"

I consider that. Was I? My answer is pretty immediate. I was. He's right. "Not intentionally."

"It's called being human, baby. We all do it." He strokes my hair. "Do you like lasagna? The place here in the building makes a hell of a lasagna."

"Are there people who *don't* like lasagna?" I ask, relieved to escape the prior topic.

"You just keep giving me reasons to like you, Allie." He catches my hand. "Come on. Let's order."

I tug against his hand. "Wait. I actually need to go to the bathroom."

"All right. I'll order, you go pee, as my sister would say. She always has to pee. Just turn right and you're there." He kisses me and leaves me in the closet, and somehow, as crazy as it might sound, it feels like trust. And yet, it's just a closet and a bathroom. And I have the distinct feeling Dash Black trusts no one.

CHAPTER FORTY-FOUR

I'm warm and riding the high of this night with Dash when I travel the short walkway to the bathroom and my jaw drops. It's an architectural masterpiece. The sink is floating brown wood with a gray granite top. In front of a floor-to-ceiling window overlooking the city, the tub is this half-moon shape in the same gray, with a brown wooden table next to it. In front of a brown glass-enclosed shower sits a brown abstract statue.

Despite all the glamour, I hyper-focus on that gorgeous tub.

I don't even own a tub but rather a tiny shower in a tiny bathroom. I can't remember the last time I took a bath. Yes, I do. I have a tub in my current place, but that won't last. And as for the last bath, it was in Brandon's fancy apartment.

I decide right then that I need my own tub.

With that decision is the realization that I'm successful but I'm not sure I'm happy. Why in the world would I not be happy? I scowl at myself. This is not the night to do this. I shove aside that thought and go pee, laughing as I think of Dash and his sister, feeling a bit of envy at his relationship with her. It must be wonderful to have a close sibling. By the time I'm washing my hands I'm back in the wrong headspace. Why am I not happy? I have all I ever wanted in a career. I'm back to the difference between successful and happy. My mother's illness really drives home the need to live life to the fullest. Every day counts.

That's when it hits me that I have no idea where my phone is right now. What if my mother has some sort of health crisis? Hurrying out of the bathroom, I head down the hallway to enter the bedroom. I find Dash standing at the window, still shirtless, his shoulders bunched. Another time, I'd wonder why he's this tense right after enjoying the view, but right now, I have my mother on my mind.

Rushing forward, I scan the general sitting area for my purse, finding it half under the couch. I grab it and sit down as Dash turns to watch me retrieve my phone from inside. "My mom. She's traveling and I had my phone on vibrate at the party. I just need to make sure I didn't miss any of her calls." I check my call log to find two calls from Tyler and one from my father.

"Everything okay?" Dash asks, sitting down next to me.

"Nothing from my mother. Just Tyler and my father." I hit the text message log and read the message from Tyler: *Tonight was a work event, Ms. Wright. Call me back.*

Dash must read my expression. "Everything *still*, okay?"

"I need to call Tyler and I may quit my job."

He refills my glass. "Not that I have any problem with you telling Tyler to fuck off. But maybe you should drink that and call him in the morning."

"Except I have a real need to know if he *knew* what he was doing when he invited my father to his party." I pick up the glass and sip, the burn in my throat and rush to my head a reminder that drinking is a bad idea. "Okay, that's probably not a good idea." I set the glass down. "I haven't eaten in a very long time."

"Food is ordered. If you have to make that call tonight, eat first."

"I don't think I can do that. If you don't mind—"

"Of course, I don't mind. I just don't want you to regret what you may or may not say when you do."

"Me either," I say, "but I'm still going to make the call. I'd like to keep the paycheck Tyler offered me coming in, but I have savings. I don't like using it, but I came to Nashville, ready and willing. If I have to donate my time to work on the auction, rather than be auctioned off myself, I'm willing." And on that note, I don't give myself time to chicken out. I dial Tyler and walk to the window, dread in my belly, but cowardice is not. Been there, done that, and I'm proud of myself for what I'm doing right now, in this minute.

"Ms. Wright," Tyler answers. "It's about time you returned my call."

"Did you know?" I demand.

"You're going to have to be a little more specific with your questions."

"Did you know that I want nothing to do with my father when you invited him?"

He's silent a beat before he says. "I did not." There's a pulse of agitation on the line before he adds, "He's been out of the country and came back early to surprise you."

I want to believe him, I do, but practiced liars can speak a lie as a truth, with nary a hesitation. "How did you know he was my father?"

"While I don't like being questioned, I sense a history behind your aggression that we need to detach ourselves from. I sent an email to my clients introducing you and explaining your experience Ms. Wright. He'd previously declined the invite to the party, but he called me shortly after receiving the email to accept and ask for my help in surprising you. He also promised a healthy donation."

"If you're lying—"

"I am a lot of things, Ms. Wright," he bites out, "a liar is not one of them."

"All right then. You should appreciate me being honest and I'm about to be. I won't deal with him. I don't even want his donation for the event." I pause. "Okay. I'll take the donation because it's not about me, but the people it can help. If me not dealing with him is going to be a problem—"

"It's not. I'll handle your father."

I quite literally laugh at that idea. I have no idea if Tyler is his attorney or if he dumped my ex altogether and Tyler reps him now, and I really don't care. "He's obviously one of your clients, Tyler. We both know he's the one who will handle you."

"You underestimate me, Ms. Wright. I'll handle your father. You handle the auction. And the next time you have a problem, give me the benefit of the doubt, and I will extend you the same. Talk to me. Are we clear?"

"I hope so," I say. "I'll see you Monday." And then I do what I would never do. I just hang up.

Dash is there when I turn, offering me my drink. "I think you need this."

"Except I still have to go home on my own two feet."

"Drink the drink, Allie. I told you, I'll take care of you."

I know he means tonight, just tonight, but there's a stir of emotions and a pinch in my chest at his promise. I open my mouth to say what I shouldn't, not in this situation, "I don't want to be taken care of," but I'm saved from both emotional stupidity and foot-in-mouth disease when the doorbell rings. "That will be the food," Dash says, "I'll grab it and be right back."

He strokes my hair, a tender gesture that's already becoming familiar with Dash, and then he's headed out of the room. I down the drink and tell myself I do not do so because of his offer to take care of me. I've had those offers. They were all lies. And this is just one night.

CHAPTER FORTY-FIVE

I delete the message from my father without listening to it and down the rest of my drink, fighting the urge to check on my mother, who I know just needs a little space. I've all but talked myself into texting her anyway when Dash reappears, the scent of delicious food with him. My stomach rumbles in delight. "I'm so ridiculously hungry right now," I say, setting my phone down on the coffee table.

He eyes my glass, and I don't miss the satisfaction at my empty glass in his gaze that I really don't understand. But then, I've been drinking which means I don't have it in me to even *try* and figure it out. "Me too," he says, sitting down next to me and pulling the coffee table closer. "I didn't eat before the party." He begins unloading the takeout bag. "Two lasagnas," he says, setting a silver container in front of each of us before he sets even more items on the table, "Bread," he adds, "bottled water, and the biggest slice of cheesecake you've ever seen to share."

"In other words, I'm going to need the gym at the house," I say. "And to stay away from the bakery. It's hard not to eat cupcakes when I'm there, but my mom's health has me thinking about my own health. But even as I say that, I justify unhealthy eating with this." I raise a finger. "I do have a gym at the house. I'll pay for my sins there." I try to lift the lid on my silver bowl but it's this foil top thing that is ridiculously hard to get off.

"I've got it," Dash says, grabbing it. "They seal in the heat but make you solve a puzzle to get to the food." Only he doesn't struggle at all. He has the lid off in an instant.

I have a feeling the vodka is working me over more than I even realize.

"I've had practice," he assures me as if he's read my mind. "I order there all the time."

"You don't have to make me feel better. I've had vodka. I know what that means."

He laughs a soft, sexy laugh, and says, "It does require a magic touch. Promise."

Now I laugh. "Is that what you call not being able to open my own food container?"

He winks, and I've already come to love those winks, probably a bit too much, but I blame that on the vodka, too. "Try it," he urges. "It's really good."

"Hopefully I'll remember it in the morning."

"You better remember everything in the morning."

My cheeks heat but I still manage the rather daring reply of, "I'm pretty sure I'll remember the good parts."

"I'm pretty sure I want you to tell me what those were."

"Some things a girl keeps to herself," I say quickly, not about to start detailing more intimate matters.

"She shouldn't," he says. "Or how else will the guy know what to keep doing?"

"I think you've figured it out on your own, Dash Black."

"We'll see, won't we."

I think that means he's planning on us getting naked again which is fine and good, but I really do need to sober up if I plan to enjoy myself. With that mission in mind, and it's a really inviting mission, I take a bite of my food and it's good, *really good.* "Okay this is definitely memorable," I say. "And this place is in your building?"

"Yes," he says. "And on that, I'm a lucky man." He takes a bite.

There seems to be an undertone of him being unlucky in other areas, but I decide I'm reading too much into the comment. "Very," I agree, and we both reach for our waters before digging back in, but I almost land my bite on the front of me. Of course, I do. I slide down onto the floor. "I'm safer here," I say, glancing up at Dash. "Less distance between your shirt and my food."

He laughs, and I do love Dash's laugh. It's warm and genuine and does funny things to my chest. He joins me on the floor and moves the table slightly closer. "How long have you lived here?" I ask.

"Since the first movie," he says. "I was in a house, still near downtown, but it ended up on one of those tourist tours. It was insanity. This place came on the market and the privacy it offers won me over."

"I guess I wasn't fair to you earlier in the elevator. I do know how you handle fame, and that is humbly and well. I forget you're kind of a big star when I'm with you. You don't act like a star. Actually, Tyler is the one who acts like a diva."

"Don't get me started on Tyler. Aside from agreeing with you, that is. As for me, I'm just me. You've dealt with authors, even highly successful authors. You know we're just people."

"You're another level of success than almost all other authors," I say, and since I've somehow inhaled half my lasagna, thank you, vodka, I seal my meal and scoot the container aside. "Even more so than your father, which must make him very proud."

He slides the tray top back into place and pushes himself onto the couch, offering me his hand. I scoot to my knees and let him help me up, feeling far more steady and sharp now than I was fifteen minutes ago.

"I don't talk to my father, Allie," he says. "At all. So while some may not understand where you're at with yours, I do."

Given his career, this news surprises me, but I have heard the stories about his father, and they aren't good. "How long has it been since you talked to him?"

"Only twice in fifteen years, and one of those times was at my mother's funeral."

"Five years ago," I supply. "I googled you," I admit. "And there wasn't even any alcohol involved."

"Don't believe everything you read, Allie."

"I'm a fiction editor, or I was. I don't believe everything I read."

"Good," he says, "because I learned the hard way, the press will print anything to get a story. And as for my mother, yes," he confirms, "it was five years ago next month."

"Were you close?"

"Both me and my sister were extremely close to my mother."

"But neither of you took over her business?" I catch myself and say, "I'm sorry. I'm being nosy."

"It's fine, cupcake. We're getting to know each other," he says. "The company had gone public by the time she passed. She hated what that did to her business model, and she stepped down from the board and sold out about a year before she died. The money we inherited works for me." He lifts his martini glass and sips. "I think my sister finds it intimidates the men she dates."

I'd assumed he inherited a large sum of money but there's also no doubt that he's wildly wealthy on his own. "She's around a lot of wealthy men, who would be her equals."

"And she thinks they're all asses. Of course, she tells no one how much she's worth. She wants to work and she wants her relationships to be honest."

"Unfortunately, I understand where she's coming from. Any man who finds out who my father is, expects me to inherit his fortune."

"Now it seems, you're the one speaking from experience."

He's right, but I don't go there. I may never go there, with Dash, or anyone for that matter. "I don't want his money, Dash, and not because I'm stubborn like my mother. He showed up at my door two years ago. He said he was a changed man. He—he did some things and you know how he tried to make those things better?"

"He tried to buy you," he supplies easily.

"Yes. I can make my own money. I don't need his."

His eyes soften and he catches my hand. "Come here."

I let him ease me closer, and when he pulls me onto his lap again, I say, "Am I going to end up with my hands behind my back unable to touch you again?"

"Not unless you want me to tie you up and tease you."

There's no denying the idea of Dash in control and me at his mercy, is a delicious prospect I won't even try to deny. And so, I don't deny anything. Instead, my arms slide around his neck, and I lean into him. "Not this time, Dash. *Please.*"

"Well now, as long as you say please, you can have about anything you want."

LISA RENEE JONES

CHAPTER FORTY-SIX

With his promise that I can have anything I want if I say please, Dash's hands slide under the T-shirt I'm wearing and up my back. Molding me close, my breasts pressed to his hard chest.

"For instance," he says, his voice low, a rough sandpaper tease on my nerve endings. "I'll lick you anywhere you want to be licked if you just say please."

I'm really, truly a rather shy person and no one has ever spoken to me so boldly as Dash has this night, but I'm different with Dash I'm starting to realize. More comfortable in my own skin and sexuality. I just can't find it in me to hide from this or him. "What about where I want to kiss *you*?"

"Where do you want to kiss me?" he asks, squeezing my backside and Lord help me I can feel the thick ridge of his erection between my thighs, and through his jeans that I want to be gone now.

"Everywhere," I assure him.

His lips curve and he says, "Is that right?"

"Oh yes, but you resist me, Dash Black."

"I assure you, Allison, I'm not resisting." Somehow him calling me Allison in this moment is more intimate than Allie, and I don't know why. "I want nothing more than your hands and mouth on my body," he says. "But you'll have to allow me to kiss you everywhere first." He drags the T-shirt over my head and by the time it's on the ground his hands are on my breasts, and when my hands cover his hands, his finger strokes my nipples.

My fingers catch long strands of his light brown hair and I tilt his gaze to mine. Any control I'd thought to gain in that moment is lost when Dash pinches my nipples, sending darts of pleasure straight to my sex. I moan and he captures the sound with his mouth, kissing me with the kind of passion that a girl thinks she will never know because it can't be real.

Oh, but it is. It so is.

My hands tunnel into his hair and when his gaze lifts to mine, I find hunger there. So much hunger, and all for me. He catches my hands and presses them behind me, bracing them on his powerful thighs, his arm wrapping my waist, securing me. Watching me now, he cups my breast and leans in, licking my nipple, sensations rippling through me, my sex clenching with impossible need, need for him. Need to have him inside me, thrusting and pumping, but we are so far from there, it's brutal.

His mouth clamps down on my nipple and he suckles and licks. My head tilts back and I bite my lip, fighting the sounds that threaten to escape my lips and failing.

I moan and pant and before I know what's happening, Dash has lifted me, stood up, and set me down on the couch. He stares down at me, his lips pressing to my knee, watching me as his lips travel lower, down my thigh, and I know now, I was never, and will never control anything with this man, with or without my clothes on. Not that I want to control him. I just want to touch him, but I'm too lost in the way he's touching me right now.

His fingers slide between my thighs, stroking the delicate flesh. My lashes flutter as he says, "So wet, baby," kissing my leg again, his tongue an erotic tease, while his fingers are exploring me, driving me out of my mind.

And the way he's watching me, confident, dominant is incredibly sexy. I wonder now why I swore I'd never let another man control me.

Sensation begins to build and I breathe out, "Dash," in a plea for more, and yet, less. I don't want this to end. And more is exactly what he gives me. He leans in, his breath warm on my clit, and licks me there. I gasp, arching into the delicate touch that is gone too soon.

"Say please," he orders softly.

His satisfied smile curves his lips, but he doesn't deny me what I both want and need, which is his mouth on my body in the most intimate of ways. He licks me again, and then he's suckling me, licking me, pumping me with his fingers and I'm losing my mind, and just too far gone, to hold back. I mean he's just so damn good-looking and good at everything he does to me, and I tumble over the edge of that invisible cliff, with a jerk of my body that I cannot control. And then I'm spasming deliciously, trembling all over.

The moment I collapse, Dash's fingers are gone and he eases my legs off his shoulders, kissing my belly. "Can you be inside me now?" I ask, my voice breathless, my body weak with the burn for what I have not had.

"No more condoms, baby. I wasn't exactly planning this weekend."

"You don't need it. I'm on the pill."

His fingers curl at my hips and his body tenses. I feel his reaction like a stab in the very belly he just kissed. "Right. Either I'm not safe or I'm a slut." I try to move and he holds me steady. "Let me up, Dash. I need to go home."

"Don't do that. I don't not use a condom."

"Okay. Can you please let me up?"

"I don't think you're a slut. Not even close."

"I didn't lie about the two years. I like knowing when to expect my period."

He stares at me a moment, God, he just stares at me, and then he's standing, dragging his pants down his legs, but I feel dirty and wrong. I stand up and when I would just walk away, he captures me to him, his thick erection at my hip.

"Damn it, Allie," he says, his voice low, guttural, "don't run away."

"I'm not running away, Dash. I'm just leaving."

"Don't," he says. "That wasn't what you think it was. I wanted to ask questions I have no right to ask. Who he was, and what he was to you, when that doesn't matter. *Shouldn't* matter."

But it does. That's what he's telling me and I really don't know what to do with that information. He cups my face and stares down at me. "You're making me crazy, Allie. You know that, right?"

"You didn't say that like it was a good thing," I whisper.

"I'm not letting you leave, not when we both want you to stay."

And when I would tell him that's not an answer, he's kissing me, drinking me in, and I'm confused, trying to resist, but he's Dash, and he has this way of touching me and unraveling all the common sense I might own.

He turns with me, pulling me onto his lap, almost as if he's telling me I have control now, but we both know I don't even come close to one inkling of control. Certainly not when he's already kissing me again, molding my breasts to his chest, the scent of him like a drug, the taste of him, addiction defined. And the more he kisses me, the more I spiral with my need for him.

"I need to be inside you, Allie," he says, his voice a near growl of urgency.

My body spasms with his words, with exaggerated need, anticipating what I've wanted for what feels like a lifetime. "Yes," I whisper or maybe I don't. Maybe I think my response. We are frenzied in the shift of our bodies.

He anchors me, holds me steady and it's my hand on his shaft that guides him inside me.

He enters me, stretching me, sensations spiraling through me as I slide down the length of him, and when I have all of him, he murmurs, "About damn time, baby."

Yes, I think. *About damn time.*

I must actually say it because he smiles and nips my lips. "Allie," he says softly, almost tenderly, I think, maybe. I don't know. His hands are all over me, touching me, and everything melds together as one big sensory overload. And then he thrusts his hips, and I catch his shoulders, holding onto him, pressing into him. He's watching me, watching every reaction, every pant, and moan, as if he's trying to learn me. I touch his face, and he catches my hand, kissing it, pressing his lips to my palm.

The air pulses alive with our passion, and every shared look that seems to speak words we never say. Passion that lives and breathes, and drives us further and further into our little world that cannot last forever, I know. He knows, too, but it's now. It's right now. And we're a collision of him and me, an explosion on the edge. I ride him, his eyes all over my body, his hands with them, but it's not hard and fast. It's slow and sultry. And when our mouths collide, we're suddenly wild, almost furious, and I've never been out of my own skin, trying to climb under someone else's, but I am now. But this can't last, it won't last, and I know that ending comes so soon, too soon, and it does. My body quakes on top of his, and I bury my face in his neck. His arms close around me, holding me to him close, his hips pumping— once, twice, three times and then he's right there with me, a low guttural groan escaping his lips.

I don't know where that explosion begins or ends, but I collapse against him and him me. For long moments, I'm just there, on top of him, against him. At some point, Dash shifts our bodies, and lays us down, grabbing napkins and cleaning us up. And then he's on his back on the couch, and I'm lying there beside him, my head on his shoulder. Neither of us talks. I'm warm and comfortable, my body sated and heavy from vodka and sex. I don't have it in me to move just yet. I'll go home in a minute.

CHAPTER FORTY-SEVEN

I blink awake to the sound of the rain that is frequent in Nashville, pitter-pattering on the window, confused by the unfamiliar ceiling. I sit up only to have a sheet fall away and the realization that I'm naked. My eyes go wide and I grab the sheet again, yanking it to my chest. I suck in a breath to realize that Dash is not only standing at the window, but he's fully dressed in jeans and a T-shirt, his feet in boots, a steaming cup of coffee in his hand.

Awkwardness overwhelms me and I don't know what to do. I scan for my clothes but my dress, I remember now, is in the closet. And since I can't seem to locate a small blanket, or anything for that matter, to wrap around me, I pretty much have two options. I stay where I'm at or I hunt down my dress—*naked*.

I'm staying here.

As if he senses I'm awake, Dash turns to face me, his eyes heavy as they rake over me. "Morning, cupcake." The greeting is pleasant and familiar, at least on the surface, but there's a tick of tension beneath its surface, as if waking up to me in his bed was not expected. I glance at the clock that reads nine AM and cringe. He has a book to write. He needs me to not be here right now.

"I obviously didn't go home," I say. "And now, the awkward morning after has officially arrived and I can't make it go away." And because I want him to know I plan on getting up and out, I rotate and throw my legs off the bed. Somehow, I actually keep the sheet in place. "I'm embarrassed to say, I don't even remember how I got in your bed."

"I carried you," he says. "I think the vodka got you. You were out like a light."

I blink in surprise that should probably be an embarrassment. He carried me to his bed? Because he wanted me in his bed, or because he felt obligated not to leave me elsewhere? And Lord help me, did I drink *that* much? I'm appalled at the idea of being a lush. "I'm sorry, Dash. I don't drink much and now you know why. I don't handle it well. To be honest, I'd get up right now and try to fix this, but I really don't want to hunt down my dress while naked. Can you maybe bring it to me?"

His reply is no reply. He just studies me, sunlight flinting through his eyes, now a striking blue with a matching T-shirt stretched over his perfect chest that I can't help but remember touching. His jaw is set hard and shadowed with a sexy one-day stubble, his expression so damn unreadable, it's killing me.

"Dash?" I ask, not sure what to do right now.

He crosses the room but instead of passing me by and locating my dress, he sits down next to me and offers me his coffee. "Lots of cream and way too much Splenda. Have some."

It's an intimate gesture that doesn't say, *go home, Allie*, and I'm confused. "I think I should leave."

He sets the mug on the nightstand and shifts in my direction. "Do you want to leave?"

Do I want to leave? I repeat in my head. No. No, I don't want to leave, but I should. He was pretty clear last night on where we stand. No relationship. Just sex. Or that was the point he got across and that felt safe. It felt like something I could do and not get hurt.

"Do you want to leave, Allie?" Dash presses.

"Why does that feel like a trick question?"

"No games, Allie. I told you that."

"Don't you want me to leave?" I counter.

"I spent the last hour staring at you in my bed, and thinking about how much I should want you to leave."

That answer stabs at me way too much. Proof that one of my first impressions of Dash was correct. He has the power to hurt me. *Badly.* I need to go home. "My dress, please?"

The doorbell rings and Dash curses. "Damn it. That will be my sister. I completely forgot she was coming over until now. She bought me this damn waffle maker she's been wanting to try."

Panic and embarrassment rush over me. "Oh my God," I murmur. "*Oh my God.* I am never drinking again." I forget my nakedness and throw away the blanket, eager to escape and get dressed, but by the time I'm standing, Dash is in front of me, his hands on my shoulder. "I don't want you to leave, Allie. Not even a little bit."

I can't even digest what he's saying or any of the implications of his words. This morning is no longer just me and him. "Your sister, Dash. I work with her. I'll look bad. I'll look like a—just bad."

"You'll look like the only woman she's ever seen at my house. The *only* woman, Allie. She won't make this awkward. But if you want me to, I'll tell her I'll meet her somewhere in an hour. But that's absolutely not what I want." The doorbell rings again. "It's your decision. Just tell me what I'm doing."

I press my hands to my face and then look at him. "I'm embarrassed."

His cellphone starts ringing. He grabs it from the nightstand and answers, "I need a few minutes, Bella. Let yourself in. We may go out to breakfast."

She says something and Dash smiles before he says, "I'll tell her." He disconnects.

"*Tell her?*" I ask. "What was that? What *was that*?!"

"She asked if you were here."

My eyes go wide. "How did she know?"

"She said she knows me and she could read us, but not to worry, no one else could. Stay, Allie. And just in case I haven't been clear enough, I'll say it again. I want you to stay."

He wants me to stay, but he also spent the past hour trying to talk himself out of that idea. *And he failed*, I remind myself. He wants me to stay and beyond reason, I *want* to stay. "I have nothing but last night's dress to put on. And high heels."

"Is that a yes to staying?"

"Yes," I whisper. "Yes, I'll stay."

Relief washes over his face as if he actually thought I'd say no. "Wear my sweats. And my T-shirt looks good on you. But do it quickly because you're sitting here naked, baby. I can't take it. Find something in my closet or my drawers that works. Nothing is off-limits. And you can have that coffee. I'll get another one. I also left some Advil on the nightstand for you."

God, he thinks I'm a lush. "Thank you. Are we really doing this?"

"Yeah, baby," he says, stroking my hair. "We are. Get dressed. I'll see you downstairs." He kisses me hard and fast on the mouth and heads for the door. A moment later, he's gone, and the door is shut. I'm naked and alone in his room, about to rifle through his closet. With his sister downstairs.

What is this man doing to me?

CHAPTER FORTY-EIGHT

I pick up the coffee cup and drink. That's where I'm at right now. I'm naked and drinking Dash's coffee while he's not even in the room. But somehow that feels more respectable than going downstairs in his clothes, with his sister present and preparing breakfast that is now for three, not two. Nope. I can't do that. It's just not an option. I have to wear my dress. I take another sip of the coffee, and hunt down my bra and panties, which I find in the sofa cushions, and put them on. My belt is under the coffee table but my thigh highs are missing and after a fairly detailed search, I abandon ship where they're concerned.

Time is ticking and Dash is expecting me downstairs, so I grab my purse and dart for the closet, where I discover my dress hanging on a hanger. I don't give myself any time to think about Dash doing that or why or the flutter in my belly at my clothes hanging with his clothes. A night has become the day after. That is all. I will not let myself start thinking this is bigger than it is.

Once my dress is back on my body, I feel a bit more in control. I mean, yes, I wore it last night, but it's not like Dash's oversized clothes hanging on me is more obvious than this. I fold the T-shirt and leave it on a shelf and drape my belt with it. The belt is so very last night. I have clothes on my body at least and I dart into the bathroom, opening drawers and hunting for toothpaste to finger brush my teeth. I hit the jackpot and discover an extra brush and I don't even hesitate to rip open the package.

In about five minutes, I have my teeth and hair brushed, and I've washed my face. I have a small amount of makeup with me and I put it to good use. I'm almost human. But now the conundrum. I stare down at my bare feet and pink-painted toes. Heels or no heels?

"I liked you better in my shirt."

I whirl around to find Dash in the doorway. "Hi," I say, reverting back to my impressive vocabulary.

His lips curve. "Hi."

"I'm trying to be less obvious," I explain.

He catches my hand and walks me to him. "She knows you stayed the night. Just go with it. Let's eat." He starts walking, taking me with him.

"I have no shoes, Dash," I object, but it's a weak objection. It's this or heels and heels really feel like a weird choice for waffles with his sister, in his kitchen. But then again, so do my bare feet, but Dash ignores my protests and keeps moving. In other words, bare feet it is. And I'm officially living the most awkward morning after ever. Aren't sisters protective of their brothers?

I have a memory of me and Dash talking about everyone wanting his sister's money. That means his money, too. I like Bella quite a lot, but she's human, and I can all but read her thoughts already and they go something like this: *Who does this barefooted brown-haired bitch think she is? She probably wants his money.* In other words, I'm screwed, and without more than two sips of coffee.

CHAPTER FORTY-NINE

Once Dash and I are in the hallway, outside the bedroom, he laces his fingers with mine. "She's just my sister, Allie. Relax."

He's just given me the exact reason I can't relax as a reason to relax, but I nod anyway as kind of a vow to try and do as he wishes. We start walking again and the whole holding hands thing kind of feels like a relationship thing and we're not in a relationship. Are we? I mean I *am* meeting his sister. No. No, I've already met his sister. And I was here when she came over so this encounter just kind of got forced on us all.

A few more steps and we clear the hallway, the scent of fresh delicious waffles baking or cooking, I don't know the proper waffle term, fills the air with the promise of happiness in my mouth. I adore waffles which is why my mother always makes them for me. To hell with my bare feet. If I'm offered a waffle, I'll eat a waffle.

Bringing the kitchen into view, Bella is behind the island, looking beautiful, relaxed, and casual in a T-shirt and leggings. Her gaze lifts and lights at our approach, no anger or judgment in sight.

"There she is," she greets. "Morning, Allie. I have fresh coffee ready and waiting." She walks to the thermal pot, pours the contents in a cup, and by the time Dash and I are on the opposite side of the island, she sets my new cup in front of me.

"That's my version of the cinnamon churro latte they have at the office," she explains.

"Thank you," I say. "And good morning, Bella." I lift the mug to my lips.

She smiles a knowing smile and wiggles a brow. "Yes, it is."

I set the mug down before I drink. "Okay, let's just get the elephant in the room dealt with. I feel really weird right now."

"Why?" she asks dramatically. "You two are grown adults. And if you want to roll around in the sheets together you have every right."

My cheeks heat and I press my hand to my face, peaking through my fingers at her. "Did you really just say that?"

"Yep." She points at the cup. "Now try the coffee."

I drop my hand and stop fighting the moment. I sip the warm beverage and approve. "It's just like the one at the office."

Dash nudges my arm. "You're supposed to say better."

"Better," I say quickly. "It actually is. I'm not saying that because your brother just told me to."

She scowls at Dash. "Stay out of this. It's just your kitchen. I'm in it now." She refocuses on me. "You like waffles, right?"

"Love them," I promise. "Which is why my mother makes them every time we have Sunday brunch."

"Perfect. You two sit and get comfortable. I'm about ready to get the food on the plates." She turns back to the stove.

"Mom loved to cook," Dash explains. "She taught Bella and it's kind of her hobby."

"Did she teach you?" I ask, my nerves starting to fade.

"She tried," he admits. "I sucked."

"He really didn't try," Bella chides from over her shoulder.

My lips curve. "I somehow think your sister is right."

"Hmmm," he says. "Probably, but I try never to tell her she's right. She starts thinking that's always the case."

I love how they are together, teasing and having fun, with an obviously close bond, and I wonder about the brother I read about and that Dash lost. Was he Bella's brother, too?

She returns to the island with two plates, setting one in front of me and Dash, waffles covered in strawberries and whipped cream. "This looks and smells amazing," I declare.

"They are amazing," she says. "Because my mama taught me right." She motions to Dash and then me. "This will be the first Saturday Dash isn't on his computer, typing while I cook. I kind of love your influence though his publisher wants his book early."

"I'm not turning it in early," Dash snaps, picking up his fork.

I take a cue and pick up my fork as well, suddenly feeling I need to eat rather quickly. "I'll go home after we eat so you can focus."

He scowls. "Better yet, you can stay and read the damn piece of shit."

Bella brings her plate to the end of the island and sits down next to me, her brows dipped. "Wait. You want her to read your work in progress?" She motions between us with her fork. "What insanity is this? You never let anyone read your work in progress."

"That's what I said," I agree readily.

Dash has another opinion. "Yeah, well, she's an ex-editor at my ex-publisher. She knows books and she's read my books."

"He just needs to read it from the beginning," I repeat yet again. "He'll figure out what's wrong if anything is wrong. I think he's just letting the Hollywood thing get in his head." I dig into my food. "Did I mention this looks marvelous?" I say again.

"Thank you," she says. "And I think you're right on Dash. The pressure is getting to him."

Dash sips his coffee and says nothing while Bella turns the attention on me. "Any chance you might stay in Nashville, Allie?"

"My mom and stepdad are here," I say, leaving out my mother's cancer, which she may or may not know about. "So it's tempting, yes. But I have a dream job in New York that I'd be kind of crazy for leaving, and the other Allison is supposed to be coming back to work."

Her brows dip. "Allison is coming back? Really? She left so suddenly. But I didn't really know her." She eyes Dash. "But maybe, right? Because of Tyler?"

I glance at Dash. "Because of Tyler?"

"They were involved. It was a toxic relationship very few people know about which is between us."

"Of course," I say, thinking of the necklace. It could have come from Tyler, but somehow that just doesn't feel right. Why would Tyler of all people send it to the office where his personal life could become public? He reads more private than that to me.

"I actually thought it ended long before she left," Dash adds, before I can ask him to define toxic, "but hell if I know," he continues. "Tyler and I haven't talked much since I moved my business to Bella."

"Tyler was your agent?" I ask.

"And attorney," he confirms. "Most of the attorneys there at Hawk Legal work as agents."

"I joined the firm a few years ago, right about the time Dash started writing," Bella explains. "I hooked him up with Tyler. I was new and green and his sister. We all thought it would be weird if I represented him. Turns out, it works. I can beat him into submission much easier than anyone else," she teases. Her cellphone buzzes with a text where it sits on the island. She grabs it, reads a message, and types. "Sorry. I have a client playing a gig at Jason Aldean's place tonight and a record label is scouting him. He's a nervous wreck."

"Oh wow," I say, sipping my coffee. "That's exciting. And I love Jason Aldean. I can't believe I've been in New York City so long I've never even been to his bar. It's on Broadway, right?"

"Smack in the middle of the action," she confirms. "You should come tonight." She points at Dash. "He has to stay here and write, but you can come with me."

"I'm not turning the book in early, Bella," Dash says. "And if Allie wants to go, I'll take her."

I think his sister just asked me out on a second date, and I fear Dash has been cornered. I glance over at him. "You need to work and so do I."

"I'm going to write this afternoon while you read the first half of the book. We don't have to be at the bar until around ten."

Bella's cellphone buzzes with a message again and she grabs it, reads the text, and says, "Okay I have to take him a waffle and calm his crazy talented ass down." She stands up. "And you two can figure out tonight. I'll leave VIP passes at the door." She hurries around the kitchen, plates an extra waffle, and then motions to the kitchen. "You know how this works, big brother. I cook. You clean up." She waves at me. "See you tonight, Allie." She winks, just like Dash winks, and heads for the door.

Dash waits for her to exit, and then turns us in our rotating stools to face each other. "Is it a date?"

A date.

I draw in a breath with the certainty that Dash chose his wording with purpose and I'm not sure what to think about any of this. "What happened to no relationship, Dash?"

"Don't overthink."

"You spent an hour thinking about why I shouldn't be here this morning."

"And I ended up here, asking you to stay again tonight."

My eyes go wide. "I thought we were just going to the bar?"

"It'll be late when we leave the bar. We might as well just come back here."

My heart is racing. This is not a good idea, I know this, and I still say, "I have to go by my place and get some things."

CHAPTER FIFTY

My father tries to call me while Dash and I are hunting for my thigh highs I don't even remember taking off. Did we take them off? And why? Why was that necessary? I grab my phone, glance at the caller ID, and hit decline. Dash, who is presently on the floor digging under the couch arches a brow. "Father?"

"Yep. Any luck?"

He pushes to his feet. "No," he says. "Where the hell are they?"

"I give up. They're gone and my coat is at Tyler's and it's freezing outside, per my phone which likes to deliver bad news."

Obliviously reading my comment he says, "If you talk to him, it's over. If you don't, he may keep calling."

"He has a short attention span. He'll be gone soon." Dash's hands are on his hips and he's just looking at me.

"If your father called, would you talk to him?" I challenge.

"He wouldn't call," he says and that ends that topic. "I'll get you one of my coats." He walks away and I sigh. We're both a mess, two troubled souls, who most likely will cut each other until we emotionally bleed. Or maybe we'll just have sex. I don't know what is in our future.

Dash returns and helps me put on his jacket, and with it swallowing me whole, we head downstairs. Half an hour later, we arrive at my new temporary home, in his fancy sports car. "I completely forgot that my car is broken," I say as Dash pulls into the garage next to my college ride. "It's ancient. I don't know why my mother kept it and I don't want to buy a car for a few months."

"I'll look at it," he promises, after being rather quiet on the short ride over, which doesn't read as regret over the invitation. I'm not sure what's on his mind. Maybe his book?

"Are you good with cars?"

"My stepfather is a NASCAR mechanic so he taught me a few things."

"NASCAR? My gosh, you live in a family of exceptionalism."

"Look in the mirror, cupcake. So do you."

"My father doesn't count. My mother's a nurse. My stepfather's a fireman chief."

"Heroes," he says.

"Yes," I say, pride filling me, but I've got Dash talking and I want to know more. "How did your mom and stepdad meet?

"My mother sponsored a car. She loved NASCAR."

"Do you?"

"I loved going with her. The sport itself, not so much now."

In other words, it hurts. I touch his face and he catches my hand and kisses it, giving me a smile that doesn't quite meet his eyes, before opening his door to exit. I'm out of mine before he can help me and at the door, punching in the code. Dash opens the door and I enter, setting my purse on the counter. "I'll grab my stuff," I say. "There's wine and diet soda in the fridge. The remote is on the coffee table. Are you sure you're okay with me showering? I'm not as fast as you are at getting ready, I'm sure."

"It's fine," he says. "I brought my laptop." He pats the briefcase at his hip.

"Good. You can get your words in." Unsure why I do it, I close the space between us, push to my toes, and kiss him. "Read it. Start at the beginning." With that advice, I leave him there.

I hurry into the bedroom, shower quickly and while my hair is partially drying, fill an overnight bag, and end up in the bathroom, staring at myself in the mirror. My cheeks have color, my lips are swollen. I look like a woman who's been fucked and fucked well. I'm not sure I've been that woman until now.

And I'm not sure what I'm doing with Dash, but I remind myself that he has the luxury of knowing I'm going back to New York. I can't read anything into my overnight stay. We are good in bed together. Why wouldn't two adults enjoy each other? It doesn't mean we have to get married. With that thought, I shake myself, and finish packing, then quickly dry my hair and do my makeup, throwing on leggings and a sweater.

I find Dash standing in the living room, staring at the fireplace, the television above is not even on.

"Dash?"

He rotates and faces me. "This is at least a two-million-dollar home, Allie. You know that, right?"

I set my bag on the kitchen island. "I kind of guessed that."

"And you think he gave you this, why?"

"HR told me it was for insurance purposes. He has to have someone in it. There's a wine cellar and vault downstairs. Allison was—"

"Fucking him, Allie. She was fucking him."

I swallow hard with the inference that there is something in my future with Tyler. And he's wrong. "There's nothing between me and Tyler. *Nothing*."

He closes the space between me and him and catches my arms.

He's jealous. Dash is jealous and I'm back to where I am with a lot of things with Dash. I don't even know what to do with that information.

"He's my boss. Nothing more, I swear. And my landlord. That's all, Dash."

He drags me closer. "And if he wants to fuck you?"

"He doesn't."

"And if he wants to fuck you? And before you answer, don't be naive. You're smarter than that."

"I don't want Tyler, Dash. Just you."

His fingers tangle in my hair and he stares down at me. "We're together until we decide otherwise."

I know where this is headed, I know how this ends, and it's not good for me, but I have no ability to deny this man. He's jealous and once again, as if feeling this once wasn't enough, as proof of how fucked up I truly am, *I like it.*

"Yes," I whisper, and his mouth is on my mouth, his hands on my body, and everything about him right now is pure possession. We're urgent with each other, tearing at each other's clothes. His sweater lands on the floor and so does mine, followed by my bra. In a matter of what seems like seconds, I'm naked and sitting on the kitchen island and Dash is buried inside me, stretching me, pumping inside me. My hands catch my weight on the island, my breasts naked between us, bouncing with every thrust and bump—his eyes all over me. It's hard, passionate, intense, and I tumble into bliss all too quickly.

Dash groans with my orgasm, his gorgeous face contorted in pleasure, his head tilted back in an animalistic display of pure masculine pleasure as he quakes to release. He pants out a breath and leans into me, and now his hands are on the island, holding his weight. He kisses me. "*God, woman.* And that's all I have to say right now. Let's get out of here. Tell me you're ready."

"I am," I say, because the truth is, I am always ready when it comes to Dash.

CHAPTER FIFTY-ONE

It's somehow two in the afternoon when we arrive back at Dash's place, both of us are still stuffed from breakfast. We end up cleaning the kitchen together and I make a pot of coffee. It's almost three when we settle onto his living room floor, both with our MacBooks open, with the fireplace going and the pot of coffee I made has filled our cups. It's almost as if we're together, and I have to remind myself that we just said we are, in fact, just that.

I've spent an hour on my work, watching Dash struggle with words, when his cellphone rings where it rests on the table.

"Bella," Dash says, answering the call. He listens a moment and replies with, "Next Saturday then. Yeah. No. Don't go there right now. Be my agent. Make this work." She says something else to him I can't hear and they disconnect. "There was a mix-up in the booking. It's all next weekend, not this weekend but we can still go to Aldean's."

"No, we can't," I say. "You need to get a grip on this book, Dash. I'll make you a deal. I'll read it from the beginning, if you read it from the beginning."

"That's going to take us both hours."

"Okay."

He grimaces. "You're so fucking stubborn."

"Me? You're stubborn. You want help. You have it."

"All right. I'll read it, if you'll read it. How do you feel about pizza?"

"Like I need to workout. I'm eating like shit."

"Done. I have a full gym. We'll workout later." He grabs his phone. "What kind of pizza?"

"Feta if they have it and pineapple."

"That's weird," he says.

"It's very good."

"We'll see. I'll be testing it."

"And I'll be reading. Send me the file. I'll text you my email."

He dials the pizza joint, and the minute my email hits his instant messenger, he shoots me the file. I grab both our coffee cups, refill them, and settle in for my new Ghost Assassin read. Thirty minutes later our cups are empty and I'm already into what looks to be an amazing read when the pizza arrives. Dash greets the pizza delivery person and grabs us both bottles of water.

"Okay, it's pretty decent," Dash says, after inhaling a slice of my feta and pineapple.

"Told ya," I say. "Now shhh. I'm reading a good book right now."

"Don't tell me it's good if it sucks."

"I wouldn't do that, Dash. It started out with a bang. I like it. I feel spoiled getting this early look. Nothing is wrong so far. *Nothing.*"

He doesn't look convinced, but we finish off our pizza and this time he refills our coffee cups. About an hour later, I laugh at a scene that is truly brilliant. Dash's gaze rockets to mine. "You're really gifted at taking a scene that is so damn brutal and adding humor to make it palpable, Dash." I want to ask him if his father has read his books, or attended his movie premieres, but I respect the topic and even understand it. When he wants to talk about it, if he ever wants to talk about what happened with his father, he will.

It's hours later, and the sun has set, the city alive with multicolored lights just outside the window, when I finish the book. I close my MacBook and Dash does the same.

"Tell me what you think. Is anything wrong?"

"You tell me what you think."

"No," I insist. "You tell me."

"I can't think of anything I'd do differently. I tried to find what was bothering me and now I'm not sure it's bothering me at all."

"Because it's really good. I can't wait to find out what happens next. Can you please write it quickly?"

He studies me a long beat that turns into two before he kisses me hard and fast. "I need to write. Are you okay with that?"

"Of course I am. I have a ton of work to do. Write the book."

He smiles and then turns back to his MacBook and I watch a master go to work.

CHAPTER FIFTY-TWO

Our work time is productive. I organize all the donations and the appraisals, while Dash bangs out so many words, he now feels he might actually be able to make an early deadline, though he doesn't plan to tell that to Bella.

"She can be surprised," he tells me, calling it "our secret."

I fall asleep with him holding me from behind and those words in my head "our secret." I decide I like the idea of us sharing a secret together rather than keeping secrets from each other. And we both have secrets. Maybe too many for our own good.

I wake to a buzzing sound, a blast of sunlight that tries to burn out my eyeballs. The buzzing sound is my cellphone and I grab it to find my mother's number on caller ID. I jolt to a sitting position, my heart pounding with irrational fear. Dash is now sitting up next to me and I drag the sheet up my body even as I answer the call. "Mom? Are you okay?"

"I was going to ask you the same thing. I thought we were having brunch today? It's already ten."

"You said next Sunday."

"This is next Sunday."

"No. You said a week from Saturday you were home."

"Did I? Well, I'm home, honey," she singsongs. "Are you coming over?"

"Yes. Yes, of course. I'm going to shower now. I'll be there soon." I disconnect and glance at Dash. "I was supposed to be at my mom's for brunch." I squeeze my eyes shut. "And I have no car."

"I'll take you," he says easily. "No problem. Don't fret."

I study him a moment. "I—Dash I don't mean to make this awkward, but—"

He frowns. "You don't want me to take you?"

"No," I say quickly, daring to add, "just the opposite. My mom and stepdad are huge fans of your books and the movies. Would you—" I hesitate, afraid of how he'll read this. We said, no forever, which usually means no family. A rule we've already broken with his sister so maybe—

He arches a brow. "Would I what?"

"You want to come? I mean it's waffles again, but really good waffles," I say, quickly adding, "and we don't have to tell my mom and stepdad we're involved. I can say you're a friend I met through my job. My mom knows I want to do things for her right now."

He laughs. "So you did me?"

I poke his naked chest. "That was a horrible joke."

"I *am* a friend from your job, just a very good friend who happens to know what sounds you make when you orgasm." Despite all we've done together, my cheeks heat. He pushes me down on the bed and leans over me. "What are you, and they, going to say when I call you cupcake?"

"They'll know what's going on."

"Alright then," he says. "Let's go shower. *Cupcake.*" He winks and pushes off of me, and by the time I'm sitting, he's walking toward the bathroom, naked. He's so very perfectly naked and his ass is so very perfectly— well perfect. I have no other words. As for the brunch, I'm not sure what I just got myself into, but I decide I'll try to figure it out in the shower—*with Dash.*

CHAPTER FIFTY-THREE

It's eleven-fifteen when Dash and I arrive at my mother's place. "Pull in at the side of the house so she can't see your car," I say. "It kind of stands out and I want to surprise her inside, not out."

He obliges and parks outside the garage. "What else?" he says.

"I'm sorry in advance. They're going to act like crazy ass fans, Dash."

"I love my fans," he says. "So let's go do this." He exits the car, and I do the same, meeting up with him at the front bumper. Me in black jeans and an olive-colored sweater while Dash looks incredibly delicious, personifying my own personal idea of "the hot, famous author" look in black jeans and a black turtleneck sweater.

We head for the back entrance of the upper-middle-class home, my mother and stepfather worked hard to own, when my mother could have easily gotten rich off my father. I'm proud that she didn't. I'm proud of who she is and I can only aspire to live my life as honestly as she has. And as for my stepfather, Barry is an honorable man. A good man. Nothing like my father and apparently Dash's father, as well.

Once we're at the door, I don't bother to knock. I open it and lean in, calling out, "Hello, hello! Coming in."

"In the kitchen, honey," my mother shouts back and I smile, stepping inside and motioning Dash forward, excited because she will be excited about meeting him.

Dash and I walk through the mudroom and turn right into the kitchen.

We find my mother behind the shiny white oversized island, mixing something in a big bowl, her gaze downturned. Unbidden, my chest pinches, and I suck in a breath at the sight of her, still looking so unlike herself. My mom is fifty-seven, petite, athletic, a dedicated runner, and until her cancer, she looked much younger than her years. But now—now her muscle tone is gone and her body is just so thin. Dash must sense my reaction, his hand settling on my shoulder.

I catch it, hold onto it, it's right then that my mother glances up, and her face lights with my arrival. "Allie," she smiles. "Who's your friend?" Her brow furrows. "Wait. You, sir, look *familiar.*"

"This is Dash, Mom. Dash Black."

My stepfather enters the room through the other side of the kitchen. Barry is a big man, over six feet tall, fit, and good-looking. He's also ten years younger than my mom, which was a problem for me at first, but he won me over with his charm, manners, and adoration for my mother. "Holy hell," Barry exclaims. "You're Dash Black."

"She just said that, honey," my mother chimes in.

"*The* Dash Black," he replies, turning his attention back to Dash. "You write the Ghost Assassin books. Holy hell," he says again.

Dash laughs. "Yes. Holy hell."

I laugh now, too. "Dash this is my stepfather, Barry, and—" I motion to my mother, "my mom."

"Cassie," my mom says. "Call me Cassie. Dash Black, in our kitchen. I don't even know what to say right now."

"Nice to meet you both," Dash says, nodding at my mother, and when Barry moves forward and extends his hand, he and Dash shake on the greeting.

"How the hell are you here?" Barry asks, his hands settling on his hips.

WHAT IF I NEVER

"I convinced Allie I had to have some of those waffles," Dash replies, always the charmer, and now is no different. "I've been hearing about them from Allie."

I round the island and hug my mother and she whispers, "Oh my God. He's so good-looking."

I laugh and whisper back, "Yes. Yes, he is."

Mom and I break apart and Dash rubs his hands together. "What can I do to help?"

"Tell me what happens next," Barry says. "That's what you can do."

From there, there is laughter, food, and conversation. Eventually, we're all sitting around the island, chowing down on waffles, and drinking coffee. It's a bit surreal. At present, Dash is talking to Barry and my mother, answering questions that flow left and right, and I just watch him. He's good with them. Actually, he seems to get along with everyone. No, seems is not accurate. He *does* get along with everyone oh so well, except Tyler. But I've seen a darker side to the man, a tormented part of Dash Black, the part he hides behind easy conversation and what I think might be practiced humor. There's a part of him that doesn't just hurt. It bleeds.

He must sense me watching him because his gaze lifts and meets mine, a question in his eyes. I smile a soft smile and mouth, "Thank you."

He winks and my stomach flutters. I'm falling for this man. I'm falling hard and I don't know if I can stop it from happening. I don't know if I even want to try.

An hour later, I know it's time to go. "Dash has a deadline," I announce. "I need to get him back to work."

Dash slides his arm around me and says, "My little cupcake here is a slave driver."

He did it. He called me cupcake. And my mother's smile is instant and glowing.

A good fifteen minutes later, Dash and I settle into his car and I glance over at him. "You called me cupcake."

"I just couldn't resist."

"Do you know the questions I now have to answer?"

"She's smiling. That's what matters." His voice sobers, turns serious. "She's good, Allie. Your mom is good. You can relax."

My belly tenses. "I know. In my mind, I know." My hand balls at my chest. "Here, not so much."

"It'll happen." He rotates in his seat toward me. "Listen, baby, I have to fly out to LA tomorrow to deal with an investment turned to shit. I'll be gone at least a few days if not most of the week. Stay with me again tonight. I'll drop you at work on my way to the airport."

He's leaving.

This news takes me by surprise and I'm not sure why. He has a life outside his apartment and me. "I better not. You need to work and so do I. And I have nothing to wear tomorrow at your place."

"I had one of my best writing days in months with you by my side yesterday so the 'need to work' protest fails. And we can swing back by your place and get you some clothes." He catches my hand. "Come on, cupcake. Stay with me."

For some reason, for an obvious reason really, his trip out of town reminds me that it will be me leaving soon, and all of this is just temporary. I could reject him for that reason or I can choose to enjoy him while I can. *No regrets*, I think. That's one of the words of advice my mother gave me when she was handed her diagnosis. *Live without regrets, Allie.* I have regrets. Many regrets. Staying home tonight isn't going to be one of them.

CHAPTER FIFTY-FOUR

"I'll take a look at your car while you pack," Dash offers, once we're inside my garage.

"Thanks," I say, "but I'm not expecting good news. It's old and it's been sitting at my mom's place for years."

"Don't be doom and gloom, just yet," he says, lifting the hood. "Go pack. I got this."

I hurry inside and head to the bedroom, picking out an outfit for work tomorrow, and filling an overnight bag. The necklace is in my nightstand and I decide to show it to Dash. I stuff it in my bag and head to the kitchen. Dash is just headed back inside.

"That was fast. Is that good or bad?"

"It's not good," he says. "I think you have engine trouble. I pushed it to the driveway so I can have it towed to a mechanic friend of mine."

"I really appreciate that, but I'm not sure it's worth the money."

"He won't charge me to look at it. We can talk about what to do about it when I hear back from him. And you can drop me at the airport tomorrow and use my car this week."

"What? No. I'm not driving your fancy sports car. It's brand new."

"It's just a car, baby. I don't mind and at least it's safe."

"I'm safe. It's not. I'm not doing that. I'll get a rental."

He steps in front of me and cups my face. "Use my car, Allie. I want you to."

"No. Dash, no."

"We'll fight about it at my place when we can argue naked."

"I'll lose that argument."

His lips curve. "That's the point." He kisses me hard and fast and says, "All ready?"

I give up the battle for now and let him change the subject, but only because now seems as good a time as any to show him the necklace. "I am, but I want to show you something first. You never asked how I ended up at Hawk Legal and it's kind of a strange story."

He leans on the island beside me. "Strange how?"

"I was doing a temp job at the Frist Art Museum just to plump up my diminishing savings account and a delivery arrived for Allison W. We all assumed that was me."

"But it was the other Allison."

"Yes. Exactly. Easy to explain since we worked a few blocks apart. But I want you to see what it is." I unzip the bag I've set on the counter and pull out the velvet box. "It's a highly personal gift that came with a note just as personal." I open the lid and display the stunning necklace. "It's expensive and the card, well you can read it." I pull the card from my bag and show it to him.

Dash accepts the card from me and reads it out loud, "*Forgive me.*" He frowns. "And no name."

"No," I say. "I guess the person assumed she'd know who it's from, but most people would still sign their name as a personal gesture. It's weird and so was her rapid departure. I know it's probably crazy, but I'm a little worried about her. And I don't know what to do with the necklace. It's a personal gift, and telling anyone about it at the office feels wrong."

He glances at the necklace. "It looks expensive. Is there a brand?"

"Nothing on the necklace or the box," I say, "but I've developed an eye for expensive at Riptide. I agree. It's valuable." I hesitate. "You said her and Tyler were a thing. Could it be from him?"

"Was the delivery meant to be received at Hawk Legal?" he asks.

"Yes. That was the address on the delivery."

"Then no. Despite how contrary this sounds, considering his personal relationship with Allison, Tyler doesn't like his personal life to touch his professional life."

"Which is my impression of Tyler, it is, but as you just said, she was an exception to his norm. Maybe he thought he'd convince her not to leave." I frown. "No. That makes no sense. She'd been gone weeks by the time I received the necklace. Though I do believe the necklace arrived at the museum and got stuffed somewhere before it made it to me."

"Have you tried to call her?"

"Yes. I did. And I texted her, too, and received no answer. Though I did make it a business call. Maybe I should just leave a message about the necklace?"

"I don't see why not."

"And maybe Tyler can get in touch with her? And if I talk to him, do I tell him about the necklace? If it's not from him, that's also a bit of an invasion of her privacy, right?"

"You could probably go to HR, but then again, that would probably still end up with either Tyler, or one of his parents, which means it still ends up with Tyler. Ask him to call her over the auction."

"Yes. I'll try that. She literally went on vacation right before she took leave, too. It's all strange and not returning calls—I mean I guess I of all people can understand a personal leave, but I still talk to my employer. I'm still aiding their success."

"She was living here and moved," he says. "It's quite possible she left and isn't coming back."

"I feel a little guilty over the appeal I find in her leaving my temporary job behind. I guess there's a part of me that just wants to stay close to my mom, when I know that's insanity. My job really is a dream job. And if my mother thought for one minute I stayed for her, she'd be upset."

"There's nothing wrong with putting family first," he says. "I'm here because Bella is here." He catches my hand and walks me to him. "And I'm fairly certain your mother will think you stayed for me, cupcake." There's warmth in his voice and eyes and I'm both confused and terrifyingly pleased he's even touched this territory.

"Because you just had to call me cupcake. You knew what that would do."

"Yes," he says. "I did. And I plan to keep calling you cupcake while eating as many of those waffles as she'll make me."

This seems like a good time to remind him that neither of us does the whole forever thing, but I don't. And I tell myself it's because a nickname and a few waffles do not make a forever relationship.

CHAPTER FIFTY-FIVE

Half an hour after leaving Dash at the airport, I pull into the parking garage of the Hawk Legal building and exit the car. It's a warm day, much warmer than the days before this one, which is good since I still don't have my coat. Another fancy sports car pulls in next to me but I don't wait to compare engines. I'm just glad the one I'm driving has one. I hurry to the building, and the impatient side of me that doesn't want to wait on the slow-ass elevator, decides to take the stairs to the lobby. A few minutes later, I'm on another elevator and headed to my floor.

I'm still early enough to beat the receptionist filling in for Katie and I settle behind my desk. I've been working a few minutes when Katie walks into my office and sets a cup on my desk. "I thought you might like that. How did the party go Friday night?"

"It was—interesting. I did get some donation promises so we'll see if they come through."

The phone on my desk buzzes. "My office, Ms. Wright."

The formal command comes from none other than Tyler. I punch the reply button, "On my way, boss."

I release the button and Katie's eyes go wide. "What was that?"

"We had a little issue Friday night." I stand up. "You should probably wish me luck."

She pushes to her feet. "Please tell me you're not about to leave."

"I'll work on the auction until it's done," I say, avoiding a more direct reply. "I'll check-in with you after the meeting." I head to the door and leave her gaping after me.

Nerves erupt in my belly, but my backbone is stiff. Dash is right. I don't need this job. My savings balance would like me to keep it, but it's not necessary. The truth is, staying here until January isn't even necessary either. I just want to stay. I cross the lobby and the elevator bank to enter Tyler's own lobby. This time there's a pretty blonde behind the desk who I assume to be his assistant.

"You must be Allison," she says. "Go on back."

I nod and do just that, marching to Tyler's office. The door is open and I walk inside. His gaze lifts and he drops his pen. "Come in and shut the door."

I inhale and do as he says, shutting the door, and crossing to sit in a chair across from him.

"Nice car you rode in with this morning, Ms. Wright. It looks a bit like the one my client Dash Black drives. You are aware that we have a strict policy against dating clients?"

I refuse to be rattled. I didn't read that in the paperwork and I actually did read the documents. "My personal life is my personal life. Which is why my father showing up at your business event wasn't expected."

"He's been told to stand down."

I laugh and not with humor. "And you think my father will listen?"

"I told you—"

"You're Tyler Hawk, god of all rich and powerful people?"

A muscle in his jaw tics. "I told him to stand down. I suggest you do the same."

He's right, I know. He's my boss. He deserves respect. I draw in a breath and say, "I'm sorry. It's bad between us and the bad is recent. And he's a manipulator. You have to see that."

"I do," he agrees. "And for the record, I had no idea who you were when I hired you. I hired you, not your father."

My anger is instantly deflated. "Thank you for saying that."

"It's the truth. As I told you, I am a great many things, Ms. Wright. One of them is not a liar."

"Look," I say, "I know this all exploded and badly, but I do want to do this job. I'm making progress and excited about the outlook. I want you to know that."

"And if it does, and you so desire, the job, and perhaps even the house, could be yours long term."

"Because you don't think Allison is coming back?"

"Because you can make your own path and establish your own worth."

"But she'll want the house back."

"Are you saying you want to stay?"

"I don't know what I want right now."

He studies me a long moment and leans closer. "That's a dangerous place to be when you're playing in someone else's playground."

I don't have to ask whose playground he's talking about. "Is that what happened to Allison?"

He goes ramrod still, seconds ticking by before he eases back into his leather chair. "What do you want to know, Ms. Wright?"

"I'm a little worried about her. She won't return my or Katie's calls. And I have something of hers I think she might want."

His eyes narrow. "What would that be?"

"It's highly personal. Can you try to reach her for me?"

A beat passes before he says, "I'll see what I can do."

"Thank you." I stand and head to the door.

"Ms. Wright," he says, as my hand touches the knob. I turn to face him. "That playground is a minefield. There's more to Dash Black than meets the eye."

He's not wrong, of course. I've seen the shadows in Dash's eyes, I've felt the wall between us at times, but I've simply passed the point of no return. I'm swimming in the dark water of Dash Black's life, most likely water filled with dangers, but my own life isn't exactly a crystal clear, blue perfect ocean, as proven by my father showing up Friday night.

Which is exactly why I don't comment on Tyler's warning. I turn and find my coat on the hanger of his door, which somehow feels as personal as this conversation, which is a bit too personal for my comfort. I grab my coat and leave his office.

CHAPTER FIFTY-SIX

My mother calls me almost the minute I'm at my desk and of course, she wants to talk about Dash. "I need to know what is happening with you and that gorgeous man."

Just like that, my irritation over everything that happened with Tyler and my father ticks down a notch with the smile in her voice.

"He is gorgeous, isn't he?" I ask.

"We were very surprised by his visit. And that cupcake nickname, honey. It's adorable."

Adorable. She just had to use that word. "Don't read into it, Mom. It's new and I go back to New York in January."

"Unless you don't," she says. "I vote that you stay here and marry Dash Black."

I face-palm and navigate her questions about me and Dash for about ten solid minutes, which is still easier than talking to her about my father. She doesn't need to know he's in town. It won't do anything but upset her. When we finally hang up, I type a text to Dash: *My mother called. She loves the way you call me cupcake.*

Of course, he won't get that message until he's on the ground, but I still smile as I press send and get to work.

***

I eat lunch in my office as I manage what turns out to be an excellent donation day. The auction is coming together. I'm sipping my afternoon coffee when my desk phone rings. "Allison Wright," I greet.

"This is Marshall," the man on the other line says. "I'm trying to reach Allison, the other Allison."

"She's on leave. Can I help?"

"On leave," he repeats. "That makes absolutely no sense to me at all."

"I'm sorry. I—who are you to Allison?"

"Her brother. Who can tell me what is going on?"

I'm sitting up straighter now. "I don't know. I'm filling in for her and I've left her a few messages myself. She doesn't reply to messages or calls. And no one seems to know how to reach her."

He's silent a moment. "Okay. Thanks." That's all he says and then he hangs up.

My brows dip and I dial Tyler's office. "Ms. Wright," he answers.

"Marshall, Allison's brother, just called. He's looking for her."

"He's always looking for her. He's a troubled man. Ignore him."

"If he's troubled is that a good idea?"

"He's not a serial killer. Just a pain in the ass."

"But he can't reach her. Should that concern us?"

"She feels about him the way you feel about your father."

I digest that with what can only be understanding. "Did you try and call her?"

"Patience is a virtue. One I've mastered. Have you?"

I don't know what that means, but I let it go. "I'll pretend Marshall didn't call."

"Good decision." He ends the call.

My cellphone buzzes with a text. I return the receiver to the office phone to the cradle and grab my cellphone to find a text from Dash: *I need a cupcake. One that tastes like you.*

I smile and type: *Then come back.*

As soon as I can, I promise, he replies. *Headed to a meeting. It will be late when I call.*

I sigh and set my phone down on my desk, the call with Marshall bothering me. Everything about Allison bothers me. My mind goes to my talk with Tyler. *There's more to Dash Black than meets the eye.* There's more to Allison leaving than meets the eye, too, and I'm not sure what to do about it. I don't even know what I think is wrong. Just—*something*. Something is wrong.

CHAPTER FIFTY-SEVEN

With Dash gone, I'm in no rush to go home to an empty house, that was *her* house. Hours after I talk Katie into going home, I order takeout and eat a salad at my desk. I spend a lot of time I should be working thinking about my life. I decide that feeling wildly confused about my life has become my new reality. I admit that fact. Perhaps that's why I start digging through files, looking for answers to the other Allison's life. I'm on empty, coming up dry, but right as I'm about to give up, a small piece of paper flutters to the ground. I grab it and find a handwritten phone number in a man's script.

I quickly key it into my search bar only to have it come up as an unlisted personal number. My fingers thrum on the desk. It's probably a work thing which means I could call it and find out. But what if it's not. My heart is racing with what I'm about to do for reasons I can't explain. I've called hundreds of Allison's contacts. *This is no different*, I tell myself. Only it is because I grab my cellphone to ensure the office number doesn't show up, and dial it anyway. A man answers. "Allison?"

His voice is familiar and yet not, which has me believing it's someone famous I just can't place. "Yes, but not the Allison you think. I'm filling in for her at Hawk Legal and—"

"Why are you calling me? Is there something wrong with Allison?"

"I don't know what's going on with her at all. Do you? I've been trying to reach her—"

"Don't call this number. Ever." He disconnects.

I blink in confusion. What just happened?

Nothing good, I think, but I still have nothing to go on but a gut feeling that something is wrong with the other Allison. My cellphone rings with an unknown number and I answer. "Allison Wright."

Turns out it's a client of Bella's. I talk to them for a good half hour, log a donation, and finally disconnect. My cellphone rings again and I quickly glance at the caller ID, expecting Dash, only to find another unknown caller. I answer the line. "Allison Wright."

There are a few beats of silence and the line goes dead. I'm officially creeped out. I toss my takeout bowl in the trash and start gathering my things. A few minutes later, I walk through the ghost town of an office, with a creepy sensation floating down my neck. I step into the elevator and it's about to close when someone catches the door. I hold my breath, not sure who I expect.

Tyler steps into the car and I blow out a relieved breath. "If you're trying to get free rent, Ms. Wright, it's already yours." He punches the garage button I've forgotten to punch.

"It's kind of weird that you give me free rent. Why?"

"You know why."

"How long was Allison in the house?"

"A year."

"And before her?"

"My grandmother," he surprises me by saying. "I inherited the house and her wine collection."

Guilt stabs at me. "I'm sorry," I say quickly. "I shouldn't have been nosey."

"I know you can't help yourself."

The elevator lands on the garage floor and the doors open. Tyler proves himself a gentleman and holds the door for me. I step outside and turn to him. The minute he joins me I say, "I'm worried about her Tyler. Really worried. Beyond reason. Please tell me you tried to call her."

"I did," he says. "She'll call me back."

"And if she doesn't?"

"Then we'll talk. I know why she left. I know why she'll come back. You need to chill the fuck out."

I blink at the informal, human-like response. "Right. You're right. I think I'm in worry mode because of my mom."

"I thought your mom was doing well?"

"She is, but I can't seem to realize that."

"Of course you can't. She's your mother. Contrary to what you might think of me, I love my mother as well. I'd be the same way. Speaking of a parent. My father has been in Europe dealing with our international clients. He's returning tomorrow. Expect him to want to meet you at some point. This is still his rodeo. I'm just one of the horses."

"Of that I doubt."

"You haven't met my father." He motions me to the car.

"Let me walk you to Dash's car."

"You just couldn't help yourself. You had to bring up Dash, right?"

He just looks at me. I almost laugh for no good reason, but I am glad for the company. We walk to the car and I click the locks. Once I've opened the door, he gives me a nod. "Goodnight Ms. Wright." He turns and walks toward the fancy sports car parked next to Dash's that I'd seen arrive this morning.

"Allie!" I call out.

He raises a hand and climbs inside his car.

***

Once I'm on the road, I consider my conversation with Tyler.

I decide he's worried about Allison, too, but that could be more about his relationship with her, and perhaps a fear that she's really done with him. Though it's hard to see Tyler fretting over such things.

Half an hour later, I walk inside his grandmother's house, switch on the alarm, but still feeling a little unsettled, I also search the house. It's crazy, I know, but I just can't stop feeling uneasy. Once I've established I'm alone and safe, my thoughts shift to Dash. It's almost nine at night and he hasn't called which means he probably *won't* call. I digest this reality with a fairly brutal stab of disappointment. I've just sat down on the bed and kicked off my shoes when my cellphone rings. Disappointment fades into relief as I greet him with a simple, "Hi."

"Hey, cupcake. Sorry I called so late. It's been a hellish day that ended in a meeting over drinks that added the hell to hellish. I'm probably going to have to go to court over this mess. I'm meeting with an attorney tomorrow."

"It's a bad investment?"

"Yeah, and a dispute over the stock I'm trying to unload. I'll tell you all about it later."

"Did you write at all today?"

"On the plane but shit words. I'll probably trash them all. So much for I might turn in the book early. Bella wants me to meet with some studio before I leave about a development deal."

"That's amazing. And exciting."

"I don't know. I mean yes, it could be, but I don't love the Hollywood scene. How was your day?"

"Busy. I worked late. I just got home. Allison's brother called today. He acted worried about her."

WHAT IF I NEVER

"Allison's brother is a lunatic. I was at the office one day when he showed up there drunk as fuck."

"Oh. Hmmm. Tyler did say something about him being a problem." My mind starts racing and lands on a heavy thought. "Dash, you don't think—I mean—"

"Don't go there, baby. Her brother is a drunk, but he loves his sister. He didn't hurt Allison."

"Right. Of course. Setting him aside. There was this other incident. I called a number I found in my desk drawer, *her* drawer, thinking it was a prospect, but the man who answered acted suspiciously. Long story short, he told me never to call him again. And before you say I'm worrying for nothing, she hasn't called Tyler back. And like me, I think he's worried about her, too."

"More like, he has a bruised ego because she blew him off. That's not something he's used to."

"And while I get that, I don't feel good about this, Dash. I just have a bad feeling. Which brings me to what I consider an important question. What would you do if you felt like I do?"

"I don't know what I'd do. If you don't hear anything from her by the time I get back, I'll talk to Tyler and see what I feel about all of this after I do."

"You don't even get along with Tyler."

"We have a history, but it's not all bad. We respect each other," he pauses and adds, "with limits."

Maybe less than Dash thinks, is my first thought, but I decide that's not a talk to have after his "hellish" day. "Thank you for this, Dash. When do you think you'll be back?"

"I hope Wednesday night, but it might be longer."

"Wednesday would be good."

"Plan on picking me up and coming home with me."

"Is that a request or a demand?"

"Which do you prefer?"

"I'll tell you Wednesday night,"

"Preferably naked," he says. "Talk to you tomorrow, cupcake."

We disconnect and I fall back on the mattress. I wonder if the man I called tonight is the man that sent the necklace. And I wonder if he ever made her feel flutters in her belly, the way I do with Dash. And if so, what changed? Why did he have to ask for forgiveness?

CHAPTER FIFTY-EIGHT

Dash isn't coming home until Friday.

This, after several days of him predicting Wednesday as the day he'd be home, but just not being able to make it happen. In the meantime, Tyler seems to be avoiding me, and that, and all other things work-related, is as usual. As for Tyler's father, by Wednesday I have yet to meet the man, though I've heard whispers of his presence. It's that day, after a heck of a lot of phone work, that I'm just about to go grab lunch when Bella pokes her head in the door. "Have you eaten?"

"No. I was about to go to the restaurant."

"Want to go with me?"

"I'd love that." I quickly call up to reception and tell them I'm taking a break.

A few minutes later, Bella and I are at a table, food unloaded and ready to eat. "I see you're driving Dash's car."

"I am," I say, feeling my cheeks heat. "My car, that really isn't my car anymore—my mom still had my college junker for some reason—died on me. He generously let me borrow his."

"He doesn't let anyone drive his car, which is always a prized possession, especially as new as that one. But he let you."

"Don't read into it, Bella. Dash knows I leave in January. I think he feels safe with me for that reason."

"I see how he looks at you."

She's the second person who's said something like that to me. I don't ask what she means because I don't want either of us to read into her assessment. "We're attracted to each other. I won't pretend we're not and now I'm changing the topic and turning it back on you. Are you dating anyone?"

"God, no. I've decided I'm not meant to find a partner in life. I seem to be drawn to players. You'd think Dash and I shared a father, but then again, I've kind of lived his father through his eyes. I read a book about that. We are creators of habit and radiate to what we know even if it's bad."

"But your father—"

"Is wonderful. I know. Maybe that means there's hope for me."

"I get it though. I don't know if you figured this out at Tyler's party but my father is Rob Wright."

"Wait. What? He's your father?"

"Yes. And I feel about him about the way Dash does his father. But the point is, that if a man finds out my father is my father, it shifts the dynamic. Even after I tell them I don't want his money and I'll give it away, they think they can change my mind. My mother didn't even take his money."

"He must have really hurt you, or was it her? Your mother?"

"Both," I say. "At different times and in different ways."

"The good news is this: you don't have to worry about any of that money and power stuff with Dash," she says. "He's got his own money and fame. He doesn't need his father's. But on the same note, I like that he doesn't have to worry that you want his money, either. If you'll walk away from your birthright, you'll walk away from him if he gives you too much shit." She sobers then and says, "We've had struggles he and I. We're kind of fucked up. There are probably reasons beyond the obvious why we're both loners. But I like to think we're both worth saving."

There is torment in her eyes, real pain, that I've only glimpsed in Dash, but I now know he simply hides it better than Bella. Her phone buzzes with a text and she glances at her screen.

"Damn it. I have to go. I have another client melting down. Tell me again why I like my job? Sorry, Allie."

"No worries. We'll do it again."

"I'd like that," she says, squeezing my hand before she grabs her tray and heads to the trash.

I repeat her words in my head. *I like to think we're both worth saving.*

Dash needs saving. That's hard to process as real and I doubt he'd agree.

CHAPTER FIFTY-NINE

By Thursday, I'm so busy that I still haven't had time to get a lockbox which amounts to, I'm still carrying around the necklace. I vow to go after hours today. With this in mind, I'm actually about to pack up my files and head out when, for the first time since our encounter in the parking garage, Tyler reappears, this time in the doorway. "We're having cocktails tonight at Nova with my father. Be there in an hour."

I blink. "I—what? Tonight? And why me?"

"He does it with all new employees."

"I'm temporary."

"Are you?"

"Probably."

"One hour," he says. "Don't be late." He disappears into the hallway.

I dial Bella's cellphone, which Dash gave me last night at her request. "Allie!" she answers. "I see Dash actually did what I said and gave you my number. Small miracles."

I don't even have a friendly greeting in me right now. "I'm suddenly having drinks with Tyler and his dad. What do I need to know?"

"Oh *that*. Jack Hawk does that with every new employee. It's a test. No one knows the criteria. It will be weird and intimidating, but just be yourself. You'll do fine. Oh, and after a schedule mess, my client is at Jason Aldean's place tomorrow night. Will Dash be back in time?"

"I'm picking him up at six. He'll be here. I'm sure he'll still want to go."

"Great. Now go get that meeting over with. Once is all you have to endure."

***

I walk into Nova five minutes early to be led to a small round table in the outdoor area, where a fireplace adds a cozy effect. Tyler and his father are already present and both men stand to greet me.

"Ms. Wright," Tyler greets. "Meet my father, the master of our universe."

I draw in a breath as my gaze touches piercing gray eyes, and a man so like Tyler, it's almost spooky. Jack Hawk is tall, fit, athletic even, and appears far younger than what must be his fifties.

"Nice to meet you, sir."

"Jack," he amends. "I'm not quite as formal as my son."

Tyler's lips twitch in what I believe to be irritation while his father motions for me to sit.

I quickly claim the seat between them and hang my purse on the back of my seat.

"How about a drink?" Jack asks.

"Coffee," I say. "I have to drive home and I'm not a good drinker."

"Well, nothing wrong with being a bad drinker." He motions to the waitress and orders my coffee.

Once that's done, Jack fixes me in a stare, and it's crazy how much he looks, sounds, and even moves like Tyler. "I hear you're filling in for Allison," he comments.

"I am. It worked out well, her leave and my leave."

"I attended a Riptide auction last year. I do believe I saw you there. What is your role with the company?"

"Jack of all trades, no pun intended," I laugh. "I've been training under the principals and do pretty much anything and everything."

"A versatile person is a keeper," he says. "Tyler takes after his old man. He knows how to see that in people, as do I. I hear your mother just recovered from cancer."

"She did," I say. "I just can't seem to let go yet, which is why I'm here until after the holidays."

"Unless you decide to stay."

"Allison is coming back and I know you all are looking forward to her return."

His lips press together in a barely perceivable way, but I notice. "That doesn't mean there isn't room for one more if it's the right one more."

From there, the conversation flows like a job interview, with Tyler my unexpected advocate, which makes for a far more comfortable conversation. I'm not alone. I'm with him which is appreciated. We're about twenty minutes in when Tyler's phone rings.

"I need to take this," he says, and before I can process me being left alone with Jack, it happens. I have no idea why this shoots a dart of nerves in me but it does.

"I actually should pop into the ladies' room," I say, reaching for my purse, and Lord help me, I strike again. It falls to the ground. Thankfully it doesn't spill and I grab it, only to have Jack reach down and hold up the velvet necklace box. "What's this?"

I swallow hard and before I can stop him, he's opened the lid. His eyes narrow on the necklace and lift to me. "It's beautiful. Why don't wear it instead of carrying it around?"

"It's not mine. It belongs to—a friend. I told her I'd ship it to her and didn't have time to get to it today." The lie does not flow easily, but rather, like a lie—awkward and heavy.

He shuts the lid and hands it back to me. "Too bad. It would look lovely on you, Allison."

There is something a little too warm in his voice and I quickly accept the velvet box and slide it back into my purse.

"What did I miss?" Tyler asks.

My attempted bathroom escape was initially to avoid Jack, but there is no escaping my spilled purse debacle. I hold my breath, expecting Jack to bring up the necklace that Tyler may well have sent Allison but he doesn't. "I was just about to ask Allison to update us on the auction."

The transition from the necklace to the auction is a clunky one for me, but I eventually fall into the conversation with the energy worthy of my hard work. It's a good hour later when we all stand to depart.

"I'll walk you to your car," Tyler offers.

Jack extends his hand and I press my palm to his, only to have him hold onto it. "I suspect I'll see you soon, Allison." For another beat, he's still holding me, until finally, he releases me.

Tyler's eyes glint at his father before he motions for me to walk ahead of him. Once we're outside, he steps to my side. "Where are we going?"

"Around the corner. You don't have to walk me."

"I'm walking you," he says, as stubborn as when Dash had said the same to me.

I sigh with resignation and start walking with him falling into step with me, but he says nothing, not a word. It's not until we're standing at the driver's side of Dash's car that he says, "What happened between you and my father when I took that call?"

"Nothing really."

"Try again."

I hesitate and reach in my purse, showing him the necklace box and watching him closely as I open the lid. There's no recognition in his face, no reaction. His gaze lifts to mine. "Is that for the auction and if so, why are you carrying it around?"

"It fell out of my purse and your father saw it, and no, it's not for the auction. It was delivered to Allison W. with a note, but I got it at the museum. That's how I ended up at your offices, asking for her."

His expression doesn't change, but I swear his energy read likes an invisible flinch. "What did the note say?"

"That seems private and—"

"What did the note say?"

"*Forgive me.*"

His chest expands and his jaw tics. "Don't walk around with something so obviously expensive, Ms. Wright. It's not a smart or safe idea."

The latter comment feels a bit like deflection, despite the fact that he's really not wrong. "Did she call you?"

"No," he says. "She didn't call me, but we'll assume she's occupied."

"Do you know who sent the necklace? Maybe we can call him and check on her?"

"No. No, I don't know who sent the necklace."

"Should we be worried?"

"She's a free woman, Ms. Wright. And she's made a choice. Unless you want to get in my car, and go to my home with me, get in your car so that I know you're safe. Therefore I can leave."

I open my mouth to argue and he says, "Don't," and there's something in the way he says it that cuts and not me. *Him.* He cared about Allison, and I'm not sure he knew, until now, just how much. I've sideswiped him in the worst of ways. I get in my car and lock the doors. He's already walking away. And he seems to know that Allison walked away. *Because freedom is a right and a choice*, I remind myself.

I start the car, but I'm uncomfortable in every possible way.

CHAPTER SIXTY

It's finally time for Dash to arrive home and I'm alone in an empty airport wing, awaiting his flight, so nervous it's really kind of ridiculous. It's not like we haven't been naked together, many times at this point, and talked and texted every day. Just last night we spent an hour talking about his week and my weird encounters with both Tyler and Jack Hawk. For a moment, I calm myself by thinking back to that conversation:

"He didn't act like he'd ever seen the necklace before," I tell him.

"I told you Tyler would not have sent that necklace to the office, which was the sender's intent."

"I think maybe he loved her," I say, thinking about Tyler's reaction to the note sent with the necklace.

"I think it's a little more complicated than that with Tyler. He likes control. He doesn't have it. That's a problem for him."

"Maybe. He did say she was a free woman and chose to leave, I'm paraphrasing slightly, I think."

"And she didn't choose the way he wanted."

"What happened between you and Tyler?"

"That's a complicated story, Allie."

I come back to the present with the same conclusion I'd had last night. Dash has secrets or perhaps not secrets, but things he's just not ready to tell me, and perhaps never will. But then, don't I have the same? How do I judge him when I'm guilty of the same?

It's right then that Dash's plane taxis to a halt under a private hanger. My heart is exaggerating every beat again at this point, and I pace about a bit, before returning to the window.

Finally, Dash is walking across the tarmac, and my God, the man is the kind of sin that drives a girl crazy. In black jeans, and a black leather jacket, with so much swagger, he puts swagger in the swagger, and my heart is literally in my throat. I don't remember any man ever affecting me in such an over-the-top way. Willing my pulse to calm, I move center to the door where he can see me when he enters the building.

The door opens and his eyes find me instantly, a smile sliding over his face, and then we're moving toward each other. We come together in an embrace and he's kissing me, a long, deep kiss that is highly inappropriate, but neither one of us seem to care. The smell of him, the feel of him, and I'm alive when I wasn't just moments before.

"Miss me, baby?" he asks when we come up for air. "Because I damn sure missed you."

"I missed you, too," I say, surprised at how much I mean those words.

"Then how about we go home, order takeout, and get naked?"

I don't miss the way he references home as if it's my home, too, when of course, he doesn't mean it literally. "You do remember we have the Jason Aldean thing tonight, right?"

"We have hours until then." He leans in near my ear, and says, "Plenty of time for me to lick you in all those places you like to be licked."

I'm reminded of how dirty Dash can be, a lot more than he's shown me, I am certain. There's a lot about this man I don't know, but I truly hope to find out.

CHAPTER SIXTY-ONE

By the time Dash and I enter his apartment, we're all over each other. It doesn't take long and we end up naked on his living room floor, and then in the shower together. At this point, we haven't eaten, and Dash suggests we go out to a taco joint he knows and loves. With this in mind, both of us dress for Aldean's. Dash in black jeans, black biker-style boots, and a T-shirt. Me in a black jean skirt with a flare, and a black lacy top. I've just sat down on the couch in the bedroom and pulled on my boots when Dash sits down on the coffee table in front of me.

In his hand is a necklace-sized velvet box and my heart is racing all over again. "You've been obsessing over another woman's necklace sent to her by another man. I thought you needed something that said me and you, not them." He opens the lid and displays a delicate chain with a sparkling pendant in the center.

I smile and laugh when I realize it's a cupcake. "Oh my God. It's gorgeous and it's really a cupcake. How did you find that?"

"I got lucky," he says. "I went into the store for a necklace and they had a cupcake. It was like it was meant to be."

He went into a store, shopping for me. My heart is mush. I mean I know that we're both kind of a mess for our own reasons, we are. We're probably going to break each other, but right now, in this moment, I feel as if maybe, just maybe, we need each other. And isn't that what matters?

"I love it, Dash. I really do." My hand settles on his jaw. "Thank you."

He catches my hand and kisses it, and when he does, when our eyes meet again, there's a shift between us I cannot explain. There is something happening between me and this man that I am so beyond stopping. Maybe he is, too. We're riding a wave that will eventually crash and I just don't know if that will be into each other or someplace dark and lonely.

"Let me help you put it on," he offers.

"I'd like that." I stand up and he pulls the necklace from the velvet.

I lift my hair and turn around. Dash steps behind me and connects the chain. "Done," he says.

Letting my hair fall down my neck, I turn to face him. "How does it look?"

He cups my face. "Beautiful, baby. Absolutely beautiful."

CHAPTER SIXTY-TWO

Dash and I Uber to Jason Aldean's place from the taco spot with the knowledge that we'll be drinking and only have a short walk back to his place from the bar.

The tacos are fabulous, but not so fabulous is the line to get inside Aldean's which is absolutely ridiculous. But thanks to Bella, and our VIP passes waiting on us, Dash and I end up inside rather easily. Hand in hand, we head to the table his sister has reserved for the three of us. Bella, dressed in an adorable, belted navy-blue dress and boots, greets me with a hug. "How was that thing you had with Jack and Tyler?"

"Weird," I say as Dash and I claim a seat across from her. "I don't know how else to explain it."

"That sounds about right," she says, flagging a waitress and motioning to us, but not without her recommendation. "I suggest the lemons drops."

"She always suggests the lemon drops," Dash comments dryly.

"Then they must be good," I say, eyeing the waiter. "I'll take a lemon drop."

Dash shakes his head at us and orders a beer. The three of us then fall into easy conversation until Bella's gaze lifts toward the door. "The record producer is here. Wish us luck." Just that fast, she's up and gone.

There's another band on now, and Dash and I enjoy the music, with me doing a whole lot of singing along. It's finally time for Bella's guy to take the stage and just before he starts his first number, Bella reappears and kneels beside our table. "I need you two to get up and dance. It encourages others to do the same. It makes my client look good." She assumes our agreement, and slides into her seat, turning to watch the stage.

Her client, a good-looking youngish man with dark hair, and a guitar hanging across his body steps to the microphone. "Hi there, Nashville," he greets. "I'm Tony Michaels, and since we're in Aldean's place, let's play a little Aldean." The music starts and the crowd goes nuts as he begins to sing "Dirt Road Anthem."

Bella waves at us to get up and dance. Dash grabs my hand and pulls me to my feet and onto the dance floor. To my complete surprise, Dash doesn't just know how to country dance. He knows how to do it well. He's twirling me around the floor and it's not long until we're two among many. The dance floor is jam-packed. "You're pretty good," I say. "I thought you were from Boston."

"And now Nashville is home." He leans in, his lips near my ear. "Just like Nashville is your home."

My chest tightens with the implications of his words. This is home. He is home. "Yes," I find myself whispering, and meaning, with all my heart. "Yes, it is."

And it's pretty clear that we're no longer talking about dancing. We're talking about me staying here. We're talking about *us*. The song blends into Aldean's "I Don't Drink Anymore," and Dash and with him, the mood, shift to more fun and good times. Dash and I are now *both* singing along. Dash twirls me around and my gaze lands on the bar on the opposite side of the dance floor. My lips parting as I realize that Tyler, of all people, dressed in jeans and a T-shirt, which is so oddly not him to me, but somehow works on him, is standing right there, watching us.

Dash twirls me again and I say, "Tyler's here."

"When a record studio is involved, that doesn't surprise me."

"He's in jeans."

Dash laughs. "You say that like he's wearing a clown suit."

"I feel like he is."

He laughs again, and I forget about Tyler. The singer is really good, and I haven't been dancing in so very long. And I've never been dancing with Dash Black. For the first time in a long time, I just let myself have fun. For the next hour we dance, we break and drink, and we dance some more, all without seeing Tyler again. I must drink more than I realize though because this time, when Dash and I head to the dance floor, I feel the vodka in my light-headedness. I sway and Dash catches me. "You okay, baby?"

I have a moment when I realize how normal him calling me "baby" has become. And I like it. So much. I like *him. Too much* for my own good. "I think I better go to the bathroom and freshen up," I say. "Lemon drops are the devil. No more. Ever."

He doesn't laugh. He strokes hair from my face and tilts my gaze to his. "I told you, Allie, I got you, baby."

A million emotions I blame on vodka wash over me, but he doesn't expect the response I don't have. That's something I love about Dash. He doesn't live the "I get what I give" mentality. He gives. Even if he doesn't get. He slides an arm around me and I ease under his shoulder, feeling a little more stable now than minutes before. I think maybe all that was wrong was that I got up too fast, and with the heat of so many bodies in this place, paired with the drinking, it was just a bad combination.

I leave Dash at the door and head into the bathroom. I'm definitely a lot better now. I freshen up and step outside to join Dash. What I find is not just Dash, but Dash and Tyler. Standing only a few feet away, toe-to-toe, both stiff, shoulders rolled forward, it's clear—this is not a friendly meeting. They look like they're about to throw blows.

CHAPTER SIXTY-THREE

I'm at Dash's side, grabbing his arm in as many seconds as it takes me to close the space between me and him, and whatever is going on between him and Tyler.

"What is this?" I demand. "What is happening right now?"

"Stay out of this, Allie," Dash orders, trying to pull me behind him.

"This is where the coin flips, Dash," Tyler bites out. "This is where I do to you what you did to me. You're not good for her. Step away before she gets hurt."

Dash sways toward him and I step in front of him, my hands on his chest. "Walk away, Dash. What he says doesn't matter. What we say, me and you, is all that matters." But he's not looking at me. He's looking at Tyler, and his expression is pure fury.

"What are you going to do?" Tyler demands, pressing Dash, and that is not a good idea right now. "Hit me?" he continues. "Does she know that about you? That you like to hit things?"

I have no idea what that means and I don't even care right now. I just want this to end but it's not even close to over.

"You're pushing me, Tyler," Dash says, his voice low, lethal, "and not to a place either of us want to go."

I rotate in front of Dash, back to his chest, and point at Tyler. "*You*, walk away. Neither of you can afford to have this go any further."

"I'll take you home," he says, when I know he knows that he's going too far, punching at Dash without ever lifting a fist, but he just won't stop. He keeps going. "It's better that way," he adds, "I know it and so does Dash."

275

Dash grabs my arm and turns me to him. "Me or him, Allie. Choose now."

"We already had this conversation. There is no choice to make. There was never a choice to make. It was always you. It's still you."

He stares down at me, seconds ticking by, in which, thank God, Tyler keeps his mouth shut, but suddenly Dash releases my hand. Then he's stepping around me and Tyler, and walking away. I move to go after him, but I'm halted as Tyler catches my arm. I whirl on him, seething. "Let me go, Tyler. This is not your business."

"If he fucks you up, you'll pack up and leave. So yes, it's my business."

"I don't know what this is tonight, or what happened before I walked up. I don't even care what set you off. We both know it's not about that. It's about you and Dash, and you and Dash alone, and I don't appreciate being made into a game piece. I have too much going on in my life to be in the middle of this war. I quit. I'm done."

I jerk at my arm and he doesn't let go. "You're choosing wrong."

"It's my choice to make, right or wrong. Not yours."

His jaw clenches and he releases me.

And I'm already moving, rushing after Dash, my heart racing. I push through the crowd, lifting to my toes, trying to see over the crowd, but I can't find Dash. I finally make it to the door and explode onto the sidewalk, looking left and right. Dash is walking to my left and he has a good lead on me. So much so that I launch into a run. He's cleared the main strip now, and I'm breathless when I catch his arm, but at least there aren't people all around us now. At least we have some semblance of privacy.

"Dash, stop. Stop, *please.*" I step in front of him, press my hands to his chest. "I would have come right away, but Tyler grabbed my arm and I had to go off on him. Why are you leaving me?"

"He was right. I'm not good for you." He literally sets me aside and starts walking again.

"Don't do this!" I call after him. "This is about you and him, not me and you. Don't make it what it isn't. Don't let him control you by using me."

He stops walking but he doesn't turn around.

I hurry forward and step in front of him again, but this time, I don't touch him. "Don't do this," I say again, softly. "Tonight was a great night. The best night. We had so much fun. I had so much fun with you, Dash. I *always* have fun with you." He draws a breath and just stands there, looking at me and that pushes my buttons. Now my temper flares and my hands go out to my side. "I don't even know what this is about, but as I told Tyler, it's not about me. And still, I've tried to fix this and I did nothing wrong. So you know what, Dash? If you walk away, it's because you want to. You don't get to blame it on Tyler. So whatever, Dash. Go on. Keep walking."

I try to step around him and he catches my arm. "Let's go," he captures my hand and starts walking with me in tow. I let him lead me forward, but my anger is here now and it's not going away. And so is his. We walk in silence, but that silence screams of what is to come. And it's not going to be gentle or quiet.

CHAPTER SIXTY-FOUR

Angry sex wins.

The minute Dash and I are inside his apartment, we're all over each other, kissing each other, hands all over each other. I end up against the door, my shirt and bra shoved to my waist. His hands all over my breasts, and not gently, an erotic tug of my nipples, as painful as it is good. The bite of anger between us is a live charge, driving every taste, and every touch. Dash turns me to face the door, forcing me to catch my weight with my hands, yanking my skirt to my waist, and then impatiently ripping my panties away. We're back to where we were that first night together and I knew then, as I know now, this is all about control. He needs it. He wants it. And I respond, God how I respond. I am hot and aching, and in need of him now, everywhere, anyway I can get him.

His fingers are between my legs, stroking my sex, and then his palm is on my backside, with a sharp smack, that smites my skin, and leaves me gasping a mere moment before he drives inside me. I pant with the punch of pleasure, the pump of his cock, and then he's thrusting into me, over and over, hard and deep, but it's just not enough. I want to yell at him. I want to touch him. I want to feel him deep inside me, over and over again.

He drags me off the door, against him, my back to his chest, leaning around me, he catches my face with his hand—he kisses me, wildly, deeply, and this right now, is all lust and demand, possession and control, but I don't care. I want it all right now. I don't know where he starts and I end. Where I start and he ends.

Somehow, I have no idea when it happened, one of my hands is back on the door, and one of his hands closes on the front of my throat, holding me there—an erotic grip that doesn't hurt but I feel the pressure every time he pumps into me. I wonder if he knows his palm is on the necklace. I wonder if that's why he's doing this. I worry that it will break but he just keeps thrusting and pumping and my body blurs my fears. I'm angry. I'm aroused. I'm a million things I can't name. Something about his hand on my throat —*oh God.*

My body betrays me.

Without warning, I tumble into orgasm, crying out as he drives into me, a low guttural groan roaring from somewhere deep in his chest. With all that explodes between us, I all but collapse into the door, but Dash's arm slides around my waist, catching me, holding me up. His face is buried in my neck, and for a few seconds, he holds me like that. Until finally, he says, "I'll get you something."

I nod and he pulls out of me.

My legs and my emotions are mush and I rotate to lean on the door and slide down the surface to sit on the floor. My hand goes to the necklace, and relief follows as I find it still secure at my neck. Dash returns quickly, squatting in front of me and offering me a towel. I take it from him and stick it between my legs, but I could really care less about anything right now but him and us.

"What was that back there, Dash?"

"You weren't wrong. It was history ignited between me and Tyler. I should have never let it become about you. I'm sorry." He offers me his hand and helps me to my feet. "I don't want you in his house, Allie. I want you here. Stay here."

Because he doesn't want me at Tyler's place. That's what I take from that. And that's when I know I'm not alright, *we're* not alright. Not even close. I'm now thinking about my thoughts earlier tonight. About how we would either crash into each other or just plain crash. I was right, but the crash is now.

"I'm back to being a game token for you and Tyler," I say. "And I don't like it. And he wasn't wrong. I'm going to get hurt."

"I want you here with me, Allie. I wouldn't ask you to move in with me to one-up Tyler. You can't believe that."

He catches my arm and tries to pull me to him. I press on his chest. "No, Dash. I'm too attached to you already. I'm too attached and that wasn't the plan. We're both a mess, both fucked up and we don't even want to tell each other why. But do we want to live together for a couple of months? I'm going home." I try to pull my arm away.

He drags me to him and this would be so much easier if being pressed to him didn't feel so damn good. But it's now or later, and now will hurt less. "Don't go," he says softly. "I need you to stay."

"We are not good for each other, Dash. I was wrong when I said this wasn't about me tonight. It was. And we are too fucked up not to fuck each other up even worse. And you might survive that, but judging from how much this hurt me tonight, I don't think I can. You won't just hurt me. *You'll destroy me.*"

He stares at me a beat that turns into three before his hand falls away, his tone resolute. "I'll drive you home."

"We walked because we've been drinking. I'll call an Uber."

"I'll ride with you and don't tell me no. I'm riding with you, Allie."

LISA RENEE JONES

CHAPTER SIXTY-FIVE

The ride to my house, my very temporary house since I just quit my job, is quiet, but the ping pong of emotions between me and Dash screams through the silence. The car pulls to the front of my place and I get out. Dash follows me and I turn and hold up a hand. "You're not coming in."

"I'm coming in."

"No. No, you are not. If you come inside, I'll forget why that's a mistake because that's what you do to me. You make me forget everything." I press my hands to my head and then drop them. "I need to think, Dash, and I need to do it when the vodka isn't driving every damn thing I say and think. And you're too damn famous for us to fight this out when the Uber driver could record us. Go home."

"That's what you want?"

No, I think, but that's not what I say, and it's not what is right. "It's the only way it can be," I say, and I sound strong, but I'm shredded inside.

He draws a deep breath and turns and gets in the car. It kills me even if it's what I know is right. I turn and walk to the front door. The Uber idles, unmoving, and I know Dash is making sure I get inside safely. *I'll take care of you*, I hear him say in my head. *Until you're gone*, I think. I enter the house, turn on the alarm and sink against the door. That's when the tears come, an avalanche of tears. I cry for me and Dash. I cry for what could have been and never will be. I cry for my mother, who has won a battle but will always have a monster on her shoulder. She will always act brave, but underneath, she will fear the moment that monster attacks again.

And I will, too. I cry and I cry some more, until I can't cry anymore. My nose is stuffy. My face is wet and I'm on the floor.

I haul myself to my feet and walk into the bedroom. I didn't even get my things from Dash's place. All my favorite makeup, my big bag, and more, are still there. I walk into the bathroom and stare into the mirror. I look like a volcano erupted on my face I have so much mascara all over the place. I wash my face and start reapplying my makeup, telling myself it's because I can't stand to see myself looking so puffy and pathetic over a man. Not because Dash might show up at my door.

He left. I told him to leave.

I'm half done with my face and it feels pointless. I have to take it all back off to go to bed. I shut the toilet and sit down. I'm exhausted in so many ways. My cellphone buzzes from somewhere, the bed where I think I threw it. I hate how much I hope it's Dash, but I still get up and hunt it down. I grab it from the mattress and read a message from Tyler: *If you want to know the real Dash, here is your chance. Go here now. I'll meet you there. You'll need me, and you'll understand why when you get there.* There's an address.

I have no idea what this means, but I don't seem to care. It's Dash. And it doesn't sound good. I rush into the bathroom and look in the mirror. I'm still a mess, but I don't care about that either. My purse is my target and I grab it and slide it on cross-body, but I pause. What if this is Tyler stirring up more trouble? I dial his phone. He answers on the first ring. "What is this?"

"You helping me save the damn fool from himself. If you care about him and you obviously do, go to the address and go now." He hangs up.

I try to call Dash. He doesn't answer. I'm officially worried. I pull up my Uber app and key in the address, before ordering a car. The driver will be here in five minutes. I'll be at my destination in fifteen.

CHAPTER SIXTY-SIX

I don't bother with a coat. I'm hot, so very hot, and spinning out of control.

My car arrives, and the location Tyler has given me is actually not far—downtown, but not the area of downtown anyone wants to be in at almost midnight. The driver pulls me to the front of a building stamped with graffiti and surrounded by more buildings with more graffiti. There's a huddle of a few men on the street, all of them smoking and talking. The driver looks back at me. "You sure this is right?"

I glance at the address on my phone, along with Tyler's instructions, which say to enter the building through the red door. I find the red door, but this just doesn't feel right. I dial Tyler and he answers with, "Are you here?"

"Yes, and it looks kind of scary."

"Because it is. I'm already inside. I'll come and get you." He hangs up and I glance at the driver. "Someone is coming to get me. I'll tip for your time."

"Happy to wait," the man says. "A lady like you can't be out here alone."

I don't know what that means, but I appreciate his kindness. "Thank you," I say.

Tyler arrives quickly and opens my door. "What is this, Tyler?" I ask, exiting to the street.

"You'll see soon enough." He motions me forward and I follow him to that damn red door that feels like a bad answer to a terrible question.

From there, we enter what looks like a long hallway leading underground. Loud music radiates around us, vibrating with the promise of bad things to come. I stop walking, turning to Tyler. "If this is going to hurt me—"

"I'm more worried about him getting hurt, Allison. You care about him. I can see that. And I think the bastard actually cares about you. That means you might be the only one who can get him under control." He turns and starts walking again, leaving me with only one option: to follow.

And I do.

I quickly double-step and catch up to him, wildly confused right now. The music is louder now, and I can hear voices and shouts, lots of voices, a crowd, I think. What is this? *What is this?* At this point, we reach two steel doors and Tyler opens one, motioning for me to enter whatever awaits me on the other side of this entryway. Not sure what to expect, I tentatively progress forward and find myself in what I think is an underground fight club, complete with a fight ring and crowds in chairs and standing around it.

Now, I'm really confused. Is Dash gambling on fights? Is that what this is?

Tyler steps to my side and I look to him for that answer. "I don't know why I'm here."

He points to the ring where two fighters and a referee appear to be ready to begin a new match. "Look closer," he orders.

A bad feeling overtakes me and my gaze rockets to the rings again. One of the men has painted his face red, almost like a mask, a disguise, and oh God. It's Dash. He's in the ring. He's going to fight. I turn to Tyler. "What the hell is this?"

"His reality for a long time. He began fighting in the underground clubs after his brother died. He got in trouble, almost landed in jail. That's why he joined the FBI. He needed something physical. But that plan didn't

WHAT IF I NEVER

work. He always comes back to this when he's fucked in the head."

Anger spikes hard and fast. "My God, Tyler. This isn't your story to tell me. Damn you. And you knew you were pushing him tonight. *You knew.*" I turn away from him and rush toward the ring, pushing through bodies, so many bodies, trying to stop the fight. I'm panting when I arrive ringside, and I don't know how or why, but Dash's eye rocket to mine.

The bell rings and the other fighter, a huge man that I know to be Russian, just because people are screaming, "The Russian Beast" at him, moves toward Dash. Dash doesn't move. He's staring at me. The Russian Beast hits him. And hits him again. Dash doesn't fight back. He just lets him hit him and I'm screaming, trying to get Dash to fight back, to protect himself. I can barely take it. Dash goes down, knocked to one knee and the Russian is pumping his fists in the air, and the crowd just loves it.

I'm screaming, "No! Dash! No!" Over and over again.

The Russian Beast steps back in front of Dash and prepares to hit him, but suddenly Dash flat palms him right under his chin. The Russian Beast flails and falls to one knee. Dash is on his feet somehow, his face bloodied up, but his feet are agile. He steps behind The Russian Beast and closes him in a hold, a sleep hold I realize, as everyone screams, "Sleep! Sleep! Sleep!" And that is exactly what happens. Dash releases the other man and the Russian Beast face plants on the mat, sound asleep.

The referee grabs Dash's hand and holds it up. The crowd goes nuts. Tyler steps beside me. "That is what he does. He comes in here, gets the shit beat out of himself *by choice,* and at the last minute, chokes the other guy out. It's how he punishes himself for whatever the fuck he wants to be punished for."

I want to know for what, I do, but I don't ask. I'm angry. I'm hurt. I'm angry all over again. "Stop talking, Tyler. Just *stop talking*."

"This place is illegal and one wrong hit and him or the other guy are dead."

I whirl on him. "How do you even know he's here?"

"This was a PR problem for Dash once before. I handled it and now I pay someone here to tell me if he shows up."

Dash is now at the side of the ring, and he comes through the ropes. The crowd is cheering him on with, "Red Face, Red Face, Red Face."

I tune out Tyler and watch as Dash jumps to the ground and walks straight toward me. Even with the red paint all over him, I can see that his face is a mess, his eye black and swollen. And the idea that he wanted this kind of abuse, guts me. Tears burns in my own eyes at the hate he must feel for himself to ask for this. He stops in front of me and drags me to him, and any relief I feel at his touch is quickly burned away. He leans in, his lips at my ear. "Why are you here?" he demands. "You aren't supposed to be here. You aren't supposed to see this."

"To get you out of here."

He's silent a moment, holding me there, before he says, "Leave. Leave, Allie. You were right. We're not good for each other." He inches back and stares down at me, letting me see the sharp cut in his stare.

The crowd seems to be dispersing, maybe even herded out of the room, thank God. I want this, all of this, to just be over. "Can we just leave please?"

"Go home, Allie," he says again, releasing me. And he says nothing else. He turns and walks away, and when I would follow, a big, burly man, a guard, I think, steps in front of me. I lean around him and watch as Dash climbs back inside the ring, talks to the referee, and then exits on the other side. He's gone then. I can't see him. I can't find him.

I turn away from the guard, and the ring, emotions twisted, as I head for the door, needing out of here before I'm stupid enough to cry again. Needing out of here, just to breathe. Finally, it seems, I exit into the hallway and Tyler is right there with me, keeping pace. "Where are you going?"

"Home. He's gone. I can't find him. And I can't be here."

"I'll drive you."

I wave him off. "I'll call a car."

"No one will pick up here after midnight."

"I'll call a car," I insist.

"Stubborn woman," he mutters.

I'm at the building exit and I step into a chilly night, phone in hand, as I pull up my Uber app. I do as I said, and order a car. "Done," I say, glancing at Tyler. "I ordered the car."

"They won't show. I'll drive you."

"I'm not going to let Dash find out I got in a car with you Tyler. He already has to think I came with you."

"Don't be a fool. This is not about his ego. It's about your safety."

"And yet you brought me here."

"To help him," he counters.

"You drove him to this."

"I thought he was over this shit four years ago when I cleaned up his mess. Obviously, I was wrong."

Guilt stabs at me. He wasn't wrong. I did this. I pushed Dash to this. I drove him to this.

"Stop," he orders and my gaze snaps back to Tyler as he adds, "I see what you're doing. I read it in your face, woman. And just stop. Stop blaming yourself. You didn't push him to this. I told you before and I'll tell you now: he's fucked up."

"So am I," I say. "And so are you. Don't deny that truth, Tyler. Stop judging him." I glance at my phone and grimace in defeat. "The driver cancelled."

"Can I take you home now?"

"Fine," I say. "Yes, please just get me out of here."

CHAPTER SIXTY-SEVEN

The engine to Tyler's fancy sports car is not quiet, roaring in the dark of night, while my emotions scream into the otherwise silent car. But I do not. I sit there next to Tyler, fingers curled in my lap and I am in my head, reliving Dash in that ring, staring at me, letting that monster of a man punish him. I'd been terrified for him and yet it was almost as if that's what he wanted, for me to watch him get beaten. And then after the fight, when he'd come to stand in front of me.

Go home, Allie.

Those words, so coldly spoken, echo in my head.

"You okay?" Tyler asks.

No, I think. No, I am *not* okay, but that's not Tyler's problem, and it's not really even his creation. I did this. I pushed Dash over the edge. I walked out on him tonight. "I'm angry with you, Tyler," I say, "really angry, but I don't even have enough objectivity to know if that's a fair emotion. And I won't tonight. Does Bella know about his fighting?"

"She doesn't. He doesn't want her to know. Not only did she have something big for her own career going on tonight that Dash would not want to fuck up, she lost one brother already." He glances over at me. "And right now, based on what I saw tonight, you're the person emotionally connected to Dash. Maybe the only person."

My hand goes to my necklace, the sweet gift from Dash, that meant so much to me. I was selfish and self-absorbed tonight. I didn't let myself see what was in front of me, which was Dash. In the end, Tyler protected Bella, as Dash would have wanted, and used me, when he really had no other choice. But I didn't protect Dash.

"You were friends," I say and it's not a question. Yes, he has a business interest in Dash, but no one can punch someone's buttons the way Tyler punched Dash's button tonight, without knowing them well.

"We were," he says. "On some level, we still are."

I'd argue that point, but I think I might be wrong. I don't ask what happened between them. There is much I should have heard from Dash when he was ready, that came to me without his consent.

Tyler doesn't fill in any blanks, and I don't think that's because he's respecting Dash's privacy, either. He has his own reasons, and that's fine. I get it. This is his private story, just as it's Dash's.

We arrive at my house, which is really his house, and Tyler pulls into the driveway and kills the engine. "I'll walk you to the door."

"No. I'm fine."

"Are you sure you're okay alone?"

"No," I say. "No, I'm not, but neither is he." I glance over at him. "If you talk to him—"

"I'll call you."

I nod and exit the car, walking to the door. Once I have it open, I wave at Tyler and enter. I lock up and set the alarm, and lean on the door. The house feels empty and so do I. I stand there, replaying the entire night, and I don't know how much time passes. I tell myself to go to bed, but I know I will never sleep. I sit down on the bed and pull off my boots, lying back on the mattress.

Go home, Allie.

Hearing Dash's voice in my head, I sit up and sigh. I need to calm my nerves. I grab my phone and I want to call Dash, but I know he won't answer. And I know I won't know what to even say. Texting is a coward's answer, but it's the answer I choose. But my words, my words are brave. *I want to see you. I need to see you.*

Please. I'm sorry I left. I was just scared, Dash. I'm scared of how much you mean to me.

Phone in hand, I can't just stare at it. I stand up and head through the house and down to the wine cellar. I'll pick a bottle and to hell with how expensive it is. I need help sleeping. I need to calm down. Once I'm down there, I start surveying the bottles, in between eyeing my messages that don't change. I'm reading a label when there's a sound upstairs. I freeze, holding my breath, telling myself it's just the house settling, but there it is again. A creak of the floorboard. I gently and quietly slide the bottle back into place. Tyler has the alarm code. It has to be Tyler. But coming in like this, that just doesn't feel like something he'd do.

Hands trembling, I walk to the light switch and flip it off and then head to a corner, and squat down. I dial Tyler. The call fails. Of course, it does. I'm in the cellar. I try another three times and finally it goes through. The minute Tyler answers I say, "Where are you?"

"At Dash's trying to get him to answer the door. Have you talked to him?"

My heart leaps and I disconnect, trying to use the signal I have when I have it. I dial Dash. He doesn't answer. Of course not. I text him: *Just please tell me if you're here. Are you in the house? Dash?*

My phone rings in my hand and fails, but the sound, the ring, was a mistake. I quickly put my phone on silent. It rings again with Dash's number. I answer with, "Please tell me you're in the house?"

"No. I'm not in the house, Allie. Is someone there? What is—"

There's another creak of the floor. Someone is walking around now. That's it, I'm not emotional and paranoid. I try 911. The call failed. I try again. The 911 operator answers and the call drops. The light from upstairs goes dark. I hold my breath, waiting for what comes next.

THE END...FOR NOW

Fear not! The next book, BECAUSE I CAN, available now!

Get it here:

https://www.lisareneejones.com/necklace-trilogy.html

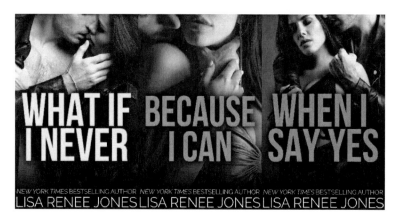

***

Don't forget, if you want to be the first to know about upcoming books, giveaways, sales, and any other exciting news I have to share please be sure you're signed up for my newsletter! As an added bonus everyone receives a free eBook when they sign-up!

http://lisareneejones.com/newsletter-sign-up/

EXCERPT FROM THE WALKER SECURITY: ADRIAN TRILOGY

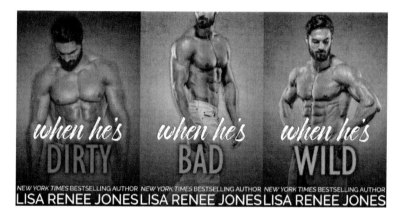

I exit the bathroom and halt to find him standing in the doorway, his hands on either side of the doorframe. "What are you doing?

"This," he says, and suddenly, his hands are on my waist, and he's walked me back into the bathroom.

Before I know what's happening, he's kicked the door shut, and his fingers are diving into my hair. "Kissing you, because I can't fucking help myself. And because you might not ever let me do it again. That is unless you object?"

That's the part that really gets me. The "unless I object," the way he manages to be all alpha and demanding and still ask. Well, and the part where he can't fucking help himself.

I press to my toes and the minute my mouth meets his, his crashes over mine, his tongue doing a wicked lick that I feel in every part of me. And I don't know what I taste like to him, but he is temptation with a hint of tequila, demand, and desire. His hands slide up my back, fingers splayed between my shoulder blades, his hard body pressed to mine, seducing me in every possible way.

I moan with the feel of him and his lips part from mine, lingering there a moment before he says, "Obviously, someone needs to protect you from me," he says. "Like me." And then to my shock, he releases me and leaves. The bathroom door is open and closed before I know what's happened. And once again, I have no idea if or when I will ever see him again.

FIND OUT MORE ABOUT THE ADRIAN TRILOGY HERE:

https://www.lisareneejones.com/walker-security-adrians-trilogy.html

GET A FREE COPY OF BOOK ONE HERE:

https://claims.prolificworks.com/free/I3n4VacJ

THE BRILLIANCE TRILOGY

It all started with a note, just a simple note handwritten by a woman I didn't know, never even met. But in that note is perhaps every answer to every question I've ever had in my life. And because of that note, I look for her but find him. I'm drawn to his passion, his talent, a darkness in him that somehow becomes my light, my life. Kace August is rich, powerful, a rock star of violins, a man who is all tattoos, leather, good looks, and talent. He has a wickedly sweet ability to play the violin, seducing audiences worldwide. Now, he's seducing me. I know he has secrets. I don't care. Because you see, I have secrets, too.

I'm not Aria Alard, as he believes. I'm Aria Stradivari, daughter to Alessandro Stradivari, a musician born from the same blood as the man who created the famous Stradivarius violin. I am as rare as the mere 650 instruments my ancestors created. Instruments worth millions. 650 masterpieces, the brilliance unmatched.

650 reasons to kill. 650 reasons to hide. One reason not to: him.

FIND OUT MORE ABOUT THE BRILLIANCE
TRILOGY HERE:

https://www.lisareneejones.com/brilliance-trilogy.html

GET A FREE COPY OF BOOK ONE HERE:

https://claims.prolificworks.com/free/FTpzSTRe

THE LILAH LOVE SERIES

As an FBI profiler, it's Lilah Love's job to think like a killer. And she is very good at her job. When a series of murders surface—the victims all stripped naked and shot in the head—Lilah's instincts tell her it's the work of an assassin, not a serial killer. But when the case takes her back to her hometown in the Hamptons and a mysterious but unmistakable connection to her own life, all her assumptions are shaken to the core.

Thrust into a troubled past she's tried to shut the door on, Lilah's back in the town where her father is mayor, her brother is police chief, and she has an intimate history with the local crime lord's son, Kane Mendez. The two share a devastating secret, and only

Kane understands Lilah's own darkest impulses. As more corpses surface, so does a series of anonymous notes to Lilah, threatening to expose her. Is the killer someone in her own circle? And is she the next target?

FIND OUT MORE ABOUT THE LILAH LOVE SERIES HERE:

https://www.lisareneejonesthrillers.com/the-lilah-love-series.html

ALSO BY LISA RENEE JONES

THE INSIDE OUT SERIES

If I Were You
Being Me
Revealing Us
His Secrets*
Rebecca's Lost Journals
The Master Undone*
My Hunger*
No In Between
My Control*
I Belong to You
All of Me*

THE SECRET LIFE OF AMY BENSEN

Escaping Reality
Infinite Possibilities
Forsaken
Unbroken*

CARELESS WHISPERS

Denial
Demand
Surrender

WHITE LIES

Provocative
Shameless

TALL, DARK & DEADLY

Hot Secrets
Dangerous Secrets
Beneath the Secrets

WALKER SECURITY

Deep Under
Pulled Under
Falling Under

LILAH LOVE

Murder Notes
Murder Girl
Love Me Dead
Love Kills
Bloody Vows
Bloody Love
Happy Death Day
The Party's Over

DIRTY RICH

Dirty Rich One Night Stand
Dirty Rich Cinderella Story
Dirty Rich Obsession
Dirty Rich Betrayal
Dirty Rich Cinderella Story: Ever After
Dirty Rich One Night Stand: Two Years Later
Dirty Rich Obsession: All Mine
Dirty Rich Secrets
Dirty Rich Betrayal: Love Me Forever

THE FILTHY TRILOGY

The Bastard
The Princess
The Empire

THE NAKED TRILOGY

One Man
One Woman
Two Together

THE SAVAGE SERIES

Savage Hunger
Savage Burn
Savage Love
Savage Ending

THE BRILLIANCE TRILOGY

A Reckless Note
A Wicked Song
A Sinful Encore

ADRIAN'S TRILOGY

When He's Dirty
When He's Bad
When He's Wild

NECKLACE TRILOGY

What If I Never?
Because I Can (December 2021)
When I Say Yes (February 2022)

eBook only

ABOUT LISA RENEE JONES

New York Times and *USA Today* bestselling author Lisa Renee Jones writes dark, edgy fiction including the highly acclaimed *Inside Out* series and the crime thriller *The Poet*. Suzanne Todd (producer of Alice in Wonderland and Bad Moms) on the *Inside Out* series: *Lisa has created a beautiful, complicated, and sensual world that is filled with intrigue and suspense.*

Prior to publishing, Lisa owned a multi-state staffing agency that was recognized many times by The Austin Business Journal and also praised by the Dallas Women's Magazine. In 1998 Lisa was listed as the #7 growing women-owned business in Entrepreneur Magazine. She lives in Colorado with her husband, a cat that talks too much, and a Golden Retriever who is afraid of trash bags.

Made in United States
North Haven, CT
21 January 2022

15058716R00183